TWO
EROTIC TALES

BY
PIERRE LOUŸS

EVANSTON PUBLISHING, INC.
EVANSTON, ILLINOIS 60201

Translated by
MARY HANSON HARRISON

Edited by
DOROTHY KAVKA

APHRODITE

THE SONGS OF BILITIS

Cover illustration and design by Dorothy Kavka

Printed on nonacid paper.

ACKNOWLEDGMENTS

Our thanks to:

Carol Heise, for the loan of her first edition translation of *Aphrodite,* privately printed in France in 1913, with no translator or publisher listed.

Heather Platt, for critiquing the final French translation, and Dr. Theo. E. Kioutas, for correcting the Greek in the text.

The unknown person who, many years ago, left the Mitchell S. Buck edition of *The Collected Works of Pierre Louÿs* in a stack of books that became summer reading for a twelve year old girl who was mesmerized by both the ancient worlds Louÿs created and the illustrations by Harry G. Spanner.

INTRODUCTION

PIERRE LOUŸS

At twenty-six years old, Pierre Louÿs had become one of the most notorious writer in 1890s France. Friend of the renowned — André Gide, Paul Valéry, Oscar Wilde, Claude Debussy, Sarah Bernhardt, Stéphane Mallarmé, Colette, José Maria de Heredia, Léon Blum, Marcel Proust, Henri de Régnier, Auguste Rodin — he was full of promise and contradiction. Although certain he would die young from tuberculosis, he was never without a cigarette dangling from his mouth; known for his sense of humor and practical jokes, he also suffered from suicidal depressions; he was a homophobe who advocated lesbianism; an anti-semite, who made the female protagonist of his first novel Jewish; a scholar, whose research was disregarded because his first work feigned to be a translation from the Greek; a libertine who squandered his inheritance, borrowing money rather than holding a salaried position.

Born Pierre-Félix Louis, Louÿs changed his name to make it sound more Greek. His early years were painful: when he was only nine years old, his mother died from tuberculosis, and five years later, his brother also died. When his elderly father died in 1889, he left Louÿs a substantial inheritance which he received when he turned twenty-one years old. Convinced by his own symptoms that he would soon also die, he squandered the money within three years on high living and prostitutes. His half-brother, Georges Louis, a well-known diplomat who was much older than Pierre, became his father figure, supporting him both emotionally and financially over the years.

In 1888, Louÿs met André Gide when they were in the same class in school. Their tumultuous relationship was finally ended seven years later by Gide for many reasons, among them the conflict between their life-styles and a need to maintain his intellectual independence. Louÿs was a loyal and generous friend, but he was a practical joker. He also considered it his duty to offer editorial advice; this and his "lax" morals upset the more puritanical Gide.

Soon after they met, Gide and Louÿs made a pact to write a page of each other's first work. In 1891, this agreement provided Gide's novel, *Cahiers d'André Walter*, with a preface by P.C. (Pierre Chrysis, one of the noms de plume Louÿs used). In turn, Louÿs' *Les Chansons de Bilitis (The Songs of Bilitis)* was dedicated to Gide.

Another good friend of Louÿs was Paul Valéry, whom he met in 1890. It was Louÿs who introduced Valéry to Gide and who was pleased when they became literary and social companions.

Louÿs was involved in starting and editing a number of literary reviews, all of which were short-lived. The most well-known, *La Conque*, first appeared in 1891. It contained the work of practically every French writer who was or was about to become famous. Lasting for only eleven issues, it was expensively priced, well designed and illustrated, and included poetry not only of Louÿs, Gide, and Valéry, but of Mallarmé, Verlaine, Moréas, Morice, de Régnier, Maeterlinck, Drovin, Quillot, Blum, Mauclair, Fazy, Bérenger, Gautier, and the English poet, Swinburne.

The strongest literary influences on Louÿs were Victor Hugo and Goethe. When he discovered Leconte de Lisle's translations of the ancient Greek writers, Louÿs learned Greek thoroughly enough to publish his own translations of Meleager and Lucian. Even before he was twenty years old, he was a member of Mallarmé's salon. Through Mallarmé, he met Henri de Régnier and through him, José-Maria de Heredia, whose salon included Léon Blum and Marcel Proust. Not only was Heredia an influence on his writing, but Louÿs fell in love with his daughter Marie, whom he wished to marry.

In 1891, while still young and largely unknown, he met Oscar Wilde who was impressed enough with the young poet to give him the manuscript of his work *Salomé* to read and comment upon. Wilde dedicated *Salomé* to "mon ami Pierre Louÿs." When Louÿs visited London, he was introduced to Wilde's circle of friends, including Sarah Bernhardt, who asked Louÿs to write a play for her, and he immediately began the outline of what would become *Aphrodite*.

Louÿs ended his friendship with Wilde in 1893 when he became aware of the nature of Wilde's relationship with Lord Alfred Douglas. Originally, Louÿs was unconcerned with homosexuality and treated it sympathetically in his translation of Meleager. Now, he may have wanted to avoid having his diplomat brother touched by any kind of scandal. He had no such reservations about lesbian love, a life-style that he endorsed from his earliest writings to his last.

Louÿs met Claude Debussy in 1892 and he remained a close friend for many years. From the beginning, Louÿs helped Debussy's career with practical, financial, and moral support. They often discussed major artistic collaborations, which never materialized.

Music was a very important part of Louÿs life and work — he was a devotee of Richard Wagner and often visited at Bayreuth. Louÿs wrote major portions of *Aphrodite* in 1893, while staying at the home of Judith Gautier, Wagner's former lover.

Also in 1893, Louÿs' brother Georges was sent as French Plenipotentiary Minister to Cairo, and this opened up travel to the Middle East and Africa for Louÿs. Gide had told him about his affair with a sixteen year old girl, Meryem ben Ali (or, *Meriem bent Atala)*, who lived in Biskra, Algeria. Typically, Louÿs decided to travel to this place that had so changed Gide's attitude about sex. He also took Meryem as his mistress, feeling he "owed it to his friendship" with Gide to do so. It was to both Gide and Meryem that *Les Chansons de Bilitis* is dedicated. According to Gide, Meryem inspired many of the poems in the work, as most of the first edition of the Chansons was written when Louÿs was with her at Constantine.

Over a six month period in 1895-1896, Louÿs published his novel *L'Esclavage* (*The Slave*) in a serialization, which he slightly revised and renamed *Aphrodite,* to be sold as a complete book. It was finally published as a novel in March, 1896. After one very favorable review by François Coppée, *Aphrodite* sold 5,000 copies in its first two weeks in print, and by September, 50 editions were sold out. At the year's end, 50,000 copies of the book had been printed. Louÿs refused permission for a translation into English and brushed off Yvette Guilbert and Camille Saint-Saëns' proposal to turn the novel into an operetta.

The next year, Louÿs traveled to Algiers where he met Zohra ben Brahim and, inspired by her, composed more poems for the Chansons. He brought Zohra back to Paris with him, where she created a sensation with her exotic looks and dress. During this same time, he began his affair with Marie de Heredia (now Marie de Régnier, the wife of Henri de Régnier) and then, surprisingly, in 1899, married her sister Louise.

Louÿs believed that in order to free his artistic soul, a man should "satisfy his natural appetites." Indeed, at one time in his life, he was sleeping with his wife, his sister-in-law, and his mistress.

Meanwhile, Debussy set some of *Le Chansons de Bilitis* to music but, although asked by Louÿs to compose music for *Aphrodite*, the composer's only other collaboration with Louÿs was a score for a special private performance of ten of the Chansons. In 1914, Debussy arranged six of these songs under the name *Six Epigraphes Antiques*, which Ernest Anserment orchestrated many years later.

Through his friendship with Coppée, Louÿs became involved with the anti-Semitic anti-Dreyfus movement. He refused to have a Jewish publisher and broke his friendship with Debussy when the composer left his wife for a Jewish woman.

Under constant pressure for money, Louÿs continued to write. *La Femme et le Pantin (Woman and Puppet)* was completed in 1898. *Les Adventures du Roi Pausole (The Adventures of King Pausole)* was published in 1901. His pulmonary problems were severe and he developed asthma, probably a by-product of the emphysema from which he also suffered. None of this kept him from his daily consumption of over sixty cigarettes.

He continued to defend sexual freedom in a series of articles to the French press. His work *Sanguines*, published in 1903, sold well initially, but did not earn enough to sustain him. Fortunately, his previous works continued to sell steadily. He began work on *Psyché*, but it was never completely finished and he ultimately destroyed some sections that were too autobiographical. Three years later, Louÿs published *Archipel,* a collection of four short stories and fourteen essays which was not a financial success. Even with his constant impoverishment, Louÿs continued spending every spare cent he had buying rare and finely made books. He amassed a library of over 20,000 books, which became his only financial asset.

After Debussy was no longer interested in composing for *Aphrodite,* Louÿs gave permission to many composers to use the work. One of the first was Arturo Berutti's *Khrysé,* performed in Buenos Aires in 1902. Camille Erlanger wrote *Aphrodite* based on a libretto by Louis de Gramont. This work premiered in 1906 in Paris; the lead was sung by Mary Garden. Other musical adaptations of the novel included an Austrian version in which Maria Jeritza made her début, and another in Buenos Aires, *Afrodita,* by Arturo Luzzati. Giacomo Puccini, who was first interested in *Aphrodite,* now looked to Louÿs' *La Femme et le Pantin* as the basis for an opera, but later backed out of his agreement. *La Femme et le Pantin* was finally put to music by Ricardo Zandonai. Called *Conchita,* the opera's title role was sung by Tarquinia Tarquini. Arthur Honegger wrote the very successful operetta *Le Roi Pausole* in 1930.

The play *La Femme et le Pantin* by Pierre Frondail, with minimal collaboration by Louÿs, and presented in 1910, also was a success, undoubtedly helped by the revealing costumes of Régina Badet who played the lead. The play *Aphrodite,* also by Frondail, was much less successful when produced in 1914, even though the statue of the goddess of love used in the set was sculpted by Rodin and the incidental music written by Henri Février. Around 1919, an expurgated three-act English version of Aphrodite, which was probably written by George C. Hazelton, was presented in New York.

But Louÿs' books were not just made into operas and plays: they also were the basis for movies such as *The Woman and the Puppet* with Geraldine Farrar, *The Devil is a Woman* starring Marlene Dietrich, and *La Femme et le Pantin* with Brigitte Bardot.

The last years of Louÿs' life were filled with illness and disappointments. His eyesight began to fail, and since he was devoting more and more time to research and critiques, this was of concern to him. For a short while in 1911, he went blind. He did regain his sight, but his eyes were never completely normal again.

Although he no longer was writing fiction and even with his bad sight, Louÿs read constantly, devoting himself to bibliographic research and literary criticism. He acquired the journals of the architect Henry Alexandre Legrand, who used a complex encryption while writing detailed memoirs of the French and Spanish courts of Louis-Philippe and Napoléon III. When Louÿs broke the code, the subsequent discoveries were not published, supposedly because Louÿs had, as a joke, declared *Les Chansons de Bilitis* a Greek translation, and editors were afraid of being part of a new "fraud." Later, the same fear of deception might have kept others from publishing Louÿs' hypothesis that Corneille had coauthored several plays thought to be Moliére's.

In 1913, after fourteen years of marriage, Louÿs' wife Louise sued for divorce. Her illnesses combined with the hopeless poverty in which they lived and Louÿs' infidelities finally became too much for her. After the breakup of his marriage, Louÿs had some short-lived liaisons with a number of actresses and then began a sporadic six-year affair with twenty-two year old Claudine Rolland. In 1916, he published *Poëtique* and the poem *Isthi*, and finished writing the poem some critics believe to be his most accomplished work, *Pervigilium Mortis.* When his brother Georges died in 1917, Louÿs, in his inconsolable grief, turned to drugs and liquor. His eyesight again worsened, and in 1918 he had to sell some of his precious book collection in order to obtain funds.

Claudine, who had become very sick, was replaced by Aline Steenackers, her half-sister. Louÿs was gravely ill himself, yet continued to rely on cocaine and liquor. Aline bore him two children and Louÿs married her in October of 1923. He continued to write as his health deteriorated — his biographers mention that some erotic, if not obscene, poetry and prose probably dates from this time. He died on June 3, 1925; he was 54 years old. A week later

Aline Louÿs gave birth to their third child. *Psyché* was published posthumously in 1927.

THE PARNASSIANS AND
THE FRENCH SYMBOLISTS

Pierre Louÿs was a member of both the salon of Mallarmé, the father of Symbolism, and that of de Heredia, the chief advocate of the Parnassians. He drew from both movements what suited his needs, especially a desire to revolt against the traditional values of a staid, bourgeois France.

The Parnassians stressed restraint, objectivity, and technical perfection in writing. They experimented with meters and verse forms, used rhyme, and often turned to mythology, exotic lands, and past civilizations such as ancient Greece for their inspiration. Rhythmic patterns and the "formal aspects of poetry" were important. There was nothing personal in their writing — the personality of the writer was not to be considered.

Like the Pre-Raphaelites in England such as Dante Gabriel Rossetti and Algernon Swinburne, the Symbolists believed in art for art's sake. They turned to their inner selves, often invoking their dreams as inspiration. These writers looked for the underlying mystery of existence through grace and exclusivity, and they constantly searched for the ultimate source of beauty. Their aesthetic principle included rarity and they published in small, limited editions of bibliographic beauty. They believed that admiration was increased when a work was protected from the masses and reserved for the artistic elite who could truly appreciate it.

Louÿs always specified that his earliest published poetry should be printed in limited editions, often of only 100 copies. The price of his early literary journals and poetry books was kept high to limit the numbers of buyers and to encourage the quality of the editions. Typically, he loved beautiful writing paper, used purple ink, and was known for his elegant "medieval" handwriting.

To Pierre Louÿs, beauty was an aesthetic ideal and more important than the classical ideal of truth and morality. The artist should actually go beyond the "boundaries of conventional morality" to provide new standards for society. Unlike Gide, he was not concerned with ideas presented in sparse, clean language, but in the music of the expression — rhythm over rhyme, the senses above reason.

APHRODITE

Aphrodite is Louÿs' interpretation of the Pygmalion legend. In the original version, Pygmalion, a nobleman and sculptor, falls in love with his sculpture of a woman and asks the goddess Aphrodite to bring her to life. In Louÿs' novel *Aphrodite*, it is a woman who must measure up to the statue of Aphrodite, and who is found lacking in comparison.

The inspiration for the work came from Sarah Bernhardt, whom Louÿs had long adored. When he met her in 1892, she asked him to write a play for her, and he began writing a tragedy he called *Chrysis*. It was about a courtesan of ancient Alexandria whose beauty becomes an obsession to a sculptor. The play was never completed. Between 1893 and 1894, Louÿs expanded on his original effort, first as a short story called "Chrysis" after the main character, and then from 1895 to 1896, as a serialized novel called *L'Esclavage*. As he prepared the serialization for publication as a book, the title became *Aphrodite*, and he added a preface which rejected the morality of 19th Century France for the ideal life of the ancients. Louÿs felt that because of their unrepressed sensuality, the ancient Greeks possessed more integrity than modern Christians.

The novel is set in Alexandria in 56 B.C. and takes place within a three-day period. Chrysis, a beautiful nineteen year old courtesan, has become bored with her life. Demetrios, a sculptor who created the statue of Aphrodite in the Temple of the Goddess, is also the lover of the Queen Berenice (who actually reigned from 57-55 B.C.). He is so handsome and powerful that all women find him irresistible.

But Demetrios loves only his statue, for no woman can match its perfection. If he desires sex, he visits Aphrodite's sacred courtesans. Yet, when he sees Chrysis, her indifference intrigues him and when she refuses his advances, he immediately wants her. She demands that he obtain three objects for her — the mirror of the courtesan Bacchis; the comb of Touni, the wife of the high priest; and the necklace from the statue of Aphrodite. He steals the mirror, murders Touni for the comb, and, although hesitating at the sacrilege, finally takes the necklace from the statue of Aphrodite he has created and whose perfection he adores.

But then Demetrios so perfectly possesses Chrysis in a dream that he no longer wants her in reality.

Chrysis, now in love with Demetrios, at his command wears the mirror, comb, and necklace and is sentenced to death. Demetrios sculpts an erotic clay model of her corpse and uses the likeness to begin a new sculpture called "Immortal Life." For all the passion in the novel, Chrysis and Demetrios never touch and Demetrios is never punished for what he has done. To Louÿs the intensity of artistic creation overcomes any crime, and desire restricted to one person becomes a form of slavery.

It is interesting to note that of the five different English versions of *Aphrodite* we consulted before beginning this translation, all were different from the original French text of 1896. More than likely, they were translated from a revised and expanded French edition. In these translations, two new chapters were added, while the most obvious stylistic change is the section when Demetrios goes to Touni to get the comb. The English versions have Demetrios and Touni actually discussing his desire to get the comb and kill her; he then makes love to her and momentarily forgets why he has come. She, having attained Demetrios, gives him permission to take the comb and put her to death. Thus the whole focus of the novel goes from the original symbolic emotional detachment of Demetrios to a romanticized version in which Demetrios is absolved of his crime by the loving victim herself.

No matter what the edition, however, all versions present the same portrait of women — every heroine is beautiful and has prodigious sexual appetites which are never slackened by any aspects of life including murder, suicide, or just physical exhaustion. His writing is that of an adoration of youth; no one is ever old, ugly, or physically handicapped. In carefully crafted prose, he glorifies sexuality and the feminine body. As his "Preface" in *Aphrodite* points out, a striving for beauty and the worship of sensual pleasures are necessary for the integration of creativity and intellect.

From the first, *Aphrodite* and then *Les Chansons de Bilitis,* were published in exquisite leather-bound collectors' editions, illustrated and hand-colored by the most talented artists in France. In the United States, the only way to obtain a copy of any of Louÿs' works was through beautifully typeset and illustrated private printings of limited editions, such as those put out by The Society of Aesthetes and The Pierre Louÿs Society. Certainly, of all his works, it is the many fine editions of *Aphrodite* and *Bilitis* that would no doubt please the bibliophile Louÿs the most if he were alive today.

THE SONGS OF BILITIS

Les Chansons de Bilitis was one of the earliest of Louÿs' works, written when he was still only twenty-three and published in December, 1894. By combining what he had learned from translating the prose poems of Meleager, and his knowledge of Lucien and Sappho, Louÿs used the voice of the young woman Bilitis for a series of his own prose poems, nominally based on her life. The original edition was made up of 93 poems and limited to only 500 copies. As the author became more well known, new editions were printed. Louÿs added periodically to the Chansons and by 1900, the final version included 75 new poems, for a total of 168.

The book was prefaced by an introduction in which Louÿs, posing as the translator "of the Greek," pedantically discusses the history of Bilitis. Her life is divided conveniently into three sections, each illustrating, with a corresponding change of tone, a different type of love: Bilitis' youthful infatuation for a young shepherd in the pastoral serenity of her home on Pamphylia, in Asia Minor; the sophisticated city of Mytilene on the island of Lesbos, where Bilitis lived passionately with another woman for ten years; and finally, at Amathus, on Cyprus, where the poetess consecrated her life to Aphrodite as a professional courtesan.

The poems conclude with the epigrams written on Bilitis' tomb. Louÿs comments about them in his "Introduction," quoting the supposed German scholar and first editor of her works, M. G. Heim. Louÿs was always a practical joker — G. Heim (Geheim) translates as *concealed* or *surreptitious* in German. Even the "Bibliography" which concluded the work as an authentication was a fabrication, although later enlarged to include real references, such as an unfavorable review by Professor Willamovitz-Moellendorf and Debussy's musical adaptations of some of the Chansons. In the "Table of Contents," some of the titles were listed as *untranslated*, with the implication that they were too risqué to be printed.

A few of the Chansons were Louÿs' reworking and adaptations of ancient poems from Greek and Latin — Meleager, Paulus Silentiarius, Philodemos, Rufinus, and even *The Odyssey* — as well as other sources, but most were original, as was the concept of the work itself.

The form of each is that of a prose poem, or "proses lyriques," in four stanzas. They are rhythmic, lyrical, and evoke a sense of the ancient world. Yet, it is their sensuality and direct invocation of sexuality that has continued to make them popular 100 years after they were first written. *Les Chansons de Bilitis* was Louÿs' first successful attempt at presenting passion as essential to creativity.

In the first section, love is presented within traditional pastoral conventions. We meet Bilitis just as she reaches puberty, and in her search for sexual fulfillment the poet calls on the symbolism associated with nature and natural love — even her lover is a shepherd, and she worships at the altar of the nymphs. Throughout all of the poems, Louÿs speaks through the voice of his heroine, Bilitis, a convention often used by writers; however, when in the second section Bilitis erotically and ecstatically sings of her love for another woman, it is only Louÿs' ability to write an eloquent, passionate depiction of love in all its aspects that prevents his stepping into the role of voyeur.

The tone of the third section is much more worldly, as Bilitis becomes a courtesan of Aphrodite. Its cruder tone may have come from Louÿs' extensive experience with prostitutes. The poems deal with subjects such as soliciting clients, jealousy, anger, drunkenness, and even rape.

Les Chansons de Bilitis is perhaps best known for its second section dealing with lesbianism than for its other themes. Louÿs was one of the few writers up to that time to portray this life-style in a sympathetic and enthusiastic manner. Recently, there was an interview on National Public Radio in which a woman discussed how difficult it was to be a lesbian in 1950s America. She related how her friends formed a group which, on the surface, seemed to be like any other woman's club: they called themselves "The Daughters of Bilitis."

ABOUT THE TRANSLATION

These translations were made directly from the French texts: *Aphrodite* from an edition printed in Paris in 1896 by Société du Mercure de France, and *The Songs of Bilitis* from various 1900 editions. Early on, the philosophical decision was made to try to keep this translation as close to the French text as possible — to try for a conservation of the tone and vocabulary of Louÿs rather than a modern impression of his works.

Certain editorial guidelines were followed: the French *tu* was translated simply as the second person *you*, rather than the now archaic English *thee* or *thou*. Vocabulary was made as accessible as possible; for example, the words usually translated as *girdle, collar,* and *croup* are in this edition, *sash, necklace,* and *buttocks.* References to drachmae, obolos, and minae were not changed because it was felt that there are no modern equivalents to the ancient coins (an obolo was one sixth of a drachma, a mina was one hundred drachmae). Words like *mulatto* and *Jewess,* even though offensive today, were kept to maintain historical accuracy.

Narrative discrepancies were not corrected. A few examples include: a priest who walks out of the Temple with an acolyte but is still there when Chrysis appears; Chrysis telling Demetrios she is not Jewish although all other references to her life make it clear that she is; courtesans dressed in 19th Century undergarments; and allusions to medieval knights and court jesters.

As we read through assorted English editions of *Aphrodite* and *The Songs of Bilitis,* we noted that each translator included in his foreword a declaration of how faithful he was to the original. Yet, because all the translations were done from the early 1900s through the 1930s (a later edition from 1950 used one of the same translations, but did not bother with attributions), some of the sexual and moral conventions of the time prevented the use of certain words and scenes. For example, one translator used the words *bosom* instead of *breast,* and *flanks* instead of *thighs.* Others, when describing a frieze depicting bestiality, described it in terms more befitting a circus than an orgy. Circumlocutions were also used when describing sexual intercourse and masturbation.

None of the editions indicated which French text was used as the basis for translation. We found chapters and dialogue inserted into the English texts that were not in the original French editions and chapters that ended paragraphs before they should. Thus, these translations of *Aphrodite* and *The Songs of Bilitis* are the first English versions that try to accurately reflect the original French editions almost one hundred years after their publication.

-Dorothy Kavka, September, 1994

SOURCES

Clive, Henry Peter. *Pierre Louÿs (1870-1925): A Biography.* Oxford: Claredon Press, Oxford University Press, 1978.

The Collected Works of Pierre Louÿs. Translated by Mitchell S. Buck. New York: Liveright Publishing Corporation, 1932. "Foreword" (pp. xii-xii); "Notes to Aphrodite" (pp. 153-155); "Notes to the Songs of Bilitis" (pp. 303-307)

Harvey, Paul. *Oxford Companion to French Literature.* Oxford: Clarendon Press, 1959 (p. 426)

Niederauer, David J. *Pierre Louÿs: His Life and Art.* Canadian Federation for the Humanities, 1981.

"Pierre Louÿs," Stanley Kunitz. Twentieth *Century Authors, A Biographical Dictionary of Modern Authors.* New York: H.W. Wilson Co., 1942 (pp.849-850)

"Pierre Louÿs," David J. Niederauer. *Encyclopedia of World Literature in the 20th Century.* Rev. Ed., New York: Ungar, 1981 (p. 334)

From *Aphrodite*, 1896 edition.

I. CHRYSIS

Couchée sur la poitrine, les coudes en avant, les pieds écartés et la joue dans la main, elle piquait de petits trous symétriques dans un oreiller de lin vert, avec une longue épingle d'or.

Depuis qu'elle s'était éveillée, deux heures après le milieu du jour, et toute lasse d'avoirs trop dormi, elle était restée seule sur le lit en désordre, couverte seulement d'un côté par un vaste flot de cheveux.

Cette chevelure était éclatante et profonde, douce comme une fourrure fauve, plus longue qu'une aile, souple, innombrable, animée, pleine de chaleur. Elle couvrait la moitié du dos, s'étendait sous le ventre nu, brillait encore auprès des genou, en boucle épaisse et arrondie. La jeune femme était enroulée dans cette toison preécieuse, dont les reflets mordorés étaient presque métalliques et l'avaient fait nommer Chrysis par les courtisanes d'Alexandrie.

Ce n'étaient pas les cheveux lisses des Syriaques de la cour, ni les cheveus teints des Asiatiques, ni les cheveux bruns et noirs des filles d'Égypte. C'étaient ceux d'une race aryenne, des Galiléennes d'au-delà des sables.

Chrysis. Elle aimait ce nom-là. Les jeunes gens qui venaient la voir l'appelaient Chrysé comme Aphrodite, dans les vers qu'ils mettaient à sa porte, avec des guirlandes de roses, le matin. Elle ne croyait pas à Aphrodite, mais elle aimait qu'on lui comparât la déesse, et elle allait quelquefois au temple, pour lui donner, comme à une amie, des boîtes de parfums et des voiles bleus.

From *Les Chansons de Bilitis*, 1900 edition.

L'ARBRE

Je me suis dévêtue pour monter à un arbre; mes cuisses nues embrassaient l'écorce lisse et humide; mes sandals marchaient sur les branches.

Tout en haut, mais encore sous les feuilles et à l'ombre de la chaleur, je me suis mise à cheval sur une fourche écartée en balançant mes pieds dans le vide.

Il avait plu. Des gouttes d'eau tombaient et coulaient sur ma peau. Mes mains étaient tachées de mousse, et mes orteils étaient rouges, à cause des fleurs écrasées.

Je sentais le bel arbre vivre quand le vent passait au travers; alors je serrais mes jambes davantage et j'appliquais mes lèvres ouvertes sur la nuque chevelue d'un rameau.

A PARTIAL LISTING OF WORKS BY PIERRE LOUŸS

APHRODITE

To
Albert Besnard
A token of profound admiration and revered friendship.
-P.L.

Pierre Louÿs

CONTENTS

Aphrodite

BOOK FOUR

BOOK FIVE

Pierre Louÿs

INTRODUCTION

The ruins of the Greek world themselves teach us how life in the modern world could be made bearable.

-Richard Wagner

The learned Prodicus of Ceos flourished toward the end of the first century (before our time) and wrote the well-known apology that St. Basil recommended for Christian mediation: *Hercules between virtue and voluptuousness.* We know that Hercules opted for the first, which permitted him to accomplish a certain number of great crimes against the Hind, the Amazons, the Golden Apples, and the Giants.

If Prodicus had left it at that, he would have written only a fable with a rather easy symbolism; but he was a good philosopher, and his collection of stories, *The Hours,* was divided into three parts, each corresponding to three stages of life, and each illustrating the moral truths that underlie the various characters. For little children, he took pleasure in using the austere choice of Hercules as an example; for young men, he doubtless recounted the sensuous choice of Paris; and to mature men, I imagine, he spoke a little like this:

"One day Ulysses was wandering about, hunting at the foot of the Delphi mountains, when along the way he met two virgins, hand in hand. One had hair like violets, with clear eyes and somber lips; she said to him: 'I am Arete.' The other one had faintly colored eyelids, delicate hands and budding breasts; she said to him: 'I am Tryphe.' And together they said: 'Choose between us.' But the artful Ulysses wisely responded: 'How could I choose? You are inseparable. The eyes that have seen you pass by, one without the other, have only taken in a barren shadow. Just as true virtue does not deprive itself of the infinite joy that sensuality carries with it, so a luxurious life would be spoiled without a certain grandeur of the soul. I will follow you both. Show me the way.' As soon as he had finished, the two visions merged and Ulysses knew that he had spoken to the magnificent goddess Aphrodite."

*

* *

The first character of this novel, whose pages you are going to leaf through, is a woman, a courtesan from antiquity; but let the reader be assured: she will not be reformed.

She will not be loved by a monk, or a prophet, or a god. In today's literature, that is an original idea.

As a courtesan, she will be as frank, as passionate, as filled with pride as any human being who has a vocation and has taken a place, freely chosen, in society. She will have the desire to rise to the top. She will never even imagine that her life would have need of an excuse or secrecy. But this demands an explanation.

Until today, modern writers who have addressed to a public less informed than young girls and high school students, have adopted a tedious strategy, the hypocrisy of which offends me: "I have painted sensuality just as it is," they say, "in order to exalt virtue." Right from the beginning of this novel, whose intrigue unfolds in Alexandria, I absolutely refuse to commit this anachronism.

For the Greeks, love was, with all its consequences, the most virtuous and the most fertile in grandeur. They never attached the concept of shamefulness and immodesty to it that the Israelite tradition, along with the Christian doctrine, have introduced among us. Herodotus *(I.x.)* tells us very simply: "Among some barbaric people, it is a disgrace to appear naked." When the Greeks or the Latins wanted to insult a man who frequented women of pleasure, they called them μοιχοσ or *moechus,* which means nothing other than *adulterer.* When a man and a woman, who were not bound to anyone else, however young, coupled, even in public, they were not considered a harm to anyone and went about freely.

We can see that the life of the ancients can not be judged by the moral ideas that come to us today from Geneva.

As for me, I have written this book with the simplicity that an Athenian would have brought to the narration of the same adventures. I hope that it is read in the same spirit.

When judging the ancient Greeks by ideas presently held, *not one single* accurate translation of their greatest writers could be left in the hands of a tenth-grade student. If M. Mounet-Sully played his Oedipus role without omissions, the police would have halted his production. If M. Leconte de Lisle had not censored *Theocritos* out of prudence, his version would have been seized the same day it was put on sale. Do we not consider Aristophanes exceptional?

But we have fourteen hundred and forty important fragments and comedies from one hundred and thirty-two other Greek poets, some of whom, such as Alexis, Philetas, Strattis, Eubulus, and Cratinus, have left us wonderful verses, and no one has yet dared to translate this shameless and sublime collection.

The teachings of a few philosophers who criticized sexual gratification are always cited in defense of Greek morals. There is a confusion here. Those few moralists indiscriminately condemned the excess of all the senses; for them, there was no difference between the orgy of the bed and that of the table. While today someone orders with impunity a six Louis dinner in a Parisian restaurant for only himself, he would have been judged no less guilty than another who made a too intimate tryst in the middle of the street, and who, by existing laws, would be forced to spend a year in prison. Moreover, these austere philosophers were generally regarded as demented and dangerous people by ancient society; they were ridiculed on the stage, beaten on the streets, used by tyrants to serve as their royal fools, and the citizens at large exiled them when they were deemed to be unworthy of capital punishment.

Modern educators, since the Renaissance to the present day, have represented, by a conscious and willful deceit, the ancient morality as the inspiration for their narrowly defined virtues. If this morality was truly great, if it were worthy to serve as a model that must be followed, it is precisely because no other better distinguishes the just from the unjust according to the criterion of beauty — to proclaim the right of every man to seek individual happiness within the limits set by the similar rights of others and to declare that there is nothing under the sun more sacred than physical love, nothing more beautiful than the human body.

Such was the morality of the people who built the Acropolis; and if I add that it has remained that of every great mind, I have only verified common knowledge, so often has it been proven that the superior intellects of artists, writers, warriors, or statesmen have never held its noble tolerance to be illicit. Aristotle made his debut by squandering his inheritance on courtesans; Sappho gave her name to a special vice; Caesar was the *moechus calvus;* — but we do not imagine Racine abstaining from the women of the theater, or Napoleon practicing celibacy. Mirabeau's fictions, Chenier's Greek verses, Diderot's correspondence, and Montesquieu's pamphlets even equaled Catullus in their daring. And from Buffon, the most severe, the most pious, the most diligent of all French writers, do we want to know which dictum he intended to recommend for romantic liaisons: "Love! Why are you the cause for happiness of all human beings and of the unhappiness of man? It is because in this passion, *only the physical* is good, and morals have no value."

*
*   *

Where does this come from? And how does it happen that the great Greek sensuality has remained, cutting through the confusion of ancient ideas, like a beam of light on the heads of the most noble?

It is because sensuality is a condition, mysterious but necessary and creative of the intellectual process. Those who have not felt the demands of the flesh to their fullest, either in loving or hating them, are incapable of comprehending the extent of the demands of the mind. Just as the beauty of the soul brightens the face, so too only the virility of the body nourishes the brain. The worst insult that Delacroix threw at those who jeered Rubens and disparaged Ingres was this terrible word: "Eunuchs!"

Better yet, it seems that the genius of the people, like that of individuals, lies in being sensual above all else. All the cities that have reigned over the world, Babylon, Alexandria, Athens, Rome, Venice, Paris, have been, as a general rule, all the more licentious as they were powerful, as if their dissoluteness was necessary to their splendor. The cities where the legislator aspired to implant an unnatural virtue, limited and sterile, saw themselves, from the beginning, condemned to total destruction. It happened like that of Lacedaemonia which, in the midst of the most amazing vigor that had ever elevated the human soul, between Corinth and Alexandria, between Syracuse and Miletus, left us neither a poet, a painter, a philosopher, a historian, nor a scientist, and hardly the popular reputation of a sort of a Bobillot who met his death, along with three hundred men, in a narrow mountain pass without even gaining victory. And that is why, after two thousand years measuring the devastation of the Spartan virtue, we can, according to Renan's exhortation: "Curse the ground where dwelled this mistress of grave errors and insult her because she is no more."

*

*   *

Will we ever see the days of Ephesus and of Cyrene return? Alas! The modern world succumbs to an invasion of ugliness. Civilizations go back toward the north, entering into the mist, the cold, and the mud. What darkness! People dressed in black circulate in the polluted streets. What are they thinking about? We no longer know; but our twenty-five years shudder at being exiled among old men.

At least, be it permitted to those who will regret forever not having known this youth intoxicated from the world that we call ancient life. It allows them to live again, through a fertile illusion, in a time when human nakedness (a form more perfect than we can perceive or even conceive since we believe it to be in the image of God) could be revealed through the features of a sacred courtesan in front of twenty thousand pilgrims spread over the shores of the Eleusis; the most sensual love, the divine love that gave birth to us, was without stain, without shame, without sin. It allows them to forget the eighteen barbarous centuries, hypocritical and ugly; to rise from the pond to the source; to come back reverently to the original beauty; to rebuild the Great Temple to the sound of magical flutes; and to consecrate enthusiastically to the sanctuaries of the true faith their hearts forever enraptured by the immortal Aphrodite.

-Pierre Louÿs

BOOK ONE

CHRYSIS

L YING on her breast, her elbows propped up, her feet spread apart and her cheek resting in her hand, she made tiny symmetrical pinpricks in the green linen pillow with a long golden hairpin.

Since she had awakened, two hours after noon and exhausted from having slept too much, she had remained alone on the disheveled bed, covered only on one side by a vast torrent of hair.

This hair was sparkling and full, sleek like a copper-colored fur, longer than a wing; it stretched out under her belly and glittered even as far as her knees in thick, rounded curls. The young woman was cocooned in this precious fleece whose bronze-colored, almost metallic reflections had given her the name of Chrysis by the courtesans of Alexandria.

It was not the glossy hair of the Syrians of the court nor the tinted hair of the Asians, nor the brownish-black hair of the daughters of Egypt. It was that of an Aryan race, of the Galilaeans from beyond the sands.

Chrysis. She loved that name. The young men who came to see her called her Chrysé-like-Aphrodite in the verses that they left hanging on her door every morning, along with garlands of roses. She did not believe in Aphrodite but she enjoyed them comparing her to the goddess, and she sometimes went to the temple to offer her, as if she were a friend, boxes of perfume and blue veils.

She was born on the shores of Lake Gennesaret in a country of shadow and sun, overrun with oldeander. Her mother went out in the evening to await the travelers and merchants on the road to Jerusalem and gave herself to them in the grass, in the midst of the pastoral silence. She was a woman much loved in Galilee. The priests did not turn away from her door because she was charitable and pious; the sacrificial lambs were always paid for by her; the blessings of the Eternal spread out over her house. But, when she became pregnant, her condition was a scandal because she had no husband. A man who was well known for having the gift of prophecy said that she would give birth to a daughter who would one day carry "the wealth and the faith of a people" around her neck. She did not understand how that could be, but she named the baby Sarah — that is to say, *Princess* in Hebrew. And that silenced those who slandered her.

Chrysis had never known about this, the soothsayer having told her mother how dangerous it is to reveal to people the prophecies that involve them. She knew nothing about her future; that is why she often thought about it. She recalled little of her childhood and did not like to talk about it. The only really distinct sensation that had remained with her was the dread and anxiety that was caused by the daily nervous surveillance of her mother who never allowed her any freedom. When the time came for her mother to leave the house, she shut Chrysis up, alone, in their room for hours on end. She remembered, too, the round window out of which she saw the waters of the lake, the bluish countryside, the transparent sky, the light air of the Galilaean country. The house was surrounded by pink flax and fruit trees. Some prickly caper shrubs straightened up their green heads as if by accident over the fine haze of the grasses. Little girls bathed in the clear stream where they found red shellfish under the tufts of flowering laurel. And there were flowers on the water, flowers over the meadow, and majestic lilies on the mountains.

She was twelve years old when she escaped to follow a troop of young horsemen who were going to Tyre as ivory merchants. She accosted them in front of a well. They had adorned their long-tailed horses with multicolored tassels. She remembered clearly how they carried her away, pale with joy, on their mounts and how they stopped a second time during the night, a night so bright that not one star could be seen.

Neither had she forgotten the entrance into Tyre: she led the way on the large saddlebags of a packhorse, holding on, her fists filled with the mane, proudly letting her dangling bare calves be seen in order to show the women of the village that she had blood down the length of her legs. The same night they left for Egypt. She followed the ivory merchants to the market at Alexandria.

And it was there, in a small white house with a terrace and slender columns, that they had left her, two months later, with her bronze mirror, some rugs, new cushions, and a beautiful Hindu slave who knew how to style a courtesan's hair. Some others had come the evening of their departure, and still others the next day.

Since she lived in the extreme eastern quarter where the young Greeks of Bruchion disdained to frequent, and like her mother, for a long time she only knew travelers and merchants. She did not see her transient lovers again; she knew how to please herself with them and to leave quickly before loving them. However, she had inspired endless passions. Caravan leaders had been seen to sell their merchandise very cheaply so as to remain where she was and ruined themselves within several nights. With their fortunes, she had bought jewels and bed pillows, rare perfumes, flowered robes, and four slaves.

She had come to understand many foreign languages and knew stories from all the countries. The Assyrians had told her of the loves of Douzi and Ishtar; the Phoenicians those of Ashtoreth and Adonis. The young Greek women of the isles had recounted the legend of Iphis to her while teaching her exotic caresses which had surprised her at first, but afterwards charmed her to the point where she could no longer go an entire day without them. She also knew the loves of Atlanta and how, following their example, flute players, still virgins, weakened the most robust of men. For seven years, her Hindu slave also patiently taught her, to the last detail, the complex and voluptuous art of the courtesans of Palibothra.

Because love is an art like music. It produces the same emotion — as delicate, as vibrant, perhaps sometimes more intense. And Chrysis, who knew its every rhythm and every subtlety, considered herself, with good reason, a greater artist than Plango herself, who was still the musician of the temple.

Seven years she lived like this, without dreaming of a life happier or more diverse than hers. But a little before she reached her twentieth year, when from a young girl she became a woman, seeing the first defining fold of a charming maturity under her breasts, she was suddenly filled with a singular desire.

And one morning as she woke up, two hours after noon, exhausted from having slept too much, she turned over again on her breast across the bed, her feet spread apart, resting her cheek in her hand and, with a long golden hairpin, pierced her green linen pillow, leaving tiny symmetrical holes.

She was deep in thought. First there were four little holes that made a square and a hole in the middle. Then four other holes making a bigger square. Then she tried to make a circle ...But it was more difficult. Then she made the pinpricks haphazardly and began to shout:

"Djala! Djala!"

Djala was her Hindu slave whose name was Djalant-achtchandrapchapala, which means: "Shimmering-as-the-image-of-the-moon-over-the-water." Chrysis was too lazy to say the whole name.

The slave entered and stayed near the door without shutting it all the way.

"Djala, who came here yesterday?"

"Do you not know?"

"No. I did not look at him. Was he good? I think that I was asleep the entire time. I was exhausted. I no longer remember anything about it. What time did he leave? Early this morning?"

"At sunrise, he said …"

"What did he leave me? Is it a lot? No — don't tell me. It doesn't matter to me. What did he say? Has no one come since he left? Will he return? Give me my bracelets."

The slave brought out an ornamental box, but Chrysis did not even look at it and, raising her arms as high as she could, she said:

"Ah! Djala. Ah! Djala! …I would like some extraordinary affair."

"Everything is extraordinary," said Djala, "or nothing. One day looks like another."

"Oh no. Long ago it was not like that. In every country in the world the gods descended to the earth and made love to mortal women. Ah! On what beds must they be expected, in what forests must they be sought, those who are a little more than men? What prayers must be said in order for them to come, those who will teach me something or who will make me forget everything? And if the gods no longer desire to come to Earth, if they are dead or if they are too old, Djala, will I also die without having seen a man who brings tragic events into my life?"

She turned over on her back, wringing her hands, one under the other.

"If someone loved me, it seems to me that I would have a great deal of pleasure making him suffer until he died from it. Those who come to me are not worthy of tears. And then too, it is my fault — it is I who call them; how could they love me?"

"Which bracelet today?"

"I will wear them all. But leave me. I want to be alone. Go sit on the steps by the door, and if anyone comes say that I am with my lover, a black slave whom I pay ...Go."

"You will not go out?"

"Yes, I will go out alone — I will dress myself alone. I will not return. Go! Go!"

She dropped one leg on to the carpet and stretched out her body until she was standing up. Djala had left, quietly.

Chrysis sauntered around the room, her hands clasped around the back of her neck, entirely engrossed in the sensuous pleasure of putting her bare feet down on the flagstones where her perspiration crystallized. Then she stepped into her bath.

Looking at herself through the water delighted her. She saw herself like a magnificent mother-of-pearl shell open on a craggy ledge. Her skin became smooth and perfect; the lines of her legs stretched out in a blue light; her entire body was more supple; she no longer recognized her own hands. Her body was so relaxed that she raised herself up on two fingers and let herself float for a moment and softly fell back on the marble, a slight eddy striking her chin. The water penetrated her ears with the provocation of a kiss.

During her bath Chrysis set about adoring herself. Every part of her body became, one after another, the object of tender admiration and of a prolonged caress. She played a thousand fascinating games with her hair and her breasts. Sometimes she even allowed herself a more direct satisfaction to her perpetual desires, and there was no resting place that appeared more favorable for the calculated slowness of that exquisite relief.

The day came to an end and she stood up in the bathing pool, got out of the water and walked toward the door. The trace of her footsteps glistened on the stone. Staggering as if she were exhausted, she opened the door wide and stopped, her arm outstretched on the latch. After Djala had seen her, she went back inside and stood wet, near her bed. She said to the slave:

"Dry me."

The Malabar woman took a large sponge in her hand and pressed it against the soft golden hair of Chrysis. Her hair, heavy with water, streamed down her back and the slave dried it, spread it out, and tossed it gently. Then, plunging the sponge into a jar of oil, she caressed her mistress up to her neck before rubbing her with a rough cloth that reddened her supple skin.

Chrysis sank shivering into the coolness of a marble seat and murmured:

"Fix my hair."

In the rays of the evening horizon, her hair, still moist and heavy, shimmered like a sudden shower illuminated by the sun. The slave took a handful and twisted it. She made it turn upon itself like a giant metal serpent, pierced as if by arrows of erect golden hairpins. She coiled the hair around a narrow green band, crisscrossed three times to magnify the reflections of the silk. Chrysis held, far from her, a mirror of polished copper. She gazed distractedly at the black hands of the slave as they moved in the thick hair, turned the wisps, captured the stray strands, and sculpted the head of hair like a vase of twisted clay. When all was done, Djala kneeled down in front of her mistress and closely shaved the arched pubic mound so that to those who would see her, the young woman might have all the purity of a statue.

Chrysis became more serious and said in a subdued voice:

"Adorn me."

A small rosewood box that came from the isle of Dioscoris contained makeup of every color. With a paint brush made of camel-hair, the slave took a bit of a black paste and placed it on the beautiful curved long lashes so that the eyes of Chrysis appeared bluer. Two unhesitating strokes of a pencil lengthened and softened them. A bluish powder covered the eyelids and two spots of vivid vermilion accentuated the corners near the tear ducts. It was necessary, in order to fix the colors, to spread a cool lotion over her face and breast. With a soft feather dipped in white pigment, Djala painted white streaks the length of Chrysis' arms and on her neck; with a tiny paintbrush swollen with crimson, she covered her mouth as if with blood and grazed the points of her breasts. Her fingers, which had spread a light cloud of red powder over her cheeks, marked at the top of the thighs the three deep folds of the waist, and on the rounded buttocks, the two sometimes shifting dimples. Then with a pad of tinted leather, she gave a hint of color to the elbows and polished each fingernail. The grooming was finished.

Then Chrysis smiled and said to the Hindu:

"Sing to me."

Chrysis remained seated, stiffly arched forward in her marble armchair. Her hairpins formed a golden radiance behind her head. Her hands, placed on her throat, spread out between her shoulders the red necklace of her painted fingernails, and her white feet were brought together on the stone.

Djala, crouching close to the wall, recalled some love songs from India:

"Chrysis ..."

She sang in a monotone.

"Chrysis, your hair is like a swarm of bees settled on a tree. The warm southern wind penetrates it with the dew from the struggles of love and the moist perfume of the flowers of the night."

The young woman alternated, using a voice sweeter and slower:

"My hair is like an infinite river in the plain where the evening, set ablaze, flows away."

And they sang, one after the other:

"Your eyes are like blue water-lilies without stems, motionless on the ponds."

"My eyes are shaded by my lashes like deep lakes under dark branches."

"Your lips are two delicate flowers, where the blood of a doe has fallen."

"My lips are the edges of a fiery wound."

"Your tongue is the bloody dagger which has made a wound of your mouth."

"My tongue is encrusted with precious stones. It is red from mirroring my lips."

"Your arms are curved like two ivory shields and your armpits are two mouths."

"My arms are elongated like two lily stems where my fingers glisten like five petals."

"Your thighs are the trunks of two white elephants that carry your feet as if they were two red flowers."

"My feet are two water-lily leaves on the water; my thighs are two swollen water-lily buds."

"Your breasts are two small rounded silver shields whose points were dipped in blood."

"My breasts are the moon and the reflection of the moon on the water."

"Your navel is a deep well in a desert of rosy sand and your belly is a young kid sleeping under the breast of its mother."

"My navel is a round pearl under an inverted cup and my groin is the bright light from the crescent of Phoebe beneath the forests."

There was a silence — the slave raised her hands and bent forward. The courtesan continued:

"She is like a crimson flower, full of honey and fragrances."

"She is like a hydra of the sea, lively and luxurious, open in the night."

"She is a moist cave, a refuge, always warm, the Asylum where man rests from the march toward death."

The prostrate woman murmured very low:

"She is terrifying. It is the face of Medusa."

Chrysis placed her foot on the back of the slave's neck and said, trembling:

"Djala."

*

*   *

Little by little, the night had come, but the moon was so bright that the room was flooded with a bluish splendor.

Chrysis, naked, looked at her body where the reflections remained motionless and where the shadows fell, very dark.

She rose abruptly:

"Djala, what were we thinking about! It is night and I have not yet left. There will be only sleeping sailors on the Heptastadion. Tell me, Djala, am I beautiful?

"Tell me, Djala, am I more beautiful than ever, tonight? Do you not find me the most beautiful woman in Alexandria? Will he not follow me like a dog, he who will pass through the sidelong glance of my eyes? Will I not make of him what pleases me — a slave if it is my whim — and can I not expect, from the first whom I meet, the most vile obedience? Dress me, Djala."

Around Chrysis' arms two silver serpents entwined themselves. On her feet the soles of her sandals were held on her brown legs by strips of crossed leather. Around her belly she herself cinched a young girl's sash that did not reach to her breasts. On her ears she put large circular hoops; on her fingers, rings and signets; on her neck, three necklaces of golden phalli chiseled at Paphos by the priests.

She looked at herself for some time, naked like this among her jewels; then, drawing from a chest an enormous loosely woven robe of yellow linen that she had left folded, she wrapped it around her, draping herself from head to toe. The diagonal folds made furrows of what little was seen of her body through the light gauze. One of her elbows jutted out from under the clinging tunic and the other

39

arm, which she had left bare, carried the long train, raised in order to keep it from dragging in the dust.

She took her fan of feathers in her hand and left nonchalantly.

Standing on the steps of the threshold, her hand leaning on the white wall, only Djala saw the courtesan leave.

She walked slowly along the houses in the deserted streets where the moonlight fell. A small fluid shadow quivered behind her steps.

ON THE PIER OF ALEXANDRIA

O N the pier of Alexandria, a woman stood singing. By
her side were two flute players sitting on the white
railing.

The Satyrs pursued into the woods
 The light footsteps of the mountain nymphs.
They chased the nymphs over the mountains,
 They filled their eyes with fright,
They seized their hair in the wind,
 They grasped their breasts on the run,
And bent their warm torsos backwards
 On to the green dew-covered moss,
And the beautiful bodies, the half-divine beautiful bodies,

Flung outward from the pain . . .
  Eros cries out from your lips, Oh, women!
The desire, mournful and sweet!

The flute players repeated:
"Eros!
Eros!"

and sighed into their double reeds.

Cybele pursued across the plain
  Attis, handsome as Apollo.
Eros had struck her to the heart, and for him,
  Oh, Totoi! but not him for her.
As for being loved, cruel god, wicked Eros,
  You counsel only hatred.
Across the meadows, the vast and distant fields
  Cybele chased Attys;
And because she adored the disdainful one
  She imbued into his veins
The vast cold breath, the breath of death.
  Oh, Desire mournful and sweet!

"Eros!
Eros!"

*

*   *

Shrill cries sprung from the flutes.

  The Goat-foot pursued until the river
    The Syrinx, daughter of the spring.
  The pale Eros, who loves the taste of tears,
    Kissed her as she fled, cheek to cheek;
  And the frail shadow of the drowned virgin
    Shudders, reeds upon the waters.
  But Eros owns the world and the gods.
    He owns even death itself.
  Over the watery tomb he gathered for us

All the rushes, and with them made a flute.
It is a dead soul who weeps here, women,
The Desire mournful and sweet.

*

*   *

While the flutes continued the slow refrain of the last verse, the singer held out her hand to the passersby who formed a circle around her and received four obols which she slipped into her shoes.

Little by little, the crowd dispersed, curious themselves to watch their countless numbers pass by. The noise of footsteps and voices covered even the roar of the sea. Sailors, shoulders bent, pulled small boats onto the quay. The women fruit vendors passed by, their wide baskets full in their arms. Beggars pleaded with a trembling hand. Donkeys laden with full goatskin bottles trotted in front of the sticks of their drivers. But it was approaching sunset, and an idle throng, larger than the moving crowd, covered the pier. Groups were formed here and there and the women wandered between them. People heard the well-known silhouettes called by name. The young men contemplated the philosophers, who were contemplating the courtesans.

The courtesans were from every class and of every circumstance, from the most famous dressed in light silks and wearing shoes of golden leather, to the most miserable who walked with bare feet. The poor ones were not less beautiful than the others, only less fortunate, and the attention of the philosophers by preference leaned toward those whose grace was not altered by the artifice of tight sashes and the hindrance of jewelry. As it was the eve of the Festival of Aphrodite, these women had full license to choose the garment which made them look their best, and some of the younger had even risked wearing nothing at all. But their nudity did not shock anyone, because they would not have exposed any detail of their bodies to the sun if one of them could be singled out by the least blemish that might have given rise to the mockery of the married women.

"Tryphera! Tryphera!"

And a young courtesan with a joyful countenance jostled some passerby in order to rejoin a girlfriend of whom she had caught a glimpse in the crowd.

"Tryphera! Are you invited?"

"Where is it, Seso?"

"At the home of Bacchis."

"Not yet. Is she giving a dinner?"

"A dinner? A banquet, my dear. She is going to free her most beautiful slave, Aphrodisia, on the second day of the festival."

"At last! She finally noticed that they no longer come because of her, only for her slave."

"I think she has seen nothing. It is a fantasy of old Cheres, the ship captain from the quay. He wanted to buy the girl for ten minae; Bacchis refused. Twenty minae; she still refused."

"She is crazy."

"What do you want? It was her ambition to have a freed slave. Besides, she was right to bargain. Cheres will give thirty-five minae, and for that price the girl is freed."

"Thirty-five minae? Three thousand, five hundred drachmae for a black woman?

"She is white."

"Yes, but her mother is black."

"Bacchis declared she would not give her a cheaper price and old Cheres is so in love that he consented."

"Is he at least invited?"

"No! Aphrodisia will be served at the banquet as the last dish after the fruit. Each one will take what he desires and it is only on the next day that they must hand her over to Cheres; but I am afraid she will be exhausted ..."

"Don't worry about her! With him she will have time to recover. I know him, Seso. I watched him sleep."

They laughed together at Cheres. Then they traded compliments.

"You have a pretty gown," said Seso. "Did you do the embroidery yourself?"

Tryphera's garment was a thin material, green with a gray grayish-blue cast and entirely embroidered with large iris flowers. A garnet mounted in gold gathered it into elongated pleats at the end of her left shoulder. The robe fell back down over her shoulder between her breasts, leaving the right side of her body bare down to a mesh sash. A narrow slit that opened and closed with each step revealed only the whiteness of her leg.

"Seso!" said another voice. "Seso and Tryphera, come, if you do not know what to do. I am going to look for my name written on the Ceramic Wall."

"Mousarion! Where are you coming from, little one?"

"From Pharos. There is no one down there."

"What are saying? It is so crowded that you only need to throw in a line to catch any one of them."

"No flat fish for me. Anyway, I am going to the Wall. Come."

On the way, Seso recounted the recent plans for the banquet at the house of Bacchis.

"Ah! At the house of Bacchis!" cried Mousarion. "You remember the last dinner, Tryphera: all the things they said about Chrysis?"

"You must not repeat it. Seso is her friend."

Mousarion bit her lip, but Seso was already worried.

"What? What did they say?"

"Oh! Some wicked remarks."

"They can talk," declared Seso. "She is worth more than the three of us put together. I know that we will never see our lovers again the day she decides to leave her neighborhood and go to Bruchion."

"Oh! Oh!"

"That is true. I would do any foolish thing for that woman. There is no one more beautiful here, believe me."

The three young women had arrived in front of the Ceramic Wall. From one end to the other of the enormous white surface inscriptions, one following after another, were written in black. When a lover desired to present himself to a courtesan it was sufficient for him to write their two names along with the price which he proposed. If the man and the money were acknowledged as worthy, the woman remained standing under the proposition, waiting for the author to return.

"Look, Seso," said Tryphera, laughing. "Who is the malicious prankster who wrote that?"

And they read, in large letters:

BACCHIS
THERSITES
TWO OBOLS

"That should not be allowed — to make fun of women in such a way. As for me, if it were a remark about me, I would have already made an investigation."

But farther along, Seso stopped before a more serious inscription.

SESO OF CNIDUS
TIMON SON OF LYSIAS
ONE MINA

She paled slightly.

"I will stay," she said.

And she leaned against the wall, the passing women looking on enviously.

Some steps further on, Mousarion found an acceptable if not as generous offer. Tryphera returned to the pier alone.

Since the hour was getting late, the crowd was thinning out. However, the three musicians continued to sing and play the flute.

Catching sight of a stranger, whose belly and clothes were a little ridiculous, Tryphera tapped him on the shoulder.

"Ah, little father! I wager you are not an Alexandrian, eh!"

"Quite so, my daughter," responded the good man, "and you have guessed it. You see me totally surprised at the town and the people."

"Are you from Boubastis?"

"No. From Cabasa. I came here to sell grain and I will return tomorrow richer by fifty-two minae. Thanks be given to the gods, the year has been good."

Tryphera suddenly felt full of interest for this merchant.

"My child," he replied timidly, "you can make me very happy. I would not like to return tomorrow to Cabasa without telling to my wife and my three daughters that I have seen some famous men. You must know some of these celebrated men, don't you?"

"Some of them" she said laughing.

"Good. Tell me their names as they pass by. I am certain that I have met on the street, within the last two days, the most illustrious philosophers and the most influential officials. I despair of not knowing them."

"You will be satisfied. Here is Naucrates."

"Who is this Naucrates?"

"He is a philosopher."

"And what does he teach?"

"That one must be silent."

"By Zeus, here is a doctrine which does not demand a great genius and such a philosophy does not please me at all."

"Here is Phrasilas."

"Who is this Phrasilas?"

"He is a fool."

"Then why don't you let him go by?"

"Because others hold him in high regard."

"And what does he say?"

"He says everything with a smile, which permits him to have his mistakes understood as voluntary and his vulgarities as artful.

He turns everything to his advantage. The world allows itself to be deceived."

"This is too much for me and I do not quite understand you. Besides, the face of this Phrasilas is marked with hypocrisy."

"Here is Philodemos."

"The strategian?"

"No. A Latin poet who writes in Greek."

"Little one, he is an enemy. I wish I had not seen him."

Then, the whole crowd moved, and a murmur of voices pronounced the same name:

"Demetrios ...Demetrios."

Tryphera climbed up on a railing and in turn said to the merchant:

"Demetrios ...Here is Demetrios. You who wanted to see some celebrated men ... "

"Demetrios? The queen's lover? Is it possible?"

"Yes, you are in luck. He never goes out. Since I have been in Alexandria, this is the first time I have seen him on the pier."

"Where is he?"

"He is the one who is leaning over in order to see the wharf."

"There are two who are leaning over."

"He is the one in blue."

"I do not see him clearly. He has his back turned to us."

"Did you know that he is the sculptor for whom the queen served as a model when he sculpted Aphrodite of the temple?"

"They say he is the royal lover. They say he is the master of Egypt."

"And he is as handsome as Apollo."

"Ah! There he is turning around. I am happy that I came. I will be able to say that I have seen him. I have heard many things about him. It appears that no woman has ever been able to resist him. He has had many affairs, has he not? How does it happen that the queen has not been informed about them?"

"Like us, the queen knows. She loves him too much to speak to him about them. She is afraid that he might return to Rhodes, to his master, Pherecrates. He is as powerful as she and she is the one who wanted him."

"He does not appear happy. Why does he look so sad? It seems to me I would be happy if I were he. I would very much like to be like him, if only for one evening..."

The sun had set. The women stared at this man who was the man of their dreams. His elbows leaning on the railing, he remained, without appearing to be conscious of the commotion he caused, listening to the flute players.

The little musicians made one more round for the collection, then, gently, they threw their light flutes over their backs. The singer threw her arms around their necks and all three returned toward town.

After nightfall, in small groups, the other women reentered the vastness of Alexandria and the troop of men followed them, but as they walked all of them turned back toward Demetrios. The last woman who passed him demurely threw him her yellow flower and laughed. Silence spread over the quay.

DEMETRIOS

D EMETRIOS remained alone, resting on his elbows, on the spot abandoned by the musicians. He heard the sound of the sea, the ships slowly creak, and the passing of the wind under the stars. All the town was illuminated by a small dazzling cloud that remained over the moon and the sky was softened by the light.

The young man looked nearby; the tunics of the flute players had left two trails in the dust. He recalled their faces; they were both Ephesians. The eldest had appeared pretty to him, but the youngest was without charm, and, as ugliness caused him pain, he avoided thinking about her.

An object made of ivory gleamed at his feet. He picked it up. It was a writing tablet with a silver stylus dangling from it. The wax was nearly used up, but the words must have been traced over several times so that, the last time, they were etched into the ivory.

He saw only three words written there:

MYRTIS LOVES RHODOCLEIA

He wondered which of the two women owned this ivory tablet and if the one of them was the loved woman or some young unknown woman abandoned at Ephesus. Then, he thought for a moment of rejoining the musicians in order to give back what was, perhaps, the souvenir of some dead beloved. But he could not have found them again without difficulty, and as he already ceased to be interested in them, he casually turned around and threw the small object into the sea.

It fell rapidly, gliding like a white bird, and he heard the lapping made by the water, distant and dark. This brief noise made him feel the vast silence of the wharf.

His back against the cold railing, he tried to drive away every thought and began to look around for other things.

He abhorred his life. He left his house only at the time of day when activity had ceased and returned when the first dawn drew the fishermen and the farmers toward town. The pleasure of seeing only the shadowy world of the town and his own figure became such a sensuous joy for him that he did not remember having seen the midday sun for some months.

He was bored. The queen was dull.

Tonight, he could hardly understand the joy and pride that had filled him three years before, when the queen, seduced perhaps more by the rumors of his beauty than by the reputation of his genius, had ordered him to the palace and announced him at the Evening Gate by the sounding of silver trumpets.

Sometimes this entrance brought to the surface the memory of one of those moments that, because of its excessive sweetness, grew bitter little by little in his soul, to the point of being intolerable. The queen had received him alone in her private apartments, composed of three small, plush rooms that muted the cries of desire. She was lying on her left side, as if hiding in a jumble of greenish silks that bathed the black curls of her hair in crimson reflections. Her young body was clothed in a brazenly pierced costume that she had made to order for herself by a Phrygian courtesan. It left uncovered the twenty-two spots of her skin where caresses are irresistible, so that during one entire night, when she should have exhausted even the last dreams of a romantic imagination, there was no need to take off that costume.

Demetrios, kneeling respectfully, had taken the little foot of Queen Berenice in his hand, kissing it like an object that was precious and sweet.

Then she rose.

Simply, as if she were a beautiful slave who is used as a model, she had undone her tightened sashes, her small ribbons, her undergarments — took off the bracelets from her arms, even the rings from her toes, and she had stood, her open hands in front of her shoulders, lifting her head under a headdress of coral that trembled alongside her cheeks.

She was the daughter of a Ptolemy and of a princess of Syria, descended from all the gods through Astarte, whom the Greeks called Aphrodite. Demetrios knew this and that she was proud of her Olympian lineage. Therefore he was not troubled when the sovereign, without moving, said to him:

"I am Astarte. Take marble and your chisel and display me before the men of Egypt. I want them to worship my image."

Demetrios regarded her and surmised beyond a doubt what naive and inexperienced sensuality excited this young woman's body. "I am the first to worship it," he said and surrounded her with his arms.

The queen was not offended at this abruptness, but drew back as she asked, "You think that you are Adonis, so that you might touch a goddess?"

He replied, "Yes."

She looked at him, smiled a little, and concurred, "You are right."

It was because of this that he became insufferable and his best friends kept their distance from him, but he infatuated the hearts of all women.

When he walked through the hall of the palace, the slaves stopped, the women of the court became silent, and strangers listened to him, for the sound of his voice was so enchanting. He retreated to the queen's quarters, and still they came to make demands of him always under more inventive pretexts. When he wandered through the streets, the folds of his tunic became filled with little notes on which the passerby wrote their names with sweet nothings. He crumpled them up without ever reading them. He was bored with all of this. When his statue of Aphrodite had been put in place, the enclosure was filled at all hours of the night with a crowd of adoring women who came to read his name in the stone and offer their living god doves and roses.

Soon his house was cluttered with gifts which at first he accepted with indifference, but later stopped and refused everything when he understood what was expected of him and that they were treating him like a prostitute. His female slaves even offered themselves. He flogged them and sold them at the flesh market at Rhacotis. Then the male slaves, seduced by presents, opened his door to women he did not know and who, upon his return, he found in front of his bed, leaving no doubt as to their passionate intentions. A few objects of his toilette and of his table disappeared one after another. More than one woman in the town had a sandal or a belt of his, a cup from which he had drunk, even the pits from the fruits he had eaten. If he dropped a flower while walking, he no longer found it behind him. The women would gather even the dust crushed by his shoes.

Not only had this persecution became dangerous and threatened to kill every sensibility in him, but he had arrived at the period of his life where the contemplative man believes in the immediate necessity of dividing his life in half and no longer intermingling the things of the mind with the demands of the senses. The statue of Aphrodite-Astarte provided him with the sublime pretext for this moral conversion. All the beauty that the queen possessed, all that he could invent of the ideal surrounding the supple lines of her body, Demetrios evoked from the marble and from that day, he imagined no other woman on earth could reach the level of his dream. His statue became the object of his desire. He adored her alone and foolishly separated from the flesh the ultimate idea of the goddess, so much the more spiritual than if he had attached her to life.

When he saw the queen in person again, he found all her charms stripped away. For a time she still satisfied his aimless desires, but she was, at the same time, too different from the Other and also too similar. The moment she left his embraces, she fell back, fatigued, and slept. He gazed at her as if she were an intruder, having usurped his bed, and having taken on the resemblance of the loved woman. Her arms were more slender, her breasts more pointed, her hips more narrow than those of the True one. She did not have the three slight folds, forming lines between her groin, that he had chiseled in the marble. It ended by his growing tired of her.

His admirers knew this, and even though he continued to visit her every day, they knew that he had ceased to be in love with Berenice. And the adoration intensified around him. He did not care about it. In fact, the change that he needed was of a different magnitude. It is rare that, between two mistresses, a man does not have an interval in his life where vulgar debauchery tempts and satisfies him. Demetrios surrendered himself to it. When the necessary trips to the palace displeased him more than usual, he went at night to the garden of the sacred courtesans which surrounded the entire temple. The women there did not know him at all. Besides, so many superfluous lovers had wearied them that they no longer had any cries or tears, and, at least there, the satisfaction that he searched for was not interrupted by the wails of a cat in heat which irritated him when he was with the queen.

The conversation that he held with these beautiful sedate people was without reflection and pointless: the visitors of the day, what the weather will be tomorrow, the sweetness of the grass and of the night, were their fascinating subjects. They did not plead with him to expound on his theories of sculpture and did not give their opinions of the Achilles of Scopas. If they happened to thank the lover who chose them or find him well built and to tell him so, he had the right not to believe in their disinterestedness.

Leaving their pious embrace, he went up the steps of the temple and fell, enraptured, before the statue.

Between the slender columns, topped with Ionian scrolls, the goddess appeared alive on a pedestal of rose-colored stone laden with dangling treasures. She was nude and sexual, lightly tinted according to the colors of a woman. She held in one hand a mirror whose handle was fashioned like a phallus and with the other adorned her beauty with a necklace made of seven strands of pearls. One pearl, larger than the others, silvery and elongated, shone between her two breasts like a crescent moon between two rounded clouds.

Demetrios contemplated her tenderly and longed to believe, like the people, that they were the true sacred pearls born from the drops of water that had tumbled into the shell of the Anadyomene.

"Oh divine Sister," he said, "Oh flowery one, oh transfigured one! You are no longer the little Asiatic whom I made your unworthy model. You are her immortal Idea, the terrestrial Soul of Astarte who was the genesis of her race. You blazed within in her ardent eyes, you burned in her sullen lips, you swooned within her soft hands, you panted within her large breasts, you stretched within her clasped legs, long ago, before your birth; that which satisfied the daughter of a fisherman would prostrate you also, goddess, you, the mother of gods and of men, the joy and pain of the world! But I saw you called forth and I captured you, oh marvelous Cytherea! This is not your image, it is you, yourself, to whom I have given your mirror and whom I have covered in pearls, as on the day when you were born from the bleeding sky and the smiling foam of the waters. The dawn, dripping with dew, welcomed you up to the shores of Cyprus with a procession of blue Tritons."

He had just worshiped her thusly, when he walked onto the pier, at the time when the crowd was slipping away, and he heard the cries of the flute's mournful tune. But on this night he had refused the temple courtesans because he caught a glimpse of a couple under the branches, and he was sickened with disgust, revolted to the depths of his soul.

The gentle influence of the night began to overtake him, little by little. He turned his face into the wind passing over the sea that seemed to draw toward Egypt the fragrance from the roses of Amathus.

Lovely feminine forms took shape in his thoughts. A grouping of the three Charities embracing had been requested from him for the garden of the goddess. However, his youthfulness found it repugnant to copy the conventional pose. He dreamed of uniting, on the same block of marble, three graceful movements of a woman: two of the Charities would be clothed, one holding a fan, her eyelids half-closed from the breeze of the swaying feathers; the other dancing among the folds of her robe. The third would be nude, behind her sisters, and, with her arms raised, would be twisting the mass of her curly hair on the nape of her neck.

He created in his mind still other projects such as — to attach to the rocks of the Pharos a black marble Andromeda in front of the surging monster of the sea; to enclose the assembly of Bruchion between the four horses of the rising sun, each one looking like some irate Pegasus — and he greatly rejoiced, intoxicated by the idea that came to him, of a terrified Zagreus facing the approach of the Titans. Ah! How he was seized again by all the beauty! How he tore himself from love! How he "separated from the flesh" the ultimate idea of the goddess! How free he felt, at last!

Now he turned his head toward the quay and saw, shimmering in the distance, the yellow veil of a woman who was walking.

THE PASSERBY

S HE came slowly, her head turned to the side, on to the deserted pier where moonlight fell. A small unsteady shadow flickered in front of her footsteps.

Demetrios watched her come closer.

Diagonal folds streaked what little of her body that could be seen through the light fabric; one of her elbows jutted out from under the close-fitting tunic, and the other arm, which she had left bare, carried the long train, raised high in order to avoid dragging it through the dust.

He recognized, because of her jewels, that she was a courtesan. In order to spare himself the necessity of greeting her, he crossed over quickly.

He did not want to look at her. Wilfully he occupied his thought with the grand sketch of Zagreus. However, his eyes turned again toward the passerby.

Then he saw that she did not stop at all, that she was not concerned with him, that she did not even pretend to look at the sea, nor to raise her veil before her, nor to be absorbed in her thoughts; but that she was simply walking alone and sought nothing other than the coolness of the wind, solitude, release, the faint shiver of silence.

Motionless, Demetrios did not stop looking at her and lost himself in a curious admiration.

She continued to walk like a yellow phantom in the distance, nonchalantly, preceded by the small dark shadow.

He heard, with each step, the faint cry of her shoes in the dust along the way.

She walked until the isle of the Pharos and climbed up on the rocks.

Suddenly, and as if long ago he had loved this stranger, Demetrios ran after her, then stopped, retraced his steps, trembled, grew angry at himself, and tried to leave the pier. However, he only had exerted his will to serve his own pleasure and when it came time to make it act for his own best interests and for the orderliness of his life, he felt himself overwhelmed with impotence and riveted to the spot, his feet heavy as lead.

As he could no longer stop thinking about her, he tried to make excuses for his preoccupation with the distraction which was growing so strong. He believed his feeling of admiration for her graceful bearing was entirely an aesthetic one. He told himself that she would be an ideal model for the Charity holding the fan that he proposed to sketch the next day. Then, unexpectedly, all his thoughts became confused and a crowd of anxious questions about this woman in yellow flooded his mind.

What was she doing on this island at this hour of the night? Why, and for whom, had she gone out so late? Why had she not approached him? She had seen him, surely she had seen him while he walked across the pier. Why, without a word of greeting, had she continued on her way? Rumor had it that certain women sometimes chose the cool hours before dawn to bathe in the sea. But no one bathed at Pharos. The sea was too deep. Besides, it was unlikely that a woman would have covered herself with jewels only to go bathing ... Then, who drew her so far from away Rhacotis? Some dissolute young man, desirous of variety, who for an instant, took the large rocks, polished by the waves, as a bed?

Demetrios wanted to reassure himself. But already the young woman was returning, with the same footsteps, steady and soft, her entire face illuminated by the gentle lunar light, and she swept, with the tip of her fan, the dust from the railing.

THE MIRROR, THE COMB,
AND THE NECKLACE

SHE had a special sort of beauty. Her hair resembled two masses of gold, but it was too plentiful and fell heavily back from her forehead, making two deep waves, filled with darkness, that engulfed her ears and entwined around the nape of her neck. Her nose was delicate, with slender nostrils that sometimes quivered above full lips, painted to their curved and lively corners. The supple line of her body undulated with each step, animated from the swaying of free-moving breasts, or from the rolling of her beautiful hips over which her rounded waist bent.

When she was no more than ten steps from the young man, she turned and looked at him. Demetrios trembled. They were extraordinary eyes; blue, but deep and glowing, at the same time, moist, languid, with tears and on fire, and almost closed under the heaviness of her lashes and eyelids. They looked out, these eyes, like sirens singing; whoever traversed their light was unable to resist. She knew it and she used their power skillfully. She counted, further still, on her simulated indifference to him whom so much true love had not been able to sincerely touch.

The navigators who have travelled the carmine seas, beyond the Ganges, recount that they have seen, under the waters, rocks that are of lodestone. When ships pass near them, the nails and ironwork tear themselves away toward the submerged cliffs and unite with them forever. And what was once a rapid ship, a dwelling, a living being, becomes no more than a flotilla of planks, dispersed by the wind, returned by the tides. In this same way, Demetrios lost himself before two magnificent magnetic eyes, and all his strength was being drawn from him.

She lowered her eyes and passed near him.

He could have shouted with eagerness. His fists clenched: he was afraid of not being able to regain his poise, because he had to speak to her. But, he approached her with the usual greeting.

"I have the honor of meeting you," he said.

"And I, you," responded the passerby.

Demetrios continued:

"Where are you going, so leisurely?"

"I am going home."

"All alone?"

"All alone."

She started to resume her walk.

Then Demetrios thought that he had, perhaps, deceived himself in judging her to be a courtesan. For some time, the wives of the magistrates and of the bureaucrats dressed and adorned themselves like daughters of joy. This one might be a powerful person, well respected, and without a sense of irony he thus completed his questioning:

"To your husband?"

She leaned back, with her two hands behind her, for support, and laughed.

"I don't have one this evening."

Demetrios bit his lips and, almost timidly, risked:

"Don't look for him. You have begun too late. There is no longer anyone here."

"Who told you I was searching? I walk alone and look for nothing."

"Where did you come from then? Because you have not put on all these jewels just for yourself, and look here, a silken veil..."

"Would you have me go out naked, or dressed in wool like a slave? I dress only for my pleasure. I like to know that I am beautiful, and I gaze at my fingers while walking in order to acquaint myself with every ring."

"You should have a mirror in your hand and look only at your eyes. They were not born in Alexandria, those eyes. You are a Jewess, I hear it in your voice; it is sweeter than ours."

"No, I am not a Jewess, I am a Galilaean."

"What is your name, Miriam or Naomi?"

"My Syrian name — you will not know it. It is a royal name that no one bears here. My friends call me Chrysis; you have paid me a compliment."

He put his hand on her arm.

"Oh! No, no," she said in a mocking voice. "It is far too late for these pleasantries. Let me return quickly. It has been almost three hours since I arose, and I am dying from fatigue."

Bending over, she took her foot into her hand: "See how my thin laces hurt me? They are much too tight. If I don't uncross them this instant, I am going to have a mark on my foot, and that will be pretty when someone embraces me! Let me leave quickly. Ah! How it hurts! If I had known, I would not have stopped. My yellow veil is all crushed at the waist, look!"

Demetrios wiped his forehand; then, with the careless tone of a man who condescends to make a choice, he murmured:

"Show me the way."

"But, I do not want to!" said Chrysis with an air of great astonishment. "You do not even ask if it is my pleasure. 'Show me the way!' How he says that! Do you take me for a girl of the market who puts herself on her back for three obols without concern for who holds her? Do you even know if I am available? Are you aware of the details of my trysts? Have you followed me on my walks? Have you made note of the doors that have opened for me? Have you counted the men who believe themselves loved by Chrysis? 'Show me the way!' I will not show it to you, if you please. Stay here or go, but anywhere else than to my house!"

"You do not know who I am ..."

"You? Come now! You are Demetrios of Sais. You sculpted the statue of my goddess. You are the queen's lover and the ruler of my town. But for me, you are only a handsome slave, because you have seen me and you love me."

She again drew near, and went on with a coaxing voice:

"Yes, you love me. Oh, do not speak — I know what you are going to tell me: you love no one and that you are loved. You are the Well-Beloved, the Cherished, the Idol. You have refused Glycera, who had refused Antiochos. Demonassa, the Lesbian, who had sworn to die a virgin, went into your bed while you slept and would have taken you by force if your two Libyan slaves had not thrown her, naked, out the door. Callistion the well-named, desperate to approach you, bought the house across from you. Every morning, she appears in the open window, as little dressed as Artemis in the bath. You believe that I do not know all that? But they tell everything among courtesans. The night of your arrival at Alexandria they told me about you; and since then not a single day has passed where they have not spoken your name in front of me. I even know the things that you have forgotten. I even know the things that you do not yet know. The day before yesterday, poor little Phyllis hung herself from the bar of your door, right? Well — it is a fashion that spreads. Lydia did the same as Phyllis; I saw her this evening in passing. She was all blue, but the tears on her cheeks were not yet dry. You do not know who Lydia is? A child, a little courtesan, fifteen years old, whom her mother had sold last month to a ship captain from Samos. He spent the night in Alexandria before going up the river to Thebes. She came to me. I gave her some advice; she knew nothing about anything, not even playing knuckle-bones. I took her often to my bed, because, when she had no lover, she had no place to sleep. And she loved you! If only you had seen her! ...She wanted to write to you. Do you understand? I told her it was not worth the trouble ..."

Demetrios looked at her without hearing.

"Yes, it is all the same to you, isn't it?" continued Chrysis. "You, you did not love her. It is me that you love. You have not even heard what I have just told you. I am certain that you will not repeat a word of it. You are well occupied in knowing how my eyelids are painted, how wonderful my very mouth must be, and how soft to the touch is my hair. Ah! How many others know this! Every one of them, every one of them who has wanted me has satisfied desires with me; men, young men, old men, children, women, young girls. I have refused no one, do you hear? For seven years, Demetrios, I have slept alone for only three nights. Calculate how many lovers that makes? Two thousand five hundred, and more, because I do not talk about the ones in the daytime. Last year, I danced naked in front of twenty thousand people and I know that you were not one of them. Do you think that I hide myself? Ah! Why do that! All the women have seen me in the bath. All the men have seen me in the bed. Only you, you will never see me. I refuse you, I refuse you! Of what I am, of what I feel, of my beauty, of my love, you will never never know anything! You are an abominable man, vain, cruel, insensitive and cowardly! I do not know why one of us has not had enough hatred to kill the both of you, one after the other, you first, and then the queen."

Demetrios calmly took hold of her arms, and, without uttering a word, forced her over on her back.

She had a flash of pain, but suddenly clasped her knees together, locked her elbows, and drew further away on her back, saying in a quiet voice:

"Ah! I am not afraid of that, Demetrios! You will never take me by force, were I a loving virgin and you as vigorous as Atlantis.

You not only want your own pleasure, but you desire mine above all. You also desire to see me, to see all of me, because you think I am beautiful and, indeed, I am. Now the light of the moon is less than my twelve wax torches. It is nearly dark here. And of course, it is not customary to undress oneself on the pier. I could not get dressed again, you see, if I did not have my slave. Let me get up, you are hurting my arms."

They were silent for several minutes, then Demetrios spoke again:

"This must stop, Chrysis. You know very well that I will not force you, but let me follow you. However much pride you have, it is a vanity that could cost you dearly — to refuse Demetrios."

Chrysis continued to keep quiet.

He began again, more gently:

"What are you afraid of?"

"You are accustomed to the love of others. Do you know what they are bound to do to a courtesan who will not love?"

He grew impatient.

"I am not asking you to love me. I am tired of being loved. I have no desire to be loved. I ask that you surrender yourself. For that I will give you all the gold in the world. I have it here in Egypt."

"I have it in my hair," she replied. "I am tired of gold. I have no desire for gold. I desire only three things. Will you give them to me?"

Demetrios sensed that she was going to ask the impossible. He looked at her anxiously. But she began to smile and said slowly:

"I want a mirror of silver in order to reflect my eyes in my eyes."

"You will have it. What more do you wish? Say it quickly."

"I want a comb of carved ivory to plunge into my hair like a net into sunlit water."

"What else?"

"You will give me my comb?"

"Certainly, finish."

"I want a necklace of pearls to spread over my breast when, in my room, I will perform for you the nuptial dances of my country."

He raised his eyebrows.

"Is that all?"

"You will give me my necklace?"

"One that will please you."

She assumed a very tender voice.

"One that will please me? Ah! And here is exactly what I wanted to ask you. Will you let me choose my gifts?"

"Of course."

"Do you swear it?"

"I swear it."

"What oath do you make?"

"Command me."

"By the Aphrodite that you have sculpted."

"I make this oath by the Aphrodite. But why the precaution?"

"Well ... I was not certain ... now I am."

She raised her head again:

"I have chosen my gifts."

Demetrios felt uneasy again and asked, "Already?"

"Yes ... Do you think that I would accept any silver mirror bought from a merchant for Smyrna, or, from some unknown courtesan? I want the one that my friend, Bacchis, has. She took a lover from me last week and wickedly made fun of me in a small orgy she had with Tryphera, Mousarion, and some other young stupid girls, who repeated everything to me. It is a mirror that she holds very dear, because it once belonged to Rhodopis — she was a slave with Æsop and was bought again by the brother of Sappho. You know that Rhodopis is a very famous courtesan. Her mirror is magnificent. They say that Sappho was reflected in it and that is why Bacchis clings to it. She has nothing more precious in the world, and I know where you will find it. She told me one night when she was drunk. It is under the third stone on the altar. She puts it there every night when she goes out at sunset. Tomorrow go to her house, at that time, and fear nothing; she takes her slaves with her."

"That is crazy," cried Demetrios. Do you want me to be a thief?"

"Do you not love me? I thought that you loved me. And then, did you not swear? I thought that you had sworn. If I am mistaken, we will speak no more of it."

He understood that she was leading him to ruin, but he let himself be dragged along without a struggle, almost willingly.

"I will do as you ask," he responded.

"Oh! I know that you will do it. But at first you hesitated. I understand why you hesitate. It is not an ordinary gift. I would not ask it of a philosopher. I ask it of you. I know well that you will give it to me.

She played for a moment with the peacock feathers in her curved fan and suddenly said:

"Ah! … I also do not want an ivory comb bought from a merchant in town. You told me that I could choose, right? Well! I want … I want the carved ivory comb that is in the hair of the wife of the High Priest. It is much more precious than the mirror of Rhodopis. It comes from a queen of Egypt who lived a long, long time ago and whose name is so difficult that I cannot pronounce it. Likewise, the ivory is very old and yellow as if it were gold. Someone engraved on it a young girl passing through a marsh of lotus taller than she, and she walks on her tiptoes, avoiding the wetness … It is truly an exquisite comb … I am happy that you will give it to me … I also have small grievances against the one who possesses it. Last month I had offered a blue veil to Aphrodite. I saw it, the next day, on the head of this woman. It gave me a start, and I was angry at her. Her comb will be my revenge for the veil."

"And how will I get it?" asked Demetrios.

"Ah! This will be a little more difficult. She is an Egyptian, you know, and she does up her two hundred braids only once a year, like the other women of her race. But I want my comb tomorrow and you will have to kill her in order to get it. You have sworn an oath."

She made a small grimace at Demetrios who was looking at the ground. Then she finished very quickly:

"I have also chosen my necklace. I want the pearl necklace with seven strands that is around the neck of Aphrodite."

Demetrios jumped back.

"Ah! This time, this is too much! You are not going to have the last laugh! Nothing, do you hear, nothing! You will get neither the mirror nor the comb nor the necklace ..."

But she closed his mouth with her hand and resumed her coaxing voice:

"Do not say that. You know that you will give me this. I am very certain of it. I will get the three gifts ... You will come to me tomorrow night and, after tomorrow, if you desire, every evening. You name the hour and I will be there, in the costume that you desire, made-up according to your taste, my hair fixed to your fancy, ready to the end, for your fantasies. If you only want tenderness, I will cherish you like a child. If you search for a rare sensual pleasure, I will not refuse even the most painful. If you desire silence, I will be silent ... When you will have me sing, ah! you will see, Beloved! I know songs from all the countries. I know some which are sweet like the murmur from the springs, others which are terrible like the thunder drawing near. I know some so innocent and so pure that a young girl could sing them to her mother. I know some that they would not sing at Lampsacus. I know some that Elephantis would blush to hear, and I would only dare to recite in a whisper. On the nights when you want me to dance, I will dance until morning. I will dance completely clothed, with my tunic dragging, or under a transparent veil, or with slit undergarments ...and a corset with two openings exposing my breasts. But have I promised you to dance naked? I will dance naked if you like it better. Naked and with flowers in my hair, or naked in my flowing hair and made up like a divine image. I know how to sway my hands to and fro, to curve my arms, to shake my breasts, to move my belly, to flex my buttocks, you will see! I dance on the tips of my toes or down on the carpet. I know all the dances of Aphrodite, the ones they dance before Urania and the ones they dance before Astarte. I even know some that they do not dare to dance … I will dance for you all the passions … When this will end, everything else will begin. You will see!

"The queen is wealthier than I, but there is not, in all the palace, a room so passion-filled as mine. I will not tell you what you will find there. There are some things that are so beautiful that I could not give you an idea of them and others that are so scandalous that I know no words with which to describe them. And then, do you know what you will see that surpasses everything? You will see Chrysis whom you love and whom you do not yet know. Yes, you have only seen my face; you do not know how beautiful I am. Ah! … Ah! Ah! You will have surprises … Ah! As you play with the tips of my breasts, as you fold me over, my waist on your arms, how you will tremble in the grip of my knees, how you will swoon on my moving body. And how sumptuous my mouth will be! Ah! My kisses! …"

Demetrios glanced at her bewilderedly.

She continued, softly:

"How can you refuse to give me a poor old silver mirror when you will have all my hair, like a golden forest, in your hands?"

Demetrios wanted to touch her hair … She pulled back and said:

"Tomorrow!"

"You will have it," he murmured.

"And do you not want to take a little ivory comb for me, one that pleases me, when you will have my two arms like two ivory branches around your neck?"

He tried to caress them … She drew them behind her, and said again:

"Tomorrow!"

"I will bring it to you," he said in a very quiet voice.

"Ah! I knew that!" cried the courtesan, "and you will also give me the seven-strand pearl necklace that is around the neck of Aphrodite. For it, I will sell you my entire body which is like a mother-of-pearl shell, half-opened, and more kisses in your mouth than there are pearls in the sea!"

Demetrios, beseechingly, moved his head toward her ... Her eager gaze drew him and her luxurious lips invited him ...

When he opened his eyes, she was already in the distance. A small shadow, paler still, ran behind her floating veil.

He continued, uncertain, on the path toward town, his head bowed by an inexpressible shame.

THE VIRGINS

A somber dawn rose over the sea. Everything was the color of lilac. The burning torch, blazing on the tower of the Pharos, was extinguished with the moon. Fleeting yellow glimmerings appeared in the violet waves like faces of sirens under the mauve hair of seaweed. It was suddenly daylight.

The pier was deserted. The town was dead. It was the sullen light of early dawn which illuminates the slumbering world and brings the enervating dreams of morning.

Nothing existed, only the silence.

Just like sleeping birds, the ships were arranged lengthwise near the quay, the oars, parallel to each other, were left to dangle in the water. The perspective of the streets, delineated by the design of the houses, was uninterrupted by a chariot, a horse, or a slave. Alexandria was only a vast solitude, taking on the appearance of an ancient city, abandoned for centuries.

Now, a faint sound of footsteps resonated on the ground and two young women appeared, one dressed in yellow, the other in blue.

They both wore the sashes of virgins that swung around their hips and tied, very low, under their young bellies. They were the singer and the flute player from the night before.

The musician was younger and prettier than her friend. Pale as the blue of her robe, her eyes, almost drowned under her eyelids, smiled faintly. Two slender flutes dangled down her back from a flowery knot at her shoulder. A double garland of iris along the curve of her legs undulated under the gauzy fabric and was fastened to two silver ankle-bracelets.

She said:

"Myrtocleia, do not be sad because you lost our tablet. Will you always forget that Rhodis loves you, or can you think, silly one, that you have read the only line written by my hand? Am I one of those terrible friends who engrave the name of their sisters of the bed on their fingernail and go to couple with another when the fingernail has grown to the end? Why do you need a souvenir of me when you have me completely and alive? I am barely at the age when women marry; however, I was only half this age when I met you for the first time. You remember well. It was at the bath. Our mothers held us under our arms and guided us, step by step, toward each other. We played for a long time on the marble before we put our clothes back on. Since that day we have not left each other, and, after five years, we have come to love one another."

Myrtocleia responded:

"There is another first day, Rhodis, you know that. It was the day when you wrote those three words on my tablet, intertwining our names, one upon the other — that was the first. We can no longer find it, but it is of no importance. Each day is new for me and when you awaken in the evening, it seems that I have never seen you. I truly believe that you are not a girl: you are a tiny nymph of Arcadia, who has left the forests because Phoebus dried up her fountain. Your body is as supple as an olive branch, your skin is as soft as the summer water, the iris wraps around your legs and you wear the lotus flower as Astarte wore the open fig. In which wood, populated by immortals, did your mother sleep before your fortuitous birth? What indiscrete demigod or god of what divine river united with her in the grass? When we have left this ghastly African sun, you will lead me to your spring, far behind Psophis and Pheneus, in the vast shadow-filled forests where we can see, on the soft earth, the double tracks of the satyrs intermingled with the light steps of the nymphs. There you will search for a polished rock and you will engrave what you wrote in wax into the stone, the three words that are our joy.

"Listen! Listen! Rhodis. By the sash of Aphrodite, where all desires are embroidered, all desires are strangers to me since you are more than my dream! By the horn of Amalthea, from which all goodness of the world is let loose, the world is of no concern to me since you are the only good that I have found in it! When I look at you and I look at me, I no longer know why you love me in return. Your hair is blond like a sheaf of wheat; mine is black like the beard of a goat. Your skin is white like shepherd's cheese; mine is tanned like the sand on the beaches. Your budding breast is flushed like the orange tree in autumn; mine is spindly and barren like a pine tree in the rocks. If my face has grown more pleasing, it is because I have loved you. Oh Rhodis, you know this, my own virginity resembles the lips of Pan eating a sprig of myrtle; yours is rosy and pretty like the mouth of a little baby. I do not know why you love me, but if you stopped loving me one day; if, like your sister, Theano, who plays the flute beside you, you stay at anytime to sleep in the houses where we are employed, then, I would not even think of sleeping alone in our bed, and when you come home, you would find me strangled with my sash."

The elongated eyes of Rhodis filled with tears and a smile at such a cruel and foolish idea. She placed her foot on a post. "My flowers between my legs bother me. Untie them, adored Myrto. I have finished dancing for the night."

The singer straightened up in surprise.

"Oh! It is true. I had forgotten them already, those men and women. Every dance, they made you dance as a pair, you in this robe from Cos that is as transparent as water, and your sister, along with you, naked. If I had not defended you, they would have taken you like a common prostitute, just as they took your sister in front of you and in the same room...Oh! What abomination! Did you hear her cries and her pleading! How painful is the love of a man!"

She knelt near Rhodis and took off the two garlands, then she placed three flowers higher, placing a kiss at each spot. When she got up, the child took her around the neck and nearly fainted under the touch of her lips.

"Myrto, you are not jealous of all those dissolute people? Why do you care if they should have seen me? Theano satisfies them, I left her to them. They will not have me, dearest Myrto. Do not be jealous of them."

"Jealous! ... I am jealous of everything that comes near you. So that your robes are not yours alone, I wear them after you have worn them. In order that the flowers in your hair do not remain in love with you, I deliver them to the poor courtesans who will defile them in their orgies. I have never given you anything so that nothing will possess you. I am afraid of everything that you touch and I hate everything you look at. I would like, for my entire life, to be within the walls of a prison, where only you and I would be, where we are united so thoroughly and you are hidden in my arms so well, that not one eye would suspect you were there. I would like to be the fruit that you eat, the fragrance that gives you pleasure, the sleep that enters under your eyelids, the love that enlivens your body. I am jealous of the happiness that I give you; meanwhile, I would like to give you the very love that I get from you. It is you I am jealous of, but I do not fear your mistresses of one night when they help me satisfy your childish desires; as for the male lovers, I know that you will never be theirs. I know that you can not love a man; a man comes and goes and is brutal."

Rhodis cried sincerely:

"I would go, rather, like Nausithoe, to sacrifice my virginity to the god Priapus, whom they adore at Thasus. But not this morning, my darling. I have danced for a long time and I am very tired. I would like to be home, sleeping on your arm."

She smiled and continued:

"I must tell Theano that our bed is no longer for her. We will make her another one and put it to the right of the door. After what I have seen tonight, I could no longer kiss her. Myrto, it is truly horrible. Is it possible that people love like this? Is this what they call love?"

"It is."

"They are wrong, Myrto. They do not know."

Myrtocleia took her in her arms and they both remained silent, together.

The wind intermingled their hair.

THE HAIR OF CHRYSIS

"WAIT!" cried Rhodis, "Look! Someone is coming."

The singer looked: a woman, far away from them, walked rapidly on the quay.

"I recognize her," continued the child. "It is Chrysis. She is wearing her yellow robe."

"What, she is already dressed to go out?"

"I don't understand it. Ordinarily she does not go out before noon and the sun is barely risen. Something has happened to her. Something wonderful, without a doubt; she has such good luck."

They went over to her and greeted her:

"Hello, Chrysis."

"Hello. How long have you been here?"

"I don't know. It was already daylight when we arrived."

"Was there anyone on the pier?"

"No one."

"Not a man? Are you certain?"

"Oh! Very certain. Why do you ask?"

Chrysis did not answer. Rhodis asked another question.

"Did you want to see someone?"

"Yes … perhaps … I think that it is best that I do not see him. It is all for the best. I was wrong to return, but I could not stop myself."

"But what is happening, Chrysis, will you tell us?"

"Oh! No."

"Not even us? Not even us, your friends?"

"You will know about it later, along with the whole town."

"That is kind of you."

"I'll tell you a little beforehand if you keep it to yourselves, but this morning it is impossible. Extraordinary things are happening, my children. I am dying to tell you, but I must keep quiet. Were you going home? Come to sleep at my house. I am all alone."

"Oh! Chrysis, Chrysidion, we are so tired! In fact, we were going home, but it would be nice to sleep."

"Ah, well! You will sleep afterwards. Today is the eve of the Festival of Aphrodite. Is it a day for rest? If you wish the goddess to protect you and make you happy next year, you must arrive at the temple with your eyelids darkened like violets and your cheeks whitened like lilies. We will think about it at my house — come with me."

She gathered the pair, holding them above their sashes, and hurriedly took them away.

Rhodis, however, remained preoccupied.

"And when will we be in your bed," she resumed, "you will still not tell us what is happening and what you expect?"

"I will tell you many things, everything that makes you happy, but of that, I will say nothing."

"Even when we will be in your arms, naked, in the darkness?"

"Do not insist, little Rhodis. You will know tomorrow. Wait until tomorrow."

"Are you going to be very happy, or very powerful?"

"Very powerful."

Rhodis opened her eyes wide and cried:

"You are sleeping with the queen!"

"No," Chrysis said, laughing, "but I will be as powerful as she. Do you have something you want from me? Do you desire something?"

"Oh! Yes!"

And the child became thoughtful again.

"Well, what is it?" inquired Chrysis.

"It is an impossible thing. Why would I ask it?"

Myrtocleia spoke for her:

"In Ephesus, in our country, when young girls, of marriageable age and virgin, like Rhodis and myself, love one another, the law permits them to marry. They go together to the temple of Athena to consecrate their double sash, and then to the sanctuary of Iphinoe to offer a lock of their interwoven hair. Finally, under the portico of Dionysis where they hand over a small sharpened gold knife to the more masculine one and a white linen cloth to stop the bleeding. In the evening, the one who is the bride is taken to her new lodgings, seated on a flower-covered chariot between her "husband" and the bridesmaid, surrounded by torches and flute players. And thereafter, they have all the rights of a married couple. They can adopt little girls and involve them in their intimate life. They are respected. They are a family. That is Rhodis' dream, but here it is not the custom …"

"The law can be changed," said Chrysis, "and you two will marry each other. I am going to make it my business."

"Oh! Is it true!" cried the child, blushing with joy.

"Yes, and I will not ask which of you will be the husband. I know that Myrto has everything that is necessary to produce the illusion. You are lucky, Rhodis, to have such a friend. No matter what anyone says, they are rare."

They had reached the door where Djala, seated on the threshold, was weaving a linen towel. The slave got up to let them pass and entered, following them.

And in an instant, the two flute players had slipped off their plain garments. They washed each other with great care in the green marble washbowl that emptied into the basin. Then they tumbled into bed.

Chrysis looked without seeing them. The most insignificant of Demetrios' words repeated themselves, word for word, in her memory, endlessly. She was not conscious of Djala, while the slave silently untied and unrolled her long saffron veil, unwound her sash, unclasped her necklaces, took off the rings, the signets, the bracelets, the silver serpents, the golden pins; but, the tickling sensation from her falling hair faintly aroused her.

She asked for her mirror.

Was she seized by the fear of not being beautiful enough to keep this new lover — because he must stay captured — after the insane tasks she had demanded of him? Or did she want, by examining each of her beautiful features, to calm any such uneasiness and give her cause to be confident?

She put her mirror close to every part of her body, while touching each one of them, one after the other.

She looked critically at the whiteness of her skin, assessing her softness and the warmth of her embraces with long, drawn out caresses. She tested the fullness of her breasts, the firmness of her belly, the tautness of her flesh. She examined her hair and considered its luster. She tried the power of her gaze, the expression of her mouth, the heat of her breath, and from the side of her armpit to the bend of her elbow, she made a trail with a kiss, slowly, down the length of her bare arm.

An extraordinary emotion, of surprise and pride, of certainty and impatience, startled her at the touch of her own lips. She turned around as if she was searching for someone, but, discovering the forgotten Ephesians on her bed, she jumped into the middle of them, separated them, and embraced them with a loving fury, her long golden hair enshrouding their three young heads.

BOOK TWO

THE GARDENS OF THE GODDESS

THE temple of Aphrodite-Astarte rose up outside the gates of town, in an immense park, full of flowers and shady spots, where the water of the Nile, conveyed through seven aqueducts, maintained an abundance of greenery all year long.

This flowered-covered forest at the edge of the sea, these deep streams, these lakes, these somber meadows, had been created in the desert more than two centuries before by the first of the Ptolemies. Since then, the sycamores planted by his orders had become gigantic and, under the influence of the fertile water, the green lawns had grown into meadows. The smaller pools had widened into ponds; nature had made a park into a country.

The gardens were more than a valley, more than a region, more than a country; they were a complete world shut off by stone boundaries and ruled by a goddess, the soul and center of this universe. A circular terrace was erected around it — eighty stadia long and thirty-two feet high. It was not a barrier; rather it gave form to a colossal city with fourteen-hundred homes. An equal number of prostitutes inhabited this pious town and represented, in this unique place, seventy different tribes.

The layout of the sacred houses was uniform and each had a door of red copper (a metal dedicated to the goddess), bearing a phallus in the guise of a hammer that struck its plate carrying the image of the female sex in relief. The name of the courtesan was engraved under it along with the initials of the common phrase:

$\Omega.\Xi.E.$

KOXΛIΣ

Π.Π.Π.

On each side of the door two rooms, in the shape of two small shops, opened up; that is to say, without a wall on the garden side. The one on the right, called "the exposed room," was the place where the adorned courtesans held court from a high throne-like seat when the men arrived. The one on the left was at the disposal of the lovers who wanted to spend the night in the open air, without, however, making love on the grass.

Through the open door, a corridor gave access to a vast court-yard paved with marble, the middle of which contained an oval pool. This huge area of daylight was surrounded with the shade from a portico that protected the entrance of the seven-room house and provided a zone of coolness. At the end of the corridor, a rose-colored granite altar was erected.

Each woman had brought a miniature idol of the goddess from her homeland and, on the native altar, she worshiped the goddess in her own language, without ever understanding the others — Lakme, Ashtoreth, Venus, Ishtar, Freia, Mylitta, Cypris, such were the religious names of their deified Sensualist. Some of them worshipped her symbolically: a red pebble, a conical stone, a large prickly shell. The majority of them worshiped a primitive statue, on a pedestal of delicate wood, with slender arms, heavy breasts, voluminous hips and whose hand on her belly pointed to the delta with its curly hair. They laid a branch of myrtle at her feet, scattered the altar with rose petals, and burned a small granule of incense for each prayer granted. She was the confidant for all their sorrows, witness to all their labors, and the supposed cause of all their pleasures. At their death, the statue was deposited in the small, fragile coffin, as a guardian of their tomb.

Among these women, the most beautiful came from the kingdoms of Asia. Every year, the ships that brought the gifts from the tributaries or the allies to Alexandria unloaded packaged goods for vending and leather goatskins bottles, along with one hundred virgins, chosen by the priests, for the service of the sacred garden. They were Mysians and Jews, Phrygians and Cretans, women from Ecbatana and from Babylon, from the shores of the Gulf of Pearls, and from the holy banks of the Ganges. Some had white skin, with cameo-like faces and firm breasts; others, brown as the earth after a rain, wore golden rings that pierced their nostrils and shook their short, dark hair from their shoulders.

Others had come from further still, small beings, slender and slow, whose language no one understood and who resembled yellow monkeys: their eyes elongated toward their temples; their straight black hair, done up in a bizarre fashion. All their life these women remained timid like lost animals. They knew the movements of love, but refused to kiss on the mouth. In between brief encounters, they could be seen playing among themselves, sitting on their tiny feet, amusing themselves like children.

In an isolated meadow, the blond and pinkish-colored women of the northern peoples lived in a band, sleeping on the grass. They were Sarmatians with triple braids, robust legs and square shoulders, who made their crowns from tree branches and held hand-to-hand combat as a diversion; Scythians, flat-nosed, full-breasted, hairy, who only copulated like beasts; gigantic Teutons who terrified the Egyptians with their pale hair like that of old men, and their flesh, softer than a baby's skin; Gauls, russet-colored like cows, who laughed with no reason; Celts, young, green-eyed as the sea, who never went out naked.

Elsewhere, the Iberians, with brown breasts, came together during the day. They had thick hair done up with a studied elegance and a sinewy belly that was barely shaved. Their firm skin and their strong buttocks were greatly appreciated by the Alexandrians. They were chosen as dancers as often as they were for mistresses.

Under the expansive shade of the palms, lived the daughters of Africa: the Numidians veiled in white, the Carthaginians arrayed in black gauze, the Negresses enveloped in multicolored costumes.

There were fourteen hundred.

When a woman entered there, she never left until the first day of her old age. She gave half of her earnings to the temple and the other half went for her food and her perfumes.

They were not slaves and each one actually owned one of the houses on the Terrace, but not everyone was loved equally, and, often, the more fortunate ones purchased neighboring houses whose occupants sold them so they would not starve. These people then transported their obscene statuette into the park and searched for a flat stone to use as an altar, placing it in a corner from which they never left. The poorer merchants knew that and more willingly directed themselves to those who lay, thusly, on the moss near their sanctuaries, in the open air. Even those men themselves, sometimes, did not appear and then the needy women, united in their misery, paired by passionate friendships, became almost like conjugal lovers in households where they shared everything, to the last wool rag and where alternative acquiescences consoled the long periods of chastity.

The ones who had no friends offered themselves as voluntary slaves to their more fortunate comrades. They were prohibited from having more than a dozen of these poor women in their service. It was pointed out, however, that the twenty-two courtesans, who reached the maximum, had chosen a household with many colors among all races.

If, by chance, one of the courtesans bore a son, he was brought up within the walls of the temple to contemplate the perfect form and to serve Her divinity. — If the woman gave birth to a girl, the child was born for the goddess. The first day of her life, they celebrated her symbolic marriage to the son of Dionysis and the Hierophant deflowered her himself, with a tiny golden knife, because virginity displeases Aphrodite. Later, she entered the Didascalion, the great monument-school situated behind the temple. There the little girls learned, in seven classes, the theory and method of all the erotic arts: the glance, the embrace, the movements of the body, the complexities of the caress, the secret procedures of biting, the deep thrust of the tongue, and the kiss. The student voluntarily chose the day she would have her first experience, because desire is ordered by the goddess and must not be contradicted. On that day, they gave her one of the houses of the Terrace. Some of these children, who were not even of marriageable age, were deemed among the most inexhaustible and the most often in demand.

The interior of the Didascalion, the seven class rooms, the little theatre and the portico of the court were ornamented with ninety-two frescoes that recapitulated the teachings of love. They were, in their entirety, the life's work of one man, Cleochares of Alexandria, disciple and natural son of Apelles, who had finished them while dying. — Recently, Queen Berenice, who was very interested in the famous school and who had sent her young sisters there, had requested of Demetrios a series of marble groupings, in order to complete the ornamentation; but up to this time, only one had been placed in the children's class.

At the end of each year, in the presence of all the assembled courtesans, a competition took place that aroused an extraordinary rivalry in this crowd of women, because the twelve prizes awarded gave the right to the most supreme glory they could have imagined: entrance into the Cotytteion.

This last monument was enshrouded by such secrecy that there can be no detailed description given today. We know only that it was included in the park and that it formed a triangle on whose base was a temple of the goddess, Cotytto, in whose name terrifying and unknown orgies took place. The two other sides of the monument were comprised of eighteen houses. Thirty-six courtesans lived there, so sought after by rich lovers that they did not ever give themselves for less than two minae: they were the Baptes of Alexandria. Once a month, at the full moon, they gathered together within the enclosing walls of the temple, frenzied by aphrodisiatic drinks and girded with the canonized phallus. The eldest of the thirty-six had to take a lethal dose of the terrible erotic potion. Knowing that she would die swiftly and surely, she took part, fearlessly, in every dangerous sensual pleasure before which the living would recoil. Her body, everywhere foaming, became the center and model for the swirling orgy; in the midst of long howls, cries, tears, and dances, the other naked women grasped her, wetting their hair with her sweat, rubbing themselves on her burning skin and imbibing in new passions within the uninterrupted spasms of this furious agony. Three years the women lived like this and, to the end of the thirty-sixth month, such was the intoxication of their end.

The other sanctuaries, less venerated, had been erected by the women in honor of the other names for the many forms of Aphrodite. There was even an altar consecrated to Urania, who received the chaste vows of the sentimental courtesans; another to Epistrophia, who brought forgetfulness of unhappy loves; another to Chryseia, who attracted rich lovers; another to Genetyllis, who protected pregnant women; another to Coliade, who approved primitive passions, because anything that touched love was pious devotion for the goddess. But the individual altars were effective and virtuous only in regard to small desires. They served them from day to day, their protection was for everyday matters and ordinary commerce. The petitioners, whose prayers were granted, placed simple flowers on them; those who were not gratified smeared them with excrement. They were neither consecrated nor maintained by the priests, consequently, their desecration went unpunished.

This was completely different from the discipline of the temple.

The Temple, the Great-Temple of the Great-Goddess, the place held most sacred in all of Egypt, was a colossal edifice, three hundred and thirty-six feet in length, raised on seventeen steps to the summit of the gardens. Its golden doors were guarded by twelve hermaphroditic temple slaves, two objects symbolizing love, and the twelve hours of night.

The entrance did not face toward the east, but rather in the direction of Paphos, that is to say, toward the northwest; the rays of the sun never directly penetrated into the sanctuary of the great nocturnal Immortal. Eighty-six columns supported the lowest beam of the entablature. They were halfway tinted crimson and the upper parts were separated completely from these red vestments by an ineffable whiteness, as if imitating the torsos of women, standing.

Between the lower beam and the cornice, the lengthy band of the frieze unfurled its bestial ornamentation, erotic and fantastic, displaying female centaurs mounted by stallions, goats penetrated by slender satyrs, virgins overlaid by monstrous bulls, water-nymphs covered by stags, drunken revelers making love with tigers, lionesses captured by griffons. In the same way, the great multitude of beings flung themselves about, aroused by irresistible divine passion. The male stretched taut, the female opened herself up, the creative wellspring from which arises the first shudder of life. Sometimes a crowd of unfathomable couples wandered haphazardly around the immortal scene: Europa, leaning, supporting the handsome Olympian beast; Leda guiding the robust swan between her young, yielding thighs. Further on, the insatiable Siren exhausted the dying Glaucus; the god, Pan took, standing, a tousled woodnymph; the Sphinx raised her buttocks to the level of the horse, Pegasus, — and, at the very end of the frieze, the sculptor had represented himself, in front of the goddess Aphrodite, following her contours in the soft wax, the curves of a perfect cteis, as if all his ideal of beauty, joy, and virtue had long since taken refuge in this flower, precious and fragile.

MELITTA

"**P**URIFY yourself, Stranger."

"I will enter pure," said Demetrios.

Dipping the ends of her hair in water, the young guardian of the gate moistened first his eyelids, then his lips and fingers, so that his gaze, the kiss from his mouth and the caress of his hands might be sanctified.

And he moved on into the woods of Aphrodite.

Through the ever-darkening branches, he caught sight of the setting sun, a dull crimson, no longer a dazzling sight. It was the evening of the same day of his encounter with Chrysis; an encounter that had disorientated his life.

The feminine soul has a naturalness that a man can not understand. Where there is only a straight line, men stubbornly search for the complexity of a weaving: they find the gap and lose themselves in it. Such was the soul of Chrysis, transparent as that of a small child, appearing to Demetrios more mysterious than a problem in metaphysics. After leaving this woman on the pier, he returned home, as if in a dream, incapable of responding to all the questions that besieged him. What did she want to do with those three gifts? It was impossible for her either to wear or to sell a stolen mirror so well-known, a comb of a murdered woman, or the pearl necklace of the goddess. If she kept them with her, each day she would leave herself open to a fatal discovery. Then why ask for them? To destroy them? He knew too well that women do not enjoy keeping things a secret and that happy events only become enjoyable for them once they are known. And then, by what clever conjecture, by what prodigious clairvoyance, had she judged him capable of accomplishing those three so extraordinary actions for her?

Assuredly, if he had desired it, Chrysis, kidnapped from her home, delivered to his mercy, could become his mistress, his wife, or his slave, according to his choice. He even had the freedom to destroy her, with ease. The revolutions of the years past had accustomed the citizens to frequent violent deaths and no one would be concerned with the disappearance of a courtesan. Chrysis must have known this and yet, she had dared...

The more he thought about her, the more he took pleasure in having her so cleverly change the debate of the propositions. How many women, equal to her worth, would have presented themselves with less skill! This one, what had she asked for? Neither love, nor gold, nor jewels, but three unbelievable crimes! She interested him intensely. He had offered her all the treasures of Egypt. He sensed now that if she had accepted them, she would not have received two obols and he would have tired of her even before he had taken her. Three crimes were assuredly an unusual price, but she was worthy of receiving it since she was the woman to demand it, and he promised himself to continue the affair.

Not wanting to give himself time to waver from his firm resolution, he went to Bacchis' house the same day, took the mirror, and went off to the gardens.

Was it necessary for him to go directly to Chrysis' second victim? Demetrios did not think so. Touni, the priestess who possessed the famous ivory comb was so charming and so delicate that he was afraid of allowing himself to be swayed if he went near her without first taking a precaution. He walked back along the Grand Terrace.

The courtesans were displayed in their "exposed chambers" like flowers in an open-air market. Their poses and their costumes were no less diverse than their ages, types, and races. The most beautiful ones, following the tradition of Phryne, leaving only the oval of their face uncovered, stood enveloped from head to foot in their grand vestments of fine wool. Others had adopted the fashion of transparent garments, beneath which their beauties were mysteriously distinguished, as when crossing over limpid water the shadowy patches of green moss on the bottom can be discerned. Those whose only charm was their youth, remained nude to their waist and arched their back so that the firmness of their breast could be appreciated. But the more mature women, knowing the features of the feminine face grow old much more quickly than the body, sat naked, holding up their breasts in their hands, and spread apart their heavy thighs as if it were necessary for them to prove that they were still women.

Demetrios passed slowly in front of them and did not permit himself to admire them.

He had never succeeded in seeing a naked woman without intense emotion. He understood neither disgust in front of those past their youth, nor insensitivity before girls too young to be displayed. On this night, any woman could have charmed him. As long as she remained silent and showed no more fervor than the minimum exacted by the politeness of the bed, he did not require her to be beautiful. Moreover, he preferred that she have a plain body, for the more his thoughts dwelt upon more perfect forms, the more his desire distanced himself from them. The disruption caused by the impression from the living beauty was of a sensuality exclusively cerebral and destroyed instinctive attraction. He remembered with anguish having remained impotent like an old man for an entire hour while close to the most admirable woman whom he had ever held in his arms. And since that night, he had learned to choose less perfect mistresses.

"Friend," said a voice, "do you not recognize me?"

He turned, signaled negatively and continued on his way, because he never undressed the same woman twice. It was the one principle that he followed during his visits to the gardens. A woman who a man has not yet had, has something of a virgin about her, but what good result, what surprise is in store in a second meeting? It is already like a marriage. Demetrios did not expose himself to the disillusions of a second night. Queen Berenice satisfied his rare conjugal whims and outside of her, he took care each evening to renew the accomplice of the indispensable adultery.

"Clonarion!"

"Gnathene!"

"Plango!"

"Mnais!"

"Crobyle!"

"Ioessa!"

They shouted out their names as he passed by and some of them added a declaration of their ardent nature or offered him an aberrant act. Demetrios kept going; he was inclined, according to his habit, to help himself, at random, to any in the group — when a little girl, dressed entirely in blue, tilted her head to the side, and without getting up, said sweetly to him:

"Is there a possibility?"

The unexpectedness of this proposition made him smile. He stopped.

"Open the door," he said. "I choose you."

The little girl joyously sprang to her feet and struck two blows with the phallic hammer. An old female slave came to open the door.

"Gorgo," said the child, "I have someone; quick, some Cretan wine, some cakes and make the bed."

She turned toward Demetrios.

"Do you need an aphrodisiac?"

"No," said the young man, laughing, "have you any?"

"It is a necessity," said the child, "They ask me for it more often than you think. Come this way; take care at the steps, one is quite worn. Go into my room, I will be back."

The decor was simple, like the room of all novice courtesans. A large bed, a second bed for lounging, some rugs and some marble benches barely furnished the room, but from a large open bay, he saw the gardens, the sea, and the double roads of Alexandria. Demetrios stood gazing at the distant city.

Setting suns behind the harbors! — incomparable glories of maritime cities, calm skies, deep-red waters, onto what turbulent soul, with pain or with joy, would you not cast silence! What steps do not halt, what sensual pleasures do not suspend themselves, what voice does not extinguish itself before you!... Demetrios looked out: a surge of torrential flame appeared to gush forth from the sun, halfway plunge into the sea, and course its way directly to the curving shore of the woods of Aphrodite. From one horizon to the other, a sumptuous gamut of crimson spread over the Mediterranean, the nuances of which formed striations without transitions, from golden red to cold violet. Between this splendor in motion and the moss-green mirror of Lake Mareotis, the white mass of the town was entirely clothed with reddish-violet reflections. The orientation of its twenty-thousand symmetrical houses were marvelously speckled with twenty-thousand spots of color, in a perpetual metamorphosis, according to the diminishing phases of the western radiance. It was rapid and incendiary; then, suddenly, the sun was nearly swallowed up and the first ebbing of night wafted over the whole earth, a chilliness, with a gentle breeze, steady and clear.

"Here are some figs and cakes, a honeycomb, some wine, and a woman. The figs must be eaten in the daylight and the woman when the light of the day can no longer be seen!"

The little girl had returned, laughing. She made the young man sit down, and she sat astride his knees and, with both hands behind her head, pinned up a rose that had slid down her light brown hair.

Involuntarily Demetrios uttered an exclamation of surprise. She was completely naked and thus stripped of the billowing garment, her petite body showed her to be so young, her breasts so childlike, so narrow-hipped, so visibly immature that Demetrios was seized with pity, like a horseman ready to mount all his weight onto a fragile filly.

"But you are not a woman!" he cried.

"I am not a woman! By the two goddesses, what am I then, a Thracian, a dockhand or an old philosopher?"

"How old are you?"

"Ten-and-a-half years old. Eleven years old. You could say eleven. I was born in the gardens. My mother is Milesian. She is Pythias, whom they call 'the Goat.' Do you want me to send someone to look for her, if you find me too young? Her house is not far from mine."

"Were you at the Didascalion?"

"I am still there and in the sixth class. I will finish next year; it will not be too soon."

"What bothers you there?"

"Ah! If you knew how difficult the teachers are! They make us do the same lesson over twenty-five times! All those things are totally useless and men never ask for such things. And then, we are tired for nothing; I do not like that. Look here, take a fig — not that one, it is not ripe. I will teach you a new way to eat them, look."

"I know it. It takes longer and it is no better. I see that you are a good student."

"Oh! What I know I have learned by myself. The teachers would like to make us think that they are more skillful than us. They are more experienced, that's possible, but they have invented nothing."

"Do you have many lovers?"

"All too old; it is inevitable. Young men are so stupid! They love only forty year-old women. I see them pass by, sometimes, those who are pleasing as Eros, and if you saw what they chose — hippopotami! It makes a person turn pale. I hope that I will not live to the age of those women. I would be too ashamed to undress myself. I am so happy, you see, so happy to be still so young. My breasts will bulge out quickly. It seems to me that the first month when I see my blood trickle down, I will believe that death already is near. Let me give you a kiss. I like you very much."

Here the conversation took a turn less sedate, if not more silent, and Demetrios quickly perceived that his scruples were not needed with this petite person already so well informed. She seemed to realize that she was meager fodder for a young man's appetite so she led her lover astray by an amazing activity of furtive touches, that he could neither anticipate, nor endure, nor control and never let him relax in a loving embrace. The small body, agile and resolute, was everywhere around him, offering and refusing, slipping, turning, struggling. In the end, they grasped each other. But that half-hour was only one long frolic.

She jumped out of the bed first, drenched her finger with honey from a cup and smeared it on her lips; then, with a thousand efforts not to laugh, she bent over Demetrios, rubbing her mouth on his. Her plump curls danced on each side of her cheeks. The young man smiled and leaning on his elbow, he asked:

"What is your name?"

"Melitta. Did you not see my name on the door?"

"I did not look."

"You could have seen it in my room. They have written it all over my walls. I will soon be forced to have them repainted."

Demetrios raised his head: the four panels of the room were covered with inscriptions.

"Really, this is rather curious," he said. "May I read them?"

"Oh! If you wish. I have no secrets."

He read. The name of Melitta was found repeated several times with the names of men and with some crude drawings. Phrases, tender, obscene or comic, were bizarrely entangled. Some lovers boasted of their vigor, or related, in great detail, the charms of the tiny courtesan, or even made fun of her fair fellow courtesans. All of which was hardly interesting except as a written witness of a general luridness. But toward the end of the panel on the right, Demetrios was startled.

"Who is this? Who is this? Tell me."

"Who? What? Where?" said the child. "What is the matter with you?"

"Here. That name. Who wrote that?"

And his finger stopped under this double line:

ΜΕΛΙΤΤΑ .Λ. ΧΡΨΣΙΔΑ
ΧΗΡΨΣΙΣ .Λ. ΜΕΛΙΤΤΑΝ
MELITTA + CHRYSIDA
CHRYSIS + MELITTAN

"Ah!" she replied. "I did. I wrote that."

"But who is this Chrysis?"

"She is my best friend."

"I thought as much. That is not what I asked you. Which Chrysis? There are many."

"Mine — she is the most beautiful. Chrysis of Galilee."

"You know her! You know her! Tell me, then! Where does she come from? Where does she live? Who is her lover? Tell me everything!"

He sat down on the lounge and took the child on his knee.

"You are in love with her then?" she said.

"It does not concern you. Tell me everything that you know. I absolutely need to know."

"Oh! I do not know everything about her. I know very little. She came to my house twice and do you think that I asked her about her family history? I was too happy to have her and I lost no time in conversations."

"What was her figure like?"

"She had the form of a beautiful woman, is that what you want me to say? Must I name every part of her body in addition to its overall beauty? She is a woman, a real woman ... When I think about her, I immediately have the desire for someone."

And she grabbed Demetrios around the neck.

"You know nothing," he resumed, "nothing about her?"

"I know ... I know that she comes from Galilee, that she is almost twenty years old and that she lives in the Jewish Quarter, east of town, near the gardens. But that is all."

"And about her life, about her tastes? You can tell me nothing? She loves women, after all, she comes to you. But is she only a lesbian?"

"Of course not. The first night she spent here, she brought a male lover and I swear to you that she did not fake anything. When a woman is sincere, I see it in her eyes. That did not prevent her from returning one time, all alone ... And she promised me a third night."

"Do you know of another friend of hers in the gardens? Anyone?"

"Yes, a woman from her country. A poor woman, Chimaris."

"Where does she live? I must see her."

"She sleeps in the woods, and has for a year. She sold her house. But I know where her cave is. I can guide you there, if you want. Put my sandals on me, will you?"

Demetrios skillfully tied the braided leather straps onto Melitta's fragile ankles. Then, he held her short tunic out and she slipped it easily over her arms, and they left hurriedly.

They walked a long time. The park was immense. From a distance, a young woman under a tree called out her name while opening her cloak, then lay back down, her hand over her eyes. Melitta knew some of them who kissed her without detaining her. While passing in front of a worn altar, she picked three large flowers from the grass and put them down on the stone.

The night had not yet darkened. The intense light of summer days has something durable that vaguely lingers in the slow-ebbing twilight. The stars, timorous and watery, hardly brighter than the nadir of the sky, blinked with a gentle palpitation, and the shadows of the branches remained tentative.

"Wait!" said Melitta. "Mamma. It is Mamma!"

Alone, a woman, dressed in a triple muslin striped with blue, came toward them, walking leisurely. As soon as she saw the child she ran to her, lifted her from the ground, took her in her arms and kissed her greedily on her cheeks.

"My little girl! My little love, where are you going?"

"I am guiding someone who wants to see Chimaris. And you? Are you taking a walk?"

"Corinna delivered her baby. I went to her and dined at her bedside."

"And what did she have — a boy?"

"Twin girls, my dear, rosy as wax dolls. You can go there tonight. She will show them to you."

"Oh! It's wonderful! Two little courtesans. What did she name them?"

"Pannychis for both of them, because they were born on the eve of the festival of Aphrodite. It is a divine omen. They will be beautiful."

She put the child back down on her feet and addressed Demetrios:

"How do you like my child? Have I the right to be proud of her?"

"You can be satisfied with each other," he said, calmly.

"Kiss mamma," said Melitta.

Without a word, he placed a kiss between her breasts. Pythias repaid him with a kiss on his mouth and they parted.

Demetrios and the child took a few more steps under the trees, while the courtesan went further away, turning back to look at them. At last, they arrived, and Melitta said:

"Here it is."

Chimaris was crouching on her left heel, on a small grassy space between two trees and a bush. She had spread out under her a sort of red rag that was her last garment during the day and upon which she lay, naked, at the time of day when men passed by. Demetrios contemplated her with growing interest. She had that feverish look of certain thin brown women whose wild bodies always seemed consumed by a pounding fervor. Her powerful lips, her furious gaze, her large, livid eyelids, formed a double image, of lustful sensuality and impoverishment. The curve of her concave belly and her impatient thighs became more taut, as if to receive. Chimaris had sold everything, her combs and her pins, even her tweezers, and her hair was entangled in an inextricable disorder, while a black pubescence added, to her nudity, something of the savage, brazen and hairy.

Near her, a large goat stood on his stiff hoofs. He was attached to a tree by a golden chain that had once wound four times around, glittering on the breast of his mistress.

"Chimaris," said Melitta, "sit up. There is some who wants to speak to you."

The Jewess looked, but did not budge.

Demetrios went toward her.

"Do you know Chrysis," he asked.

"Yes."

"Do you see her often?"

99

"Yes."

"Can you tell me about her?"

"No."

"Why, no? Why can you not?"

"No."

Melitta was bewildered:

"Tell him," she said. "Be assured; he loves her — he wishes her well."

"I see clearly that he loves her," replied Chimaris. "If he loves her, he wishes the worst. If he loves her, I will not speak."

Demetrios shook with anger, but held his tongue.

"Give me your hand," the Jewess said to him. "I will see there if I am wrong."

She took the left hand of the young man and turned it toward the moonlight. Melitta bent over in order to see, although she could not read the mysterious lines, their fatality attracted her.

"What do you see?" asked Demetrios.

"I see ... can I say what I see? Will you be pleased with me? Will you even believe me? First, I see complete happiness; but it is in the past. Also, I see complete love, but that is lost in the blood ..."

"Mine?"

"The blood of a woman. And, the blood of another woman. And then, yours, a little later."

Demetrios shrugged his shoulders and when he turned around, he caught a glimpse of Melitta running as fast as her legs could carry her down the path.

"She is afraid," resumed Chimaris. "However, it has nothing to do with either her or me. Let things take their course, since nothing can stop them. Before you were born, your destiny was determined. Go. I will speak no more."

And she let his hand drop.

SCRUPLES

"THE blood of a woman. Followed by the blood of another woman. And then, yours, a little later."

Demetrios repeated those words as he walked, and however he might have wanted it otherwise, her conviction oppressed him. He had never trusted prophecies extracted from the body of the victims or from the movement of the planets. Such relationships seemed too questionable to him. But the complex lines of his hands had themselves the appearance of an exclusive, individual horoscope that he regarded with some uneasiness. And so the prediction of the clairvoyant inhabited his thoughts.

In turn, he contemplated the palm of his left hand, where his life was compressed in signs, secret and indelible.

First, he saw, at the summit, a sort of ordinary crescent, whose tips were pointed toward the base of his fingers. Below that, a fourfold line, tangled and pale pink, creased and marked in two places by bright red points. Another more slender line ran down, at first parallel, then veered abruptly toward his wrist. Finally, a third, short and precise, formed the contour for the base of the thumb that was entirely covered with faint threadlike lines. — He saw all that, but not being able to read the hidden meaning, he put his hand over his eyes and changed the object of his meditation.

Chrysis, Chrysis, Chrysis. This name throbbed within him like a fever. To satisfy her, to conquer her, to wrap her in his arms, to fly away with her, to Syria, to Greece, to Rome, anywhere, provided that it was in a place where he would have no mistresses and she no lovers — that was what must be done, and now, now!

Of the three gifts that she had asked for, one was already secured; two others remained.

"First, the comb," he thought.

And he quickened his pace.

Every evening, after the sun set, the wife of the High Priest sat on a white marble bench, its back framed by the forest, overlooking the expanse of sea. Demetrios was always aware of her, because this woman, like so many others, was in love with him, and she had told him once that, on the day he desired, she would be there for his taking.

Consequently, that is where he went.

She was, in fact, there, but she did not see him coming. She remained seated, with her eyes closed, her body thrown back against the white bench and her arms placed as if by random.

She was an Egyptian. Her name was Touni. She wore a translucent tunic of vivid purple, without clasps or sashes, and the only embroidery on it marked the points of her breast with two black stars. The sheer fabric, pressed into folds, fell to the delicate rounding of her knees and tiny sandals of blue leather enveloped her slender and curved feet like gloves. Her skin was very dusky, her lips were very full, her shoulders were very straight. Her delicate and pliant waist appeared fatigued by the weight of her neck. She slept, her mouth open, dreaming peacefully.

Demetrios leaned over her, without a sound. For several moments, he breathed in the exotic fragrance of her hair; then, drawing out one of the two long, golden hairpins that glittered above her ears, he thrust it quickly under her left breast.

But, this woman would have given him her comb and even her hair as well for love.

If he did not ask it, it was because of his exacting scruple: Chrysis had, very precisely, demanded a crime — not simply any antique jewel sticking in the hair of a young woman. That is why he believed it was his duty to agree to the spilling of blood.

Yet, he might have considered that the oaths that a lover makes to women during the amorous foreplay can be forgotten in the meantime without great damage to the moral value of the lover who has sworn them. And if this involuntary forgetfulness could be used as an excuse, it would surely be in a case where the life of another innocent woman lay in the balance. But Demetrios did not see the validity of such reasoning. The affair he pursued had turned out to be so unique that the violent events disappeared into thin air. He was afraid that he would later regret having erased from the intrigue some scene, however short, that was necessary to the beauty of the totality. Often, only one sanctimonious deletion is necessary for reducing a tragedy into the banality of everyday life. The death of Cassandra, he mused, was not an indispensable fact in the plot of *Agamemnon,* but if it had not taken place, all of the *Orestea* would have been spoiled.

That is why, having cut Touni's hair, he thrust into his cloak the comb with scenes etched in ivory, and, without reflecting any further, he undertook the third of the labors commanded by Chrysis: the possession of the necklace of Aphrodite.

He did not intend to enter the temple by way of the Great Gate. The dozen hermaphrodites who guarded the entrance would have doubtlessly let Demetrios pass through, in spite of the interdiction that halted all the uninitiated in the absence of the priest.

There was, however, no reason that he prove, so naively, his future culpability, since a secret entrance led to the sanctuary.

Demetrios went into the section of the deserted woods where the Necropolis of the High-Priests of the goddess lay. He counted from the beginning tombs, turned the door of the seventh one, and closed it behind him.

With great difficulty, because of the heaviness of the stone, he raised the burial slab, beneath which plunged a marble stairway, and he descended, step by step.

He knew that he could take sixty steps in a straight line, and after that, he must follow the wall, feeling the way, in order not to bump into the temple's subterranean stairway.

The vast coolness of the earth's depths calmed him, little by little.

In a few moments, he arrived at the end.

He went up the stairs and opened the door.

MOONLIGHT

OUTSIDE the night was light and in the divine enclosure, dark. When he had, with caution and gentleness, closed the reverberating door, he felt a shiver overwhelm him, as though engulfed by the coldness of the stones. He did not dare to look up. The black silence frightened him; the darkness populated itself with the unknown. He laid his hand on his forehead like a man who does not want to wake up for fear of finding himself living. Finally, he looked around.

In the full moonlight, the goddess appeared lifelike on her pedestal of rose-colored stone, laden with dangling treasures. She was naked and sexual, vaguely painted according to a woman's coloring. In one hand, she held a mirror whose handle was a phallus, and, with the other, she adorned her beauty with a necklace made of seven strands of pearls. One pearl was larger than the others, silvery and elongated, glowing between her breasts like a nocturnal crescent moon between two rounded clouds. And they were the true sacred pearls, born of the drops of water that had tumbled into the shell of the Anadyomene.

Demetrios was lost in an inexpressible adoration. Indeed, he believed that it was Aphrodite herself. He no longer recognized his own work, so profound was the abyss between what he had been and what he had become. He held out his arms before him and murmured the mysterious words in the way the goddess is beseeched in the Phrygian ceremonies.

Supernatural, luminous, impalpable, naked and pure, the vision, wavering on the stone, swayed gently. He stared at her; but, he feared already that the caress of his gaze would make the fragile hallucination dissipate into the air. He advanced very softly, touched the pinkish toe with his finger as if to assure himself of the statue's existence, and, incapable of stopping himself as she drew him to her, he stepped up, stood close to her and placed his hands on her white shoulders while gazing into her eyes.

He trembled, he swooned, he laughed with joy. His hands roamed over her naked arms, squeezed her cold hard waist, descended down her legs, and caressed her rounded belly. Using all his strength, he pushed away from this Immortality. He looked at himself in the mirror, lifted up the pearl necklace, took it off, luminescent in his hands, and timorously put it back. He kissed the folded hand, the curved neck, the throat, the slightly opened marble mouth. Then, he drew back to the edge of the base, and, clinging to her divine arms, he looked tenderly at the exquisite bowed head.

Her hair was fixed in the oriental style and lightly veiled her forehead. Her half-closed eyes were drawn out with her smile. Her lips remained apart, as though fainting from a kiss.

Silently, he arranged the seven strands of rounded pearls over the magnificent breast and stepped down to the floor to look at the idol from a distance.

Then, it seemed that he reawakened. He recalled what he had come to do, what he had wanted to do — had all but accomplished — a monstrous thing. He felt himself flush to his temples.

The recollection of Chrysis passed through his mind like a crude apparition. He listed everything that made the beauty of the courtesan doubtful: her thick lips, her billowy hair, her indolent steps. He had forgotten her hands, but he imagined them as broad, to add an odious detail to the image that he spurned. His state of mind became like a man surprised at dawn by his own mistress having been replaced by a woman of the lower class, and who could not understand how he could have been tempted the evening before. He found neither an excuse or even a substantial reason. Evidently, for one day, he had suffered from a sort of momentary madness, a physical disorientation, an illness. He felt cured, but still in a drunken stupor.

In order to complete his recovery, he leaned back against the wall of the temple and remained standing for a long time in front of the statue. The moonlight continued to fall through a square opening in the roof. Aphrodite shone brightly and, as though her eyes could see in the darkness, he sought to meet their gaze …

… He spent all night like this. Then, daylight came and the statue took on, in turns, the rosy plum of the dawn and the golden reflection of the sun.

Demetrios could no longer think. The ivory comb and the silver mirror that he carried in his tunic had disappeared from his mind. He gently abandoned himself to a serene meditation.

Outside, a storm of bird cries chattered, whistled, and sang in the garden. He heard the voices of women talking and laughing at the foot of the walls. The excitement of morning surged forth from the awakened earth. Demetrios was filled with happiness.

The sun was already high and the shadows from the roof had shifted when he heard the jumbled noise of feet, lightly scurrying up the outside steps.

It was, without a doubt, a sacrifice being offered to the goddess, a procession of young women had come to fulfill or declare their vows in front of the statue. It was the first day of the Festival of Aphrodite.

Demetrios wanted to flee.

The sacred pedestal opened in the back in a certain way known only to the priest and the sculptor. A priest stood there, whose voice was clear and high, in order to dictate to a young child the miraculous words that came from the statue on the third day of the festival. Through this opening, Demetrios could get to the gardens. He went through it and stopped in front of the doorway bordered with bronze that opened the dense stone.

The two heavy golden doors opened slowly and the procession entered.

THE INVITATION

DURING the middle of the night, Chrysis was awakened by three knocks at the door.

She had slept all day between the two Ephesians and, except for the rumpled bed, they could have been taken for three sisters. Rhodis was curled up against the Galilaean, whose sweating leg lay heavily on her. Myrtocleia slept on her stomach, her face on her arm, with her back bare.

Chrysis untangled herself carefully, took three steps on the bed, got down, and opened the door a crack.

A loud voice came from the entrance.

"Who is it, Djala? Who is it?" she asked.

"Naucrates, he wants to talk with you. I told him that you are not free."

"Really, what stupidity! Of course, I am free! Come in, Naucrates. I am in my bedroom."

And she went back to bed.

Naucrates remained on the threshold for some time, as though he feared being indiscreet. The two musicians opened their sleepy eyes, but could not tear themselves away from their dreams.

"Sit down," said Chrysis. "This is no occasion for us to be coy with one another. I know you do not come for me. What do you want?"

Naucrates was a well-known philosopher who, for more than twenty years, had been Bacchis' lover and had never betrayed her, more from laziness than from fidelity. His gray hair was cut short, his beard pointed, like Demetrios, and his mustache ran along the top of his lips. He wore a large white garment of plain evenly striped wool.

"I come with an invitation," he said. "Bacchis is giving a diner tomorrow that will be followed by a festival. There will be seven of us if you come. Do not fail to come."

"A festival? What is the occasion?"

"She is going to set her beautiful slave, Aphrodisia, free. There will be dancers and flute players. I believe your two friends had been given orders and they should not be here. People are rehearsing at the house of Bacchis this very moment."

"Oh! It is true," cried Rhodis, "We weren't thinking about it. Get up, Myrto, we are very late."

But Chrysis protested.

"No! Not yet! That is wicked of you to take my women away from me. If I suspected that, I would have never let you in here. Oh! Look, they are already dressed!"

"Our tunics are easy to put on," said the child. "And we are not beautiful enough to spend a long time getting dressed."

"Will I see you at the temple, at least?"

"Yes, tomorrow morning, we will bring the doves. I am going to take one drachma from your purse, Chrysis, because we have nothing with which to buy them. Good-bye, until tomorrow."

They ran out. Naucrates looked, for some time at the door that closed behind them, then folded his arms and said in a hushed voice, turning back toward Chrysis:

"Good. You conducted yourself well."

"How so?"

"Just one woman no longer satisfies you. Now, you must have two. You even take them into the street. What a good example. But then, will you tell me, what remains for us, the men? You have all the women friends and, after leaving their exhausting embrace, you give only as much of your passion as they are willing to leave you. How long do you think that can be endured? If things continue like this, we will be forced to go to Bathyllus..."

"Ah! No!" cried Chrysis. "I will never admit to that! I know people make that comparison. It does not make any sense and I am astonished that you, who make a profession of thinking, you do not understand the absurdity of it."

"And what difference do you find?"

"It is not a question of difference. There is no comparison between the one and the other, that is clear."

"I do not say that you are wrong. I want to know your reason."

"Oh! That can be said in a few words — listen carefully. The woman is, as concerns love, a finished instrument. From head to toe, she is designed uniquely, marvelously, for love. She alone knows how to love. She alone knows how to be loved. Consequently, if an amorous couple is made of two women, it is perfect; if there is only one woman, it is half as good; if there is no woman, it is purely idiotic. I have spoken."

"You are hard on Plato, my girl."

"Great men are not, any more than the gods, great in every circumstance. Pallas had no business sense, Sophocles did not know how to paint, Plato did not know how to love. Philosopher, poets, or rhetoricians — those who make use of his name are no better, and, however admirable they may be in their art, in love they are ignorant. Believe me, Naucrates, I know I am right."

The philosopher nodded: "You are a little irreverent," he said, "but I certainly feel that you are not entirely wrong. My indignation was not genuine. There is something charming in the union of two young women, on the condition that everything, for the two of them, should retain the feminine, keeping their long hair, uncovering their breasts and not putting on artificial implements, as if, illogically, they envy the crude sex that they so prettily scorn. Yes, their liaison is remarkable because their caresses are all external and their sensual pleasure so much more subtle. They do not embrace with roughness, they glide over the surface, in order to taste the ultimate joy. Their wedding night is not bloody. They are virgins, Chrysis. They know nothing of brute force; in that, they are superior to Bathyllus, who claims to offer the equivalent, forgetting that you too, even for this shabby business, could compete with him. Human love is only distinguished from senseless bestial rutting by two divine functions, the caress and the kiss. These are the sole functions experienced by the women whom we are talking about here. They have even perfected them."

"No one can do better," said Chrysis, perplexed. "But why, then, do you reproach me?"

"I reproach you for the existence of one hundred thousand; already a huge number of woman experience that perfect pleasure only with their own sex. Soon, you will no longer welcome us, even as a last resort. I chide you because I am jealous."

Naucrates found that the conversation had gone on long enough and he calmly stood up.

"I can tell Bacchis that she can expect you?" he said.

"I will come," responded Chrysis.

The philosopher kissed her knees and left slowly.

*

* *

Then, she clasped her hands and spoke out loud, although she was all alone.

"Bacchis ... Bacchis ... He comes from her house and does not know! ... then, the Mirror is still there? ... Demetrios has forgotten me ... If he hesitated the first day, I am lost; he will do nothing ... But it is possible that all is done! Bacchis has other mirrors that she uses more often. Without a doubt, she still does not know...Gods! Gods! There is no way of getting the news, but perhaps ... Ah! Djala! Djala!"

The slave entered.

"Give me my knuckle-bones," said Chrysis. "I want to throw them."

And she threw the tiny four-sided bones into the air ...

"Oh! ...Oh! ... Djala, look! The cast of Aphrodite!"

She called out a rather rare cast by which each bone presented a different face. There was exactly a thirty-five-to-one chance against such an occurrence taking place. It was the best throw of the game.

Djala observed coolly:

"What did you ask for?"

"It is true," said Chrysis, disappointed. "I had forgotten to make a wish. I really thought of something, but I said nothing. Does it count all the same?"

"I do not think so. You must start over."

For a second time, Chrysis threw the bones.

"Now the cast of Midas. What do you think?"

"I do not know. Good and bad. It is a cast that is explained by another throw. Do it again with one bone."

For a third time, Chrysis demanded an answer from the game, but as soon as the bone stopped tumbling, she stammered:

"The ... the point of Chios!"

And she burst into sobs.

Djala said nothing; she, too, was upset. Chrysis cried on the bed, her hair spread out around her head. Finally, she turned around angrily.

"Why did you make me do it again? I am certain that the first throw counted."

"If you made a wish, yes. If you did not make a wish, no. Only you know," said Djala.

"Besides, the bones prove nothing. It is a Greek game. I do not believe in it. I am going to try something else."

She dried her tears and walked across the room. She took a box of white tokens from the shelf, counting out twenty-two, then, with the tip of a sculpted pearl buckle, she engraved on them, one after the other, the twenty-two letters of the Hebrew alphabet. They were the secrets of the Cabalah that she had learned in Galilee.

"It is in these that I have confidence. Here, there is no trickery," she said. "Lift up the hem of your robe; that will be my bag."

She threw the twenty-five tokens into the slave's tunic, while asking over and over again in her mind: "Will I wear the necklace of Aphrodite? Will I wear the necklace of Aphrodite? Will I wear the necklace of Aphrodite?"

And she drew the tenth secret, which said precisely what she had wished: "Yes."

THE ROSE OF CHRYSIS

I T was a procession — white, blue, yellow, rose, and green.

Thirty courtesans moved on, carrying baskets of flowers, snow-white doves with red feet, veils of the most pale azure, and precious ornaments.

An old white-bearded priest, enveloped even around his head in a stiff, unbleached material, walked in front of the youthful procession and guided the file of bowing devotees toward the stone altar.

They chanted, and their chant languished like the sea, sighed like the wind of midday, and panted like a passionate mouth. The first two carried the harps, supported in the hollow of their left hand, and curved out before them like slender wooden sickles.

One of the young women stepped forward and said:

"Tryphera, Oh beloved Cypris, offers you this blue veil that she wove herself, so that you continue to be benevolent toward her."

Another:

"Mousarion lays at your feet, Oh Goddess of the Magnificent Crown, these crowns of gillyflowers and this bouquet of bowed narcissi. She wore them in the orgy and invoked your name in the intoxication of their perfume. Oh Victorious one, receive these spoils of passion."

Still another:

"As an offering to you, Golden Cytherea, Timo consecrates this spiral bracelet. May you coil vengeance around the throat of someone you know like this silver serpent coiled itself to the top of your naked arms."

Myrtocleia and Rhodis came forward, hand in hand.

"Here are two doves from Smyrna, with white wings like caresses, with red feet like kisses. Oh Double Goddess of Amathonte, accept them from our joined hands, if it is true that the tame Adonis alone does not satisfy you and that a still sweeter embrace sometimes delays your sleep."

A very young courtesan followed:

"Aphrodite Peribasia, receive my virginity with this tunic stained with blood. I am Pannychis of Pharos; since last night I have dedicated myself to you."

And another:

"Dorothea implores you, Oh charitable Epistrophia, to banish from her soul the desire that Eros cast there, or, finally, set ablaze for her the eyes of him who refuses. She gives this branch of myrtle to you because it is the tree that you prefer."

Another:

"On your altar, Oh Pasiphae, Callistion deposits sixty silver drachmae, the remainder of four minae that she received from Cleomenes. Give her a lover more generous still, if you see the offering as a good one."

There only remained before the idol a child, blushing all over, who had placed herself at the end of the line. In her hand she held only a crown of crocus and the priest showed contempt for such a meager offering.

She said:

"I am not rich enough to give you pieces of silver, Oh Shining Olympian. Besides, what could I give you that do not already possess? Here are flowers, yellow and green, braided into a garland for your feet. And now…"

She undid the two clasps of her tunic and stood naked, the cloth having slid down to the ground.

"…Here I am in my entirety for you, Beloved Goddess. I want to enter into your gardens, to die a courtesan of the temple. I vow to desire only love, I vow to delight in love, and I renounce worldly life, and take refuge in you."

The priest then enveloped her in incense and surrounded her bareness with the veil woven by Tryphera. They went out from the nave together through the door to the gardens.

The procession seemed to be finished, and the other courtesans were starting to retrace their steps, when they saw, crossing the threshold late, the last woman.

She had nothing in her hand and they could have thought that she also had come to offer only her beauty. Her hair appeared like two torrents of gold, two waves, deep and shadow-filled, that engulfed her ears and twisted itself on the back of her neck. Her nose was delicate, with slender nostrils that sometimes quivered above her full mouth, painted to its curved, mobile corners. The supple line of her body undulated with each step, animated by the sway of her hips or the swing of her unbound breasts below which her curved waist yielded.

Her eyes were extraordinary deep blue, but bright at the same time, changeable like lunar stones, half-closed under recumbent lids. They looked out, these eyes, like the sirens sing…

The priest turned toward her, waiting, so she might speak.

She said:

"Chrysis, Oh Chryseia, begs you. Accept the meager gifts that I place at your feet. Listen, heed, love and soothe her who lives according to your example and for the veneration of your name."

She held out her hands, golden with rings, and bowed, her legs pressed together.

The faint chant began again. The strum of the harps rose toward the statue along with the swift smoke from the incense that the priest burned in a trembling brazier.

She straightened slowly, and presented a bronze mirror that hung inside her sash.

"To you," she said, "Astarte of the Night, who intermingles hands and lips and whose symbol is like the imprint of the foot of the doe on the pale earth of Syria, Chrysis consecrates her mirror. It has seen the blackened contour of my eyelids, the sparkling of my eyes after love, my hair pasted to my temples by the sweat from your struggles, Oh Combatant with fierce hands, who intertwines bodies and mouths."

The priest placed the mirror at the feet of the statue. Chrysis drew from her golden coil of hair, a long comb of reddish copper, the terrestial metal of the goddess.

"To you," she said, "Anadyomene, who was borne from the bloody dawn and from the foamy smile of the sea; to you, who tied up your wet hair with ribbons of green seaweed, nakedness dripping with pearls, Chrysis consecrates her comb. It has plunged into my hair disheveled by your movements, Oh furious, breathless Adonienne, who draws taut the loins and contracts the rigid knees."

She gave the comb to the old man and bent her head to the side in order to remove her necklace of emeralds.

"To you," she said, "Oh Hetara, who makes the blush from the timid virgin vanish and who excites the unchaste laugh, to you, who passes the wind of love, streaming from her entrails, Chrysis consecrates this necklace. It was given, in payment, by a man whose name is not known to her, and each emerald is a kiss where you have lived for an instant."

She bowed down further, one last time, put the necklace into the hands of the priest and took a step to go.

The priest restrained her.

"What do you ask from the goddess for those precious offerings?"

She smiled, shaking her head, and said:

"I ask nothing."

Then she walked along the side of the procession, stole a rose from a basket and put it in her mouth as she was leaving.

One by one, the women followed. The door closed on the empty temple.

*
*　*

Demetrios remained alone, hidden by the bronze pedestal.

During this entire scene, he had not missed one gesture or one word, and when everything finished, he stayed for a long time motionless from a new anguish, passionate and hesitant.

He had believed himself cured of his brush with insanity, and he had thought that nothing, from that time on, could throw him a second time into the passionate shadow of this exotic woman.

But he had left her out of his calculations.

Women! Oh Women! If you want to be loved, show yourselves, return, be here! The emotion that he had felt at the entrance of the courtesan was so complete and so oppressive that he could no longer think of fighting it with his own volition. Demetrios was bound like a barbaric slave to a triumphal chariot. Freeing himself was an illusion. Without him knowing how, she had taken hold of him naturally.

He had seen her coming far into the distance, because she had on the same yellow cloth as when she went along the pier. She walked, her steps slow and supple, swaying her hips gently. She had come straight towards him, as though she had divined him behind the stone.

From the first moment, he realized that he would fall at her feet again. When she drew the mirror of polished bronze from her sash, she looked at herself for some time before she gave it to the priest and the brilliance of her eyes became stupefying. When taking out her copper comb, she placed her hand on her hair while raising a bending arm, like a gesture made by the Charities, every beautiful line of her body displayed itself under the fabric and, in her armpit, the sun set ablaze a dew of sweat, sparkling and minute. Finally, in order to lift up and take off her heavy emerald necklace, she threw the pleated silk that veiled her breasts down to the sweet shadow-filled space where a bouquet could be slipped, Demetrios felt himself seized by such a frenzy — to place his lips there and tear off the rest of her tunic ... But Chrysis had begun to speak.

She spoke, and each word caused him pain. Wantonly, she seemed to insist on dwelling on the prostitution of this vessel of beauty that she was, white like the statue herself, and full of gold that streamed from her hair. She spoke about her door open to the leisure of the passerby, the contemplation of her body given up to the undeserving, and the placing of her hot checks into the care of awkward children. She spoke about the mercenary fatigue of her eyes, her lips hired out to the night, her hair entrusted to brutal hands and her divinity plowed over.

The ease of access to her in these surroundings drew Demetrios towards her, determined at least to have her for himself alone and to shut the door behind her. So true is it that a woman is only thoroughly seductive if a man has a good reason to be jealous of her.

But then, having given her emerald necklace to the goddess in exchange for that which she hoped for, Chrysis turned back toward the town, — she carried away a human will between her lips, like the tiny stolen rose whose stem she nibbled.

Demetrios waited until he was alone in the enclosure, then he left his hiding-place.

He looked at the statue with difficulty, waiting for that battle within himself. But, as he was incapable of reviving such a very violent emotion after so brief an interval, he became astonishingly calm again and without any untimely regrets.

Heedlessly, he climbed up quietly, close to the statue, lifted the Necklace of the True Pearls of the Anadyomene from the nape of the bowed neck and slid it into his tunic.

THE STORY OF THE ENCHANTED LYRE

H E walked very rapidly, hoping to find Chrysis still on the road that led to the town, fearful that if he waited any longer his courage and will would again fail him.

The path, white-hot, was so bright that Demetrios shut his eyes as against the noonday sun. He went on like this and, without looking in front of him, just missed colliding with four black slaves who walked at the head of a new procession. Just then, a tiny, melodious voice said sweetly:

"Beloved! How happy I am!"

He raised his head: it was the queen, Berenice, leaning on her elbow, in her litter.

She gave an order:

"Stop, bearers!" and held her arms out to the lover.

Demetrios found this exceedingly irritating, but he could not refuse her, and he sullenly climbed in.

Then Queen Berenice, mad with joy, crept along on her hands to the end of the litter, slithering over the pillows like a cat who wants to play.

This litter was a room, carried by twenty-four slaves, so that a dozen women could easily, randomly, lie down in it, on a dull blue rug, strewn with pillows and fabrics, and its height was such that they could not touch the ceiling, even with the tip of their fans. It was more long than wide, enclosed in front and on three sides by yellow, very thin curtains that sparkled from the light. The back wall was made of cedar, draped with a long veil of orange silk, while at the top, above this vibrant lining, a vast golden sparrow-hawk of Egypt spread out its rigid feathered span.

Beneath it, sculpted in ivory and silver, the ancient symbol of Astarte opened above the lighted lamp that struggled with the daylight in the wandering reflections. Below, Queen Berenice was lying between two Persian slaves who waved two fans of peacock feathers around her.

Her gaze drew the young sculptor to her side and she said again:

"Beloved! I am happy!"

She put her hand on his cheek.

"I have been searching for you, Beloved. Where have you been? I have not seen you since the day before yesterday. If I had not met up with you just now, I would soon be dead from sorrow. Completely alone in this huge litter, I was so bored that while passing over the Hermes bridge, I threw all my jewels into the water in order in make circles. You see, I no longer wear any rings or necklaces. I look like a little waif at your feet."

She turned around facing him and kissed him on the mouth. The two fan-bearers went to crouch a little further away, and when Queen Berenice began to speak very quietly, they put their fingers in their ears to appear as if they could hear nothing at all.

But Demetrios did not respond, paid little attention, and remained aloof. As for the young queen, he saw only the red smile of a mouth and the head of loose hair, like a black cushion to lay a weary head down on.

She said:

"Beloved, I cried during the night. My bed was cold. When I woke up, I spread out my two bare arms from both sides of my body and I did not feel you there, and nowhere did my hand find your hand, the hand that I kiss today. I waited for you every morning and since the full moon you have not come. I sent slaves into every section of the town and I killed them myself when they returned without you. Where were you? Were you at the temple? You were not in the gardens with those strange women, were you? No, I see it in your eyes that you have not been unfaithful. Then, what were you doing so far from me? Were you in front of the statue? Yes, I am certain of that, you were there. Now you love her more than me. She looks like me, she has my eyes, my mouth, my breasts; but it is she that you desire. Me, I am a poor destitute girl. You are bored with me, I can tell that. You think about your marble and your pitiful, sordid, wretched statues as if I were not the most beautiful of all of them, and at least, alive, loving and good, ready for what you want to accept, resigned to what you refuse. But you want nothing. You do not want to be king, you do not want to be a god and worshiped in a temple of your own. You scarcely want to make love to me."

She drew her feet back under her and leaned on her hand.

"I would do anything to see you at the palace, Beloved. If you no longer desire me, tell me who attracts you, she will be my friend. The ...the women of my court... are beautiful. I have a dozen there who, since their birth, have been protected in my women's quarters and have no idea that men even exist ... they will all be your mistresses if you come to see me after them ... And I have others with me who have had more lovers than the sacred courtesans and are expert in love. Say something, I also have a thousand foreign slaves: those whom you desire will be delivered. I will clothe them as I do myself, in yellow silk and gold and silver.

"But of course, you are the most handsome and the most indifferent of men. You love no one, you let yourself be loved, you give yourself away as charity to those whom your eyes set ablaze with passion. You allow me to take my pleasure of you, but like a beast permitting someone to draw milk from it while turning its gaze off into the distance. You are filled with condescension. Ah, Gods! Ah! Gods! I will end up doing without you, young conceited youth who is adored by the entire town and who can never be made to shed tears. I do not have only females in the palace. I have robust Ethiopians who have chests of bronze and arms knotted by muscles. In their embraces, I will quickly forget your girlish legs and your pretty beard. The performance of their passion will, without a doubt, be new for me and I will be refreshed from being loved. But the day when I will be certain that your absent gaze will no longer worry me and I can replace your lips, then I will hurl you from the top of Hermes' bridge to join my necklaces and my rings like a jewel worn too long. Ah! To be queen!"

She sat up and gave the impression of waiting. But Demetrios remained, as always, impassive and no more changed than if had not heard her. She began again, with anger:

"Have you not understood?"

He leaned nonchalantly on his elbow and said, in a very calm voice:

"The idea for a story has come to me."

*

*   *

"Once upon a time, long before Thrace had been conquered by your father's ancestors, it was inhabited by savage beasts and a few frightened men.

"The beasts were strikingly beautiful — there were lions burnt red as the sun and tigers striped as the evening sky, and bears pitch-black as the night.

"The people were small and snub-nosed, covered by aged hairless skin, armed with crude and rough-hewn bows. In their mountain cave, they shut themselves in behind gigantic stones that were rolled away with great difficulty. Their life was spent on the hunt. There was blood in the forest.

"The country was so dismal that the gods had deserted it. When, in the whiteness of the morning, Artemis left Olympus, her course was never the one that would have led her toward the north. The wars that were indulged in there never concerned Ares. The absence of flutes and lyres dissuaded Apollo. The triple Hecate shone, alone there, like a face of Medusa over a petrified landscape.

"Now a man came there to live. He was from a more prosperous race and he did not walk around clothed in skins like the mountain savages.

"He wore a long white robe that trailed a little behind him. At night, he loved to wander in the woods in the moonlight through the gentle clearings, holding in his hand a small tortoiseshell in which were placed two horns of the wild ox and between them three silver cords were drawn taut.

"When his fingers touched the cords, a delicious music came from them, much sweeter than the sound of the springs, or the phrases of the wind in the trees, or the movements of the wild grasses. The first time he played, three sleeping tigers awoke, so amazingly charmed that they made no effort to harm him, but approached as closely as possible and withdrew when he stopped. The next day, there were still more of them — wolves, and hyenas, and snakes erect on their tails.

"So that, after a very short time, the animals themselves began to beg for him to play for them. It often happened that a single bear came close to him and went away contented with the three marvelous chords. In return for his compliance, the wild beasts gave him his food and protected him from men.

"But the man wearied of this indolent life. He became so sure of his genius and of the pleasure that he gave to the beasts, that he no longer tried to play well. The wild beasts found themselves always satisfied, as long as he was the one playing it. Soon, he refused to give them even that satisfaction, and quite casually stopped playing. All the forest was saddened, but the bites of meat and savory fruits did not fail to appear on the threshold of the musician. They continued to bring food and they loved him even more. The heart of the beast is thus made.

"Now, one day, leaning in his open doorway, he watched the sun fall behind the motionless trees, and a lioness passed nearby. He made a move to go inside, as if he were fearful of unpleasant greetings. The lioness was not concerned with him, and simply passed by.

"Then, he asked her, astonished: 'Why do you not beg me to play for you?' She replied that she did not care about it. He asked her: 'Do you not know me?' She replied: 'You are Orpheus.' He asked again: 'And do you not want to hear me?' She repeated: 'I do not want to.' — 'Oh!' he cried. 'Oh! How I am to be pitied. It is just for you that I would have desired to play. You are much more beautiful than the others and you must understand so much better. If you listen to me for only an hour, I will give you everything you dream of.' She responded: 'I order you to steal the fresh meats that belong to the men of the plain. I order you to kill the first man that you meet. I order you to take the victims that they have offered to your gods and lay them at my feet.' He thanked her for demanding nothing more and went to do as she commanded.

"For an hour, he played before her, but after that he broke his lyre into pieces and acted as though he were dead."

*

* *

The queen sighed:

"I never understand allegories. Explain it to me, Beloved. What does it mean?"

He arose.

"I have not told it to you so that you will understand. I have recounted a story to calm you a little. Now, it is late. Farewell, Berenice."

She began to cry.

"I knew it! I knew it!"

He laid her down like an infant on her soft bed of velvety cushions, with a smile placed a kiss on her unhappy eyes, and calmly descended from the huge moving litter.

Pierre Louÿs

BOOK THREE

THE ARRIVAL

BACCHIS was a courtesan for more than twenty-five years. That is to say, she was nearing her fourth decade and in that time, her beauty had taken on several different forms.

For a long time, her mother had been the manager of her household and had advised her on life. She had given her the principles of conduct and economy that she had applied carefully in her youth. She had amassed, little by little, such a considerable fortune that, at an age when the magnificence of the bed makes up for any deficiencies in the lustre of the body, she could consume without calculating the cost.

In the same way, instead of buying very expensive slaves at the market — an expenditure that others thought necessary and that bankrupted young courtesans — she had owned, with satisfaction, only one Negress for ten years and, in preparation for the future, she had her impregnated each year so that numerous servants were created, free of charge, who would later enrich the household. As she had chosen the father with care, seven very beautiful mulatto girls were born of her slave, and also three boys, whom she had killed because male slaves arouse needless suspicions in jealous lovers. She had named the seven girls after the seven planets and had chosen separate privileges that corresponded, as nearly as possible, to their given names. Heliope was the slave of the day, Selenis, the slave of the night, Aretias guarded the door, Aphrodisia concerned herself with the bed, Hermione went shopping, and Cronomagira did the cooking. Finally, Diomede, the steward, kept the accounts and made the important decisions.

Aphrodisia was the favorite slave, the prettiest, the most loved. She often shared the bed of her mistress on the demand of lovers who were desperately attracted to her. Therefore, she was excused from all menial tasks to preserve her delicate arms and soft hands. As an exceptional privilege, she was not made to cover her head, so that she was often taken for a free woman and this very evening, she was going to be freed, at the enormous price of thirty-five minae.

The seven slaves of Bacchis, all of lofty stature and admirably trained, were such a source of pride for her that she did not go out without having them follow her, at the risk of leaving her house empty. It must have been this indiscretion that allowed Demetrios to enter her house so easily; but she still was not aware of her misfortune when she gave the banquet — the banquet to which Chrysis was invited.

*
*　*

That evening, Chrysis was the first to arrive.

She was dressed in a green robe embroidered with enormous branches from which grew roses, flowering over her breasts.

Aretias opened the door for her, without her having to knock, and, following the Greek custom, she led her into a small side room, took off her red shoes and gently washed her bare feet, because guests were spared every trouble, even of having to do their own grooming before going to diner. Then raising her robe or pushing it aside, depending on the spot, she perfumed wherever it was necessary. After that, she presented a comb and hairpins to her, to rearrange her hair, and, at the same time, some thick, dry makeup for her lips and cheeks.

When Chrysis was finally ready:

"Who are the pale imitations?" she asked the slave.

All the guests were called this, except the one who was the Guest. The one in whose honor the diner was being given had brought with him those who pleased him, and the pale imitations had only to take care to bring along their pillowy-beds and behave themselves.

Aretias responded to Chrysis' question:

"Naucrates invited Philodemos with his mistress, Faustine, who he brought back from Italy. He also asked Phrasilas and Timon, and your friend, Seso from Cnidus."

At that very moment Seso entered.

"Chrysis!"

"My dear!"

The two women embraced and lavished each other with exclamations at the happy chance that reunited them.

"I was afraid of being late," said Seso. "This pest Archytas kept me ..."

"What, still him?"

"It is always the same old thing. When I am going to dine in town, he imagines that everyone is going to have his way with me. Then, before it happens, he wants to avenge himself and that is what I must put up with! Ah! My dear! If he only knew me better! I hardly have a desire to betray my lovers. I have had my fill of them!"

"And the child? It is not obvious, you know."

"I should hope so! I am in the third month. It is growing, the little wretch. But it does not bother me yet. In six weeks I will begin to dance; I hope that will make it very difficult for it to tolerate and that it will take its leave quickly."

"You are right," said Chrysis. "Do not let your body become distorted. Yesterday, I saw Philemation, our little friend from years past, who has lived in Boubaste for three years with a grain mer- chant. Do you know what she told me? The very first thing? 'Ah! If you could see my breasts!' and she had tears in her eyes. I told her that she was still pretty, but she repeated: 'If you could see my breasts! Ah! Ah! If you could see my breasts!' while crying like a Byblis. Then, I realized that she wanted to show them and I asked to see them. My dear! Two empty sacks. And you know how beau- tiful they were. I could not see any nipples, they were so white. Do not spoil yours, my Seso. Keep them young and firm as they are. The breasts of a courtesan are worth more than her necklace."

The two women continued to talk like this while they dressed. Finally, together, they entered the banquet hall where Bacchis stood waiting, her waist grasped by a serpent-like cinch and her neck laden with golden necklaces, one on top of the other, up to her chin.

"Ah! Dear beauties, what a good idea of Naucrates it was that you two get together again tonight."

"We were both pleased that it was at your house," replied Chrysis, without appearing to understand the allusion. And, in order to immediately say something wicked, she added:

"How is Doryclos?"

He was the very rich young lover who had just left Bacchis in order to marry a Sicilian.

"I ... I have sent him away," retorted Bacchis.

"Is it possible?"

"Yes. They say that he is going to marry just for spite. But I expect him the day after his wedding. He is mad about me."

While asking: "How is Doryclos?" Chrysis thought: "Where is your mirror?" but Bacchis did not look directly at her and she could read nothing but a vague disquiet, devoid of meaning. More- over, Chrysis had time to resolve this question and, in spite of her impatience, she knew enough to resign herself to wait for a more favorable occasion.

She had begun to continue the conversation when she was interrupted by the arrival of Philodemos, Faustina, and Naucrates, which forced Bacchis to create more original compliments. She fell into ecstasies over the poet's embroidered garment and over the diaphanous robe of his Roman mistress. This young girl, knowing little of Alexandrian customs, had thought to Hellenize herself in this way, not realizing that this kind of costume was not worn at a banquet where hired dancers would appear in the same state of undress. Bacchis did not make it apparent that she noticed this mistake. She found some kind words complimenting Faustina on her thick bluish hair so soaked with glistening perfumes that she wore it up off the back of her neck, held with a golden hairpin to avoid spotting her airy silken fabric with myrrh.

They were about to take their places at the table, when the seventh guest entered: it was Timon, a young man whose absence of principles was a natural gift, but who had found, in the teachings of the philosophers of his time, some excellent reasons to improve his character.

"I have brought someone," he said, laughing.

"Who is it?" asked Bacchis.

"A certain Demo, who is from Mende."

"Demo! You don't mean it, my friend. She is a woman of the streets. Anyone can have her for the price of a dried date."

"Oh, well. I will not insist," said the young man. "I just met her at the corner of the Canopic way. She asked me to take her to dinner and I lead her to you. If you do not want her ..."

"This, Timon, is unbelievable," Bacchis declared.

She called a slave:

"Heliope, go tell your sister that she will find a woman at the door and she is to drive her away. Go."

She turned around, looking for someone.

"Phrasilas has not arrived?"

THE BANQUET

WITH these words, a pitiful little man, with a gray fore-head, gray eyes and a small gray beard, came forward with mincing steps and said, smiling,

"I was over there."

Phrasilas was an esteemed writer on several different matters, yet no one could say exactly whether he was a philosopher, a grammarian, a researcher, or a mythologist, as he approached the most serious studies with a hesitant intensity and a flittering curiosity. He did not dare write a treatise. He did not know how to construct a drama. His style had the flavor of the hypocritical, the meticulous and the vain — for the thinkers, he was a poet; for the poets, he was a wise man; for society, he was a great man.

"Well, let us go to the table," said Bacchis. And she stretched herself out on the lounge with her lover, presiding over the banquet. At her right lay Philodemos and Faustine with Phrasilas; to the left, Naucrates, Seso, then Chrysis and young Timon. All the guests reclined at an angle, resting their elbows on a silk cushion, their heads encircled with flowers. A slave brought the garlands of red roses and blue lotus. Then the meal began.

Timon felt that his caprice had thrown a slight chill over the women. Therefore, he did not speak to them first, but addressed Philodemos, saying with great seriousness:

"They claim that you are a very devoted friend of Cicero. What do you think of him, Philodemos? Is he an enlightened philosopher or merely a compiler without discernment or taste, because I have heard both opinions upheld."

"Precisely because I am his friend, I cannot respond to that," said Philodemos. "I know him too well; I know his bad side. Ask Phrasilas, who, having read little of him, will judge without error."

"Well, what does Phrasilas think of him?"

"He is an admirable writer," said the little man.

"What do you mean by that?"

"In the sense that all writers, Timon, are admirable in something, like every country and every soul. I would not know how to place more importance on the spectacle of the sea than on the dullest of the plains. Therefore, I would not classify, according to my own preferences, a treatise by Cicero, an ode by Pindar, and a letter by Chrysis, even if I knew the style of your excellent friend. I am satisfied when, after closing a book, I can take away in my memory one line that has made me think. Until now, all of those that I have opened contained that one sentence, but not one has given me a second. Perhaps each of us has only one thing to say in our lives and those who attempt to speak for a longer time have illusions of grandeur. How much more I regret the irretrievable silence of the millions of souls who have not spoken."

"I do not agree with you," said Naucrates, without raising his eyes. "The universe was created so that three truths might be told and it is our misfortune that their certainty was proved five centuries before tonight. Heraclitus understood the world; Parmenides unmasked the soul; Pythagoras determined God: we have only our silence left. I find the chick-pea very audacious."

With the handle of her fan, Seso tapped the table.

"Timon," she said, "my friend."

"What?"

"Why do you ask questions that are of no interest, either to me, who does not know Latin, or for you, who wants to forget it? Do you think you will dazzle Faustine with your foreign erudition? Poor friend, you do not deceive me with your words. I undressed your great soul last night under my covers and I know, Timon, what chick-pea concerns your soul."

"Do you think so?" the young man said simply.

But Phrasilas began a second little discourse, in an ironic and sweet voice.

"Seso, when we have had the pleasure of hearing you judge Timon, whether it be to applaud him as he deserves or to blame him, about which we could know nothing, remember that he is a spirit whose soul is unique. The soul does not exist by itself, or at least we cannot know that it does, but reflects that which is mirrored there and changes its configuration when it changes place. Last night, it was like you: I am not surprised that it pleased you. At this moment, it has taken on the image of Philodemos; that is why you just said that it contradicted itself. Now it has no need to contradict itself since it affirms nothing. You see that it is necessary, my dear, to refrain from making thoughtless judgements."

Timon shot an irritated glance at Phrasilas, but held back his response.

"However that may be," replied Seso, "here we are, four courtesans, and we intend to direct the conversation so that we do not look like rosy-pink babies who only open their mouth in order to drink milk. Faustine, since you are the newest arrival, begin."

"Very good," said Naucrates, "choose for us, Faustine. What should we talk about?"

The young Roman turned her head, raised her eyes, blushed, and, with one heave of her whole body, sighed:

"Of love."

"A good subject!" said Seso.

But no one took up the topic.

*

* *

The table was covered with garlands, herbs, cups and pitchers. Slaves brought baskets of bread as light as snow. On painted earthenware plates, there were fat eels sprinkled with seasonings, and fish — alphestes the color of wax and sacred callichtys.

They also served a pompile, a deep-reddish fish that was believed to be born from the same foam as Aphrodite, boöps, bedradones, a red mullet flanked by squid and multicolored scorpaeni. So that they could be eaten while piping hot, they were served in their tiny casseroles, then a portion of mollusk, fatty tuna, and hot octopus whose arms were tender; finally, the white belly of an electric ray, with curves like that of a beautiful woman.

This was the first course, and the guests selected, with tiny mouthfuls, the succulent morsels of each fish, leaving the rest to the slaves.

"Love," began Phrasilas, "is a word that has no meaning or means everything at once, because it designates, in turn, two irreconcilable sensations: Sensual pleasure and Pain. I do not know in which sense Faustine means it."

"I want," interrupted Chrysis, "sensual pleasure for my part and suffering for my lover's. You must talk about both or you will only half interest me."

"Love," murmured Philodemos, "is neither suffering nor pleasure. Love is something other ..."

"Oh! For heaven's sake," cried Timon, "let us make an exception tonight and have a banquet without philosophizing. We know, Phrasilas, that you can maintain, with a sweet eloquence and a honey-coated persuasion, the superiority of multiple Pleasure over singular Suffering. We know too that, after having spoken for a full hour over so difficult a subject, you would be ready, in the next hour, to support the argument of your opponent with the same sweet eloquence and the same honeyed persuasion. I do not ..."

"Allow me ...,"said Phrasilas.

"I do not deny," continued Timon, "the charm of this little game, nor even the wit that you bring to it. I do doubt its difficulty and, more than that, its interest. The 'Banquet' that you published in the past carried a less serious narrative, and too, the thoughts that you recently ascribed to a mythical person, the image of your ideal, appeared fresh and unique under the reign of Ptolemy Auletes. But for three years we have lived under the young Queen Berenice and I wonder by what reversal in the method of reasoning you, harmonious and smiling, had taken from the illustrious guide that has suddenly aged a hundred years under your stylus, like the fashion of closed necklines and yellow tinted hair. Excellent master, I lament it, because if your tales loose a little of the fire, if your experience of the feminine heart is superfluous, you are endowed, as compensation, with a comic spirit and I know the pleasure of your having made me smile."

"Timon!" cried Bacchis, indignantly.

Phrasilas stopped her with a gesture.

"Let it be, my dear. Unlike the majority of men, I remember, of the judgements where I am the subject, only the part of the oration that I find congenial. Timon has given me his; others praise me on other points. I could not live in the midst of an unanimous approval, and even the variety of sentiments that I awake is, for me, a charming flower-bed when I desire to inhale the roses without uprooting the succulents."

Chrysis made a movement with her lips that clearly indicated how little she thought of this man who was so expert at ending discussions. She turned back toward Timon, next to her on the lounge, and put her hand around his neck.

"What is the purpose of life?" she asked of him.

It was the only question that she knew to ask a philosopher, but this time she put such a tenderness into her voice that Timon believed he was hearing a declaration of love.

However, he responded with an assured calmness:

"To each his own, my Chrysis. There is not a universal purpose for the existence of beings. For myself, I am the son of a banker whose clients comprised all of the great courtesans of Egypt and, my father having amassed a considerable fortune by ingenuous methods, I nobly restore it to the victims of his beneficence, while lying with them as often as the strength that the gods have given to me allows. My energy, I had thought, is allowed to be replenished only by one activity in life. Such is the one I have chosen since it reconciles the demands of the rarest virtue with the contrary satisfactions that another ideal would not sustain as easily."

While saying these things, he had slid his right leg behind those of Chrysis, lying on her side, and attempted to spread apart the closed knees of the courtesan, as if to give a precise purpose to his existence for that evening. But Chrysis did not let him do as he pleased.

There were a few moments of silence, then Seso started the discussion again.

"Timon, you are very annoying, interrupting from the start, the only serious talk whose subject we could grasp. At least let Naucrates speak, since you have such a wicked nature."

"What will I say about love?" responded the Invited One. "It is the name that is given to pain, in order to console those who suffer. There are only two ways to be unhappy here: either desire what you do not have or possess what you desire. Love begins with the first and is finished with the second, in the most lamentable case, that is to say, as soon as it succeeds. May the gods save us from loving!"

"But to possess unexpectedly," said Philodemos, smiling, "is that not true happiness?"

"What a rarity!"

"Not at all, — if care is taken. Pay attention, Naucrates: not to desire, but make certain that the occasion presents itself; not to love, but cherish from a distance some very select persons to whom you are drawn and, to whom, in the long run, you could have a liking if chance and circumstances made you inclined towards them; never embellish a woman with those qualities that you desire, nor boast of her beautiful adornment which she keeps a mystery, but anticipate tastelessness so that you are astonished by the exquisite — is this not the best advice that a sage could give to lovers? Only those who have lived happily have known how to savor, in their precious existence, the invaluable purity of some unexpected delight."

*
*   *

The second course was nearly finished. They had been served pheasants, grouse, a magnificent blue and red phorphyris, and a swan with all its plumage, which had been cooked for forty-eight hours so as not to scorch its wings. Water hyacinths, a pelican, a white peacock appearing to have hatched eighteen rounded testes, roasted and oiled, were displayed on rounded platters; in short, provisions enough to feed one hundred people from the scraps that were left after the choice morsels had been set aside. But all of this was nothing compared to the last dish.

The masterpiece (for a long time, nothing like it had been seen at Alexandria) was a suckling pig, half of which had been roasted and the other half had been simmered in broth. It was impossible to discern the manner in which it had been killed, or how they had filled up the belly with everything it contained. In fact, it was stuffed with plump quails, breasts of fowl, larks, succulent sauces, portions of vulva and minced meat; all of whose presence, in the intact animal, appeared inexplicable.

There was a cry of admiration, and Faustine decided to ask for the recipe. Phrasilas uttered, while smiling, sentences stuffed with metaphors; Philodemos improvised a couplet where the word χοιροσ, or sacrificial pig, took on double meanings, one after the other, so that Seso, who was already drunk, laughed until she cried.

But, Bacchis had, at the same time, given the order to pour seven rare wines into seven cups for each guest and the conversation degenerated.

Timon turned toward Bacchis:

"Why," he asked, "were you so merciless towards that poor woman I wanted to bring in? She was, after all, a colleague. In your place, I would value a poor courtesan more than a rich matron."

"You are crazy," said Bacchis, as if to end the discussion.

"Yes, I have often remarked that those who are considered madmen are those who risk exclusion by telling the obvious truths. The world is full of paradoxes, right?"

"Look, my friend, ask your neighbors. What sort of wellborn man would take a woman without jewels for his mistress?"

"I have done that," said Philodemos, plainly.

And the women scorned him.

"Last year," he continued, "at the end of spring, the exile of Cicero gave me a reason to fear for my own safety, so I made a short journey. I secluded myself in a charming place called Orobia, at the foot of the Alps near the shores of Clisius, a small lake. It was a rustic village, with only three hundred women and one of them had become a courtesan so the virtue of the others would be protected. Her house was known by the bouquet of flowers hanging from her door, but she herself could not be distinguished from her sisters or her cousins. She knew nothing of makeup, perfumes, cosmetics, transparent veils and curling irons. She did not know how to take care of her beauty, depilating herself with a sticky resin as though ripping out weeds from a courtyard of white marble. It makes a person shudder to think that she walked without shoes and, due to that, I would not kiss her bare feet like we kiss Faustine's, which are softer than her hands. And yet, I found her so full of charm, that near her brown body, for one whole month, I forgot Rome and happy Tyre and Alexandria."

Naucrates nodded approvingly and said, after taking a drink:

"The grand climax of love is the instant when nakedness reveals itself. Courtesans should know this and save some surprises for us. But now it seems, on the contrary, they put all their efforts into disillusioning us. Is there anything more painful than seeing the marks of a hot iron on flowing hair? Anything more disagreeable than painted cheeks whose color clings to the kiss? Anything more pitiful than the outlined eye whose charcoal has smeared? If absolutely necessary, I could understand how honest women might use these illusory means: every woman loves to surround herself with a circle of adoring men. Those honest women do not, at any rate, expose themselves to the liberties that would unmask their natural appearance. But the courtesans, who have the bed as a goal and a resource, they are not afraid of exposing themselves as less beautiful than on the street; for them, that is unimaginable."

"You know nothing about it, Naucrates," said Chrysis, with a smile. "I know that one lover out of twenty cannot be held; but one man out of five hundred is not seduced, and before pleasing him in bed, it is necessary to please in the street. No one would look at us, in passing, if we did not put on red and black. The little peasant of whom Philodemos spoke did not have any problem attracting him because she was the only one in her village; there are fifteen thousand courtesans here — it is a different sort of competition."

"Do you not know that pure beauty needs no ornamentation and is sufficient in itself?"

"Yes. Very well, put a pure beauty, as you define her, up against, Gnathene, who is ugly and old. Put the first in a tunic full of holes in the last row of the theatre and the second in her star-covered robe in a place reserved by her slaves, and note their prices when they leave: eight obols will be given to the pure beauty and two minae to Gnathene."

"Men are stupid beasts," concluded Seso.

"No, just simply lazy. They do not trouble themselves when choosing their mistresses. The most loved are the most deceitful."

"What if," insinuated Phrasilas, "what if, on the one hand, I would willing praise …"

And he affirmed, with a great charm, two suppositions devoid of all interest.

*

* *

One by one, a dozen dancers appeared, the first two played the flute and the last two, the tambourine; the others struck their rattles together. They tightened their thin straps, rubbed white resin on their tiny sandals, and waited, their arms held out, for the music to begin... One note... two notes... a Lydian scale ... and with a fast beat, the twelve young girls surged forward.

The dance was sensual, luxurious and without apparent order, although all the steps had been choreographed in advance. They gradually furled themselves into a small space; they mingled together like waves. Soon, they formed couples, and, without missing a beat, untied their sashes and let their rose-colored tunics drop. An odor of nude women spread out around the men, dominating the fragrance of the flowers and the vapor of the half-opened meats. They thrust themselves backward, their bellies taut and their arms before them. Then, they straightened up, pushing apart their thighs and their bodies touched, in passing, the nipples of each other's shaking breasts. Timon's hand was caressed by a thigh, wild and hot.

"What is our friend thinking?" said Phrasilas in his frail voice.

"I feel perfectly happy," responded Timon. "I have never understood so clearly, until this evening, the supreme mission of woman."

"And what is it?"

"To prostitute herself — with or without skill."

"That is one opinion."

"More to the point, Phrasilas, we know that nothing can be proved; furthermore, we know that nothing exists and even of that we are not certain. Remember that, and to satisfy your venerable mania, permit me to have a thesis, at the same time debatable and trite as they all are, but interesting for me who affirms it and for the majority of men who deny it. In matters of thought, originality is still an ideal more fanciful than a certainty. You cannot ignore that."

"Give me some wine from Lesbos," said Seso to her slave. "It is stronger than the other one."

"I maintain," continued Timon, "that a married woman, in devoting herself to a man who betrays her; in refusing herself all others (or in only allowing herself a rare adultery, which comes to the same thing), in bringing into the light the infants that distort her before their birth and monopolize her after it: — I maintain that, in living like this, the honest woman loses her life, and that the day of her marriage, the young woman makes a fool's bargain."

"She considers it obeying her duty," said Naucrates, without conviction.

"A duty? Toward whom? Is she not free herself to direct a question that concerns her alone? She is a woman and, as a woman, she is generally deaf to all intellectual pleasure; and, not content to remain estranged from half of human joy, she marries, denying herself the other face of sensual pleasure. So a young girl can say to herself at the age when she feels everything so intensely: 'I will know my husband, and ten lovers, perhaps, a dozen.' Can this young girl imagine that she will die without any regrets? For myself, three thousand women will not have been enough on the day that I leave this life."

"You are ambitious," said Chrysis.

"But with what a eulogy, with what gilded verses," cried the sweet Philodemos, "must we forever praise the beneficent courtesans! Thanks to them, we escape the complicated precautions, the jealousies, the deceptions, the pounding heart of the adulterer. They save us from waiting in the rain, teetering ladders, secret entrances, interrupted trysts, intercepted letters, and misunderstood signals. Oh, dearest ones, how I love you! With you, no siege is necessary: for some insignificant pieces of money you give us and beyond, what another would grudgingly accord us as a favor after three weeks of cruelty. For your enlightened souls, love is not a sacrifice, it is a gift exchanged equally between two lovers. Likewise, the sums entrusted to you do not serve as a compensation for your invaluable tenderness, but do pay a fair price for the many charming excesses that, with the utmost willingness, you consent to take care of our needs and each night exhaust our sensual demands. Because there are so many of you, we always find among you, the woman of our dreams, the whim of our night, — all the voracious women, with their hair in every shade, their eyes in every color, their lips in every flavor. There is no love under the sky so pure that you would not know how to mimic it, or so vile that you would not dare to offer it. You are charming to the uncouth, consoling to the afflicted, welcoming to all, and beautiful, so beautiful! That is why I tell you, Chrysis, Bacchis, Seso, Faustina, that it is a just law of the gods that bestows to the courtesans the eternal desire of lovers, and the eternal envy of virtuous wives."

The dancers were no longer dancing.

A young acrobat had just entered, juggling daggers and walking on her hands between erect blades.

Since the attention of the guests was focused on the child's dangerous game, Timon looked at Chrysis, and little by little, without being seen, he stretched out behind her until he could touch her with his feet and with his lips.

"No," said Chrysis in a quiet voice. "No, my friend."

But he slid his arm around her through a large slit in her robe and he carefully caressed the beautiful skin, hot and delicate, of the reclining courtesan.

"Wait," she pleaded. "They will see us. Bacchis will get angry."

A quick glance around convinced the young man that no one was looking at him. He grew more bold, caressing her further, where a woman, after permitting a man to go so far, rarely offers resistance. Then, so as to decisively extinguish the last scruples of fading modesty, he put his money into the hand that found itself accidently open.

Chrysis no longer put up a defense.

Meanwhile, the young acrobat continued her artful and perilous tricks. She walked on her hands, between sharp swords with long pointed tips, her skirt falling back, her feet dangling over her head. Her incommodious position and, perhaps also the fear of

wounds, flooded her cheeks with warm, dark blood that magni-
fied, even more, the brightness of her wide open eyes. She bent
over at the waist and straightened again. Her legs moved, whip-
like, in the air. Her bare breasts heaved with each difficult breath.

"Enough," said Chrysis, sharply. "You have irritated me, nothing more. Let go of me. Let go of me."

And at the moment when the two Ephesians rose up to play,
according to tradition, "The Fable of Hermaphroditus," she managed to slip from the bed and left, agitated.

RHACOTIS

T HE door had barely closed when Chrysis laid her hand on the burning center of her desire, as if to press a painful spot in order to quiet the throbbing. Then she leaned against a column and, wringing her hands, cried softly.

She would never learn anything!

Along with the passing hours, the improbability of her success exploded in front of her. Suddenly asking for the mirror was a tempting way to learn the truth. Yet, if it had been taken, she would draw suspicion toward herself and all would be lost. On the other hand, she could no longer stay there without speaking; such impatience had made her leave the room.

Timon's clumsiness had only aggravated her mute rage to the point of a trembling fury that forced her to press her body against the cool column, smooth and monstrous.

She feared she was having an attack of nerves.

She called out to the slave, Aretias: "Guard my jewels; I am going out." And she went down the seven steps.

The night was hot. Not a breath of air fanned the heavy drops of sweat from her forehead. The disappointment had increased her discomfort and made her unsteady.

She walked, closely following the street.

Bacchis' house was situated at the extreme end of Brouchion, at the outskirts of the infamous town of Rhacotis, an enormous hole in the wall populated with sailors and Egyptian women. The fishermen, who slept on their anchored ships during the oppressive heat of the day, spent their nights until dawn there, and, as payment for their double intoxication from the women and the wine merchants, they left the price from the fish of the day before.

Chrysis became entangled in the side streets of this Alexandrian slum, full of voices, animation, and barbaric music. She glanced furtively through open doors, the rooms reeking from the smoke of the lamps, where naked couples united. At crossroads, on low boards placed in rows in front of houses, multicolored straw mats groaned and undulated in the shadows under the doubled human weight. Chrysis walked, unsettled. A woman without a lover solicited her. An uncouth old man pinched her nipple. A mother offered her daughter to her. An adoring peasant kissed the back of her neck. She fled, blushing with shame and fear.

This foreign town within the Greek town was, for Chrysis, full of darkness and dangers. She was unfamiliar with the strange labyrinth, the complexity of the streets, the secrets of certain houses. When she risked going there, with long intervals in between, she always followed the same direct route toward a small red door; and there, she forgot her ordinary lovers in the untiring embrace of a young muscular mule-driver whom she, in turn, had the joy of paying.

But on this evening, without even having to move her head, she felt herself being followed by two pairs of footsteps.

She quickened her pace. The pair hurried after her. She started to run; they ran behind her; then, terrified, she took another side-street, then another one in the opposite direction, then a long path that led in another unfamiliar direction.

She fled, her throat dry, her temples pounding, sustained by Bacchis' wine, turning from right to left, pale and bewildered.

Finally, a wall barred her escape: she was at a dead end. With haste, she tried to turn back, but two sailors obstructed the narrow passage with their browned hands while one of them laughingly asked her: "Where are you going, little golden arrow?"

"Let me get past!"

"What? Are you lost, young woman; do you not know Rhacotis well enough then? We will show you the town."

And the both of them grabbed her by her sash. She cried out, struggled, threw a punch, but the second sailor seized both her hands at the same time with his left hand and said simply:

"Calm down. You know that no one here likes Greeks; no one will come to help you."

"I am not a Greek!"

"You lie, you have the white skin and the straight nose. Take it easy, unless you are not afraid of being beaten."

Chrysis looked at the one who spoke and, suddenly, threw her arm around his neck.

"I love you. You I will follow you," she said.

"You will follow the both of us. My friend here will have his due. Walk with us; you will not be disappointed."

Where would they take her? She had no idea, but the second sailor pleased her by his coarseness and his bestial head. She considered him with the steady gaze of a young dog in front of meat. She bent her body toward him in order to touch him while they walked.

Quickly, they went through foreign-looking quarters, without life, without light. Chrysis did not understand how they found their way in this nocturnal maze and she could not have found her way out on her own because the side streets were so bizarrely convoluted. The closed doors, empty windows, and motionless shadows terrified her. Above her, between two adjoining houses, a ribbon of pale sky stretched itself out, flooded with light from the moon.

At last, they returned to the living. The street turned, and suddenly, eight, ten, eleven lights appeared, brightening doorways where young Nabataean women remained crouched between two red lamps that lit from below their heads draped in gold.

In the distance, they heard a growing hum approaching, then the resounding clamor of chariots, tossed packages, donkey hooves and human voices. It was the marketplace of Rhacotis, where, when all of Alexandria slept, all of the provisions were amassed to feed nine hundred-thousand mouths in one day.

They walked along the houses surrounding the square, among the green piles, vegetables, lotus roots, glossy beans, baskets of olives. Chrysis took handfuls of mulberries from a reddish-purple heap and ate them without stopping. At last they arrived in front of a low door and the sailors descended with the One for whom the True Pearls of Anadyomene had been stolen.

There was an immense room. Five hundred working men were there, waiting for dawn, drinking cups of yellow beer, eating figs, lentils, sesame cakes and olyra bread. In the midst of them, a throng of screeching women, a field of black hair and flowers of every color, moving violently, in a heated atmosphere. They were poor women, without a home, who belonged to everybody. They came there begging to stay, barefoot, bare-breasted, a red and blue rag hardly covering their belly; most of them held a baby swaddled in a light cloth in their left arm. Also, there were dancing-women, six Egyptian women, on a stage, with an ensemble of three musicians; the first two struck leather-covered tambourines with slender sticks, while the third shook a large bronze rattle.

"Oh! Sugared plums!" said Chrysis, joyfully.

And she bought two coppers' worth from a little girl vendor.

Suddenly, she felt faint; so unbearable was the smell from this den of filth that the sailors carried her out in their arms.

The outside air seemed to refresh her a little.

"Where are we going?" she begged. "Let it be quick; I can no longer walk. I am not resisting you, you see, I am going to be good. But let us find a bed as soon as possible, or otherwise I will fall down in the street."

BACCHANAL AT THE HOUSE OF BACCHIS

WHEN she arrived once more before Bacchis' door, she was infused with a delicious sensation that gives respite from desire and silences the flesh. Her brow was unfurrowed. The lines of her mouth had softened. Only one intermittent ache still wandered in the crevice of her loins. She climbed the steps and crossed the threshold.

Since Chrysis had left the room, the orgy had spread like a fire.

Other friends had entered and, for them, the dozen naked dancers were easy prey. The ground was strewn with dead flowers from forty garlands. A goatskin of wine from Syracuse poured out, from one corner, a golden river reaching to the table.

Near to Faustine, whose clothes he had stripped off, Philodemos sung from memory the verses he had written about her:

"Oh feet," he sang, "Oh smooth thighs, deep loins, rounded bottom, slit fig, hips, shoulders, breasts, wavering nape! Oh you who drive me mad, eager hands, knowing touches, lively tongue! You are Roman, you are too brown, and you do not sing the verse of Sappho, but Perseus himself was also the lover of the Indian Andromeda."

Meanwhile, Seso was on the table, lying flat on her belly in the middle of the scattered fruit; completely disoriented from the fumes of the Egyptian wine, she dipped the nipple of her right breast into a sorbet of snow and repeated with a comical tenderness:

"Drink, my little one. You are thirsty. Drink, my little one. Drink. Drink Drink."

Aphrodisia, still a slave, triumphed in a circle of men and celebrated her last night of servitude with an unruly debauch. Following the tradition of all Alexandrian orgies, she handed herself over, at the first moment, to three lovers at the same time, but her task was not limited to that, and, until the night ended, according to the law of slaves who became courtesans, she had to prove, by an infinite zealousness, that her new dignity was in no way usurped.

Alone, standing behind a column, Naucrates and Phrasilas cordially discussed the respective merits of Arcesilas and Carneades.

At the other end of the room, Myrtocleia protected Rhodis from an unrelenting guest.

As soon as they saw Chrysis enter, the two Ephesians ran to her.

"We must go, my Chrysé. Theano is staying, but we are going."

"I will stay too," said the courtesan.

And she stretched out on her back on a huge bed covered with roses.

The sound of a voice and coins being thrown drew her attention: it was Theano who, in order to ridicule her sister, had thought, in the midst of laughter and cries, to act out a satire of the Fable of Danaë, feigning a frenzied sensual pleasure with each gold coin that penetrated her. The provocative impiety of the reclining child amused all the guests, because it was long past the age when lightning would have destroyed the mockers of the Immortals. But the play deteriorated, as might be feared. A clumsy man wounded the poor little girl and she began to cry loudly.

To console her, a new diversion had to be invented. Two dancing-girls slid, into the middle of the room, an enormous glided silver bowl, filled to the brim with wine, and someone grasped Theano by her feet and made her drink, head bent down, shaking from a burst of laughter that she could no longer control.

This idea was such a success that everyone gathered around her. When the flute player was put back on her feet, they saw her tiny face bright red from the blood rushing to her head and drops of wine streaming down; there was such a widespread hilarity from all the attendants that Bacchis said to Selenis:

"A mirror! A mirror! Let her see herself like this!"

The slave brought a bronze mirror.

"No! Not that one. The mirror of Rhodopis. She is worth the trouble."

With a single bound, Chrysis stood straight up.

A surge of blood rushed to her cheeks, then calmed down, and she remained perfectly pale, her chest heaving from the pounding of her heart, her eyes riveted on the door where the slave had gone out.

This moment would decide her whole life. Her last hope was going to vanish or be realized.

All around her the festivities continued. A crown of iris, thrown from who knows where, struck her mouth and left her with the acrid taste of pollen on her lips. A man poured perfume over her head from a small vial and it ran down too quickly, wetting her shoulders. Splashes from a full cup into which a pomegranate was thrown spotted her silk tunic and penetrated to her skin. She wore magnificently all the stains of the orgy.

The absent slave did not return.

Chrysis kept her stony pallor, immobile as a sculpted goddess. The rhythmic and monotonous moan of a woman making love not far from her measured the passing time. It seemed to her that this woman had been groaning like this since the day before. She would have liked to wring something, to break her fingers, to cry.

Finally, Selenis returned, her hands empty.

"The mirror?" asked Bacchis.

"It is …it is no longer there …it is …it is …stolen," the servant stuttered.

Bacchis uttered a cry so shrill that everyone stopped and a horrible silence suddenly interrupted the tumult.

From every corner of the vast room, men and women came close together: there was only a small open space where the frantic Bacchis stood before the slave, fallen at her feet.

"Speak! …Speak! …" shrieked Bacchis.

And when Selenis did not respond, she grabbed her violently by the neck:

"It is you who stole it, right? It is you? Answer now! I will have you whipped until you speak, you miserable little bitch!"

Then, something terrible happened. The child, wild with fear, fear of suffering, fear of dying, a terror more real than she had ever known, suddenly cried out:

"It is Aphrodisia! It is not me! It is not me!"

"Your sister!"

"Yes! Yes!" cried the mulatto slave, "It is Aphrodisia who took it!"

And they dragged their sister, who had just fainted, to Bacchis.

THE CRUCIFIED WOMAN

EVERYONE repeated in unison:

"It is Aphrodisia who took it! Bitch! Bitch! Filth! Thief!"

Their hatred for the favored sister was doubly intensified by the fear for themselves.

Aretias kicked her in the chest.

"Where is it!" Bacchis asked again. "Where did you put it?"

"She gave it to her lover."

"Who is he?"

"An Orphic sailor."

"Where is his ship?"

"It sailed this evening for Rome. You will not see the mirror again. She must be crucified, the bitch, the bloody beast!"

"Ah! Gods! Gods!" wept Bacchis.

Then her grief changed into an insane fury.

Aphrodisia had revived, but paralyzed with fright and comprehending nothing of what was going on, she remained silent, without tears.

Bacchis grabbed her by the hair and dragged her over the filthy floor, through the flowers and the puddles of wine, and screamed:

"To the cross! To the cross! Find the nails! Find the hammer!"

"Oh!" Seso said to her neighbor. "I have never seen a crucifixion. Let us follow them."

They all followed close together, hurrying. And Chrysis followed too — she alone who knew the guilty one, she alone who was the cause of it all.

Bacchis went directly into the slaves' room, a square room furnished with three mats where they slept, two by two, after nightfall. At the back, propped up like an ever-present menace, stood a cross in the form of a "T" that had not been used, until now.

In the midst of the confused murmuring of the young women and men, four slaves raised the martyr to the level of the branches of the crossbeam.

Not a sound had left her mouth, but when she felt the coldness of the rough beam against her bare back, her elongated eyes opened wide, she began a staccato wailing that never stopped until the end.

They put her astride a wooden stake that was driven into the middle of the upright beam, which supported the weight of the body, to avoid tearing her hands.

Then they spread out her arms.

Chrysis watched and said nothing. What could she say? She could not exonerate the slave without accusing Demetrios, who was above all pursuit, and would, she believed, seek cruel revenge. Besides, a slave was a valuable commodity, and Chrysis' long-standing rancor found pleasure in witnessing that her enemy would destroy, with her own hands, the worth of three thousand drachmae as certainly as if she had thrown silver coins into the Eunostos. And then, why should she concern herself with the life of a servile being?

Heliope held out the first nail and the hammer to Bacchis and the martyrdom began.

Intoxication, spite, fury, every passion at once, even that instinct for cruelty that dwells in the heart of woman, shook the soul of Bacchis at the moment when she struck and she let out a cry almost as piercing as Aphrodisia's when the nail tore at her open palm.

She nailed up the second hand. She nailed her feet, one on top of the other. Then, imboldened by the spurts of blood that gushed from the three wounds, she shouted:

"It is not enough! Wait! Thief! Sow! Sailor's Whore!"

One by one, she removed her long hairpins and thrust them violently into the flesh of Aphrodisia's breasts, belly, and thighs. When she no longer had any weapons in her hand, she slapped the wretched creature and spit on her.

For some time she contemplated the finished product of her vengeance, then she returned to the great room filled with guests.

Only Phrasilas and Timon did not follow her.

*

* *

After a moment of collecting himself, Phrasilas coughed slightly, put his right hand into his left, lifted his head, raised his eyebrows and approached the crucified girl whose body was in constant spasms.

"Although I am," he said to her, "in many cases, opposed to theories that speak in absolutes, I cannot disregard that you may profit, at this surprising juncture in your life, from being familiarized, in a more sophisticated manner, with the maxims of the Stoics. Zeno, who appears not to have had a mind free from error in all things, left us some sophisms without great import in general, but from which you could draw benefit with the specific intention of calming your last moments. 'Pain,' he said, 'is a word devoid of meaning, since our will overcomes the imperfections of our perishable body.' It is true that Zeno died at the age of ninety-eight without having had, the biographers say, one illness, even a slight one, but this is not an objection that can be held against him, since he did know how to keep himself in constant good health, we could only logically conclude that he would have been deficient of character if he had become ill. Besides, it would be an abuse to compel the philosophers to personally practice the rules of life that they propose and to unceasingly cultivate the virtues that they judge to be superior. Briefly, so as not to prolong excessively a discourse that would risk enduring longer than yourself; force yourself to elevate your soul, as much as you are able, my dear, above your physical sufferings. Whatever misfortune, whatever cruelty that you may be experiencing, I beg you be assured that I truly take a part of it. They reach their end; be patient — forget. Among the diverse doctrines that attribute immortality to us, now is the hour when you can choose the one that will best lay to rest your regret at dying. If the doctrines speak the truth, you will have lightened even the dread of the transition. If they speak falsely, what do you care? You will never know that you made a mistake."

Having thus spoken, Phrasilas readjusted the fold on the shoulder of his garment and shuffled away, with a troubled step.

Timon remained alone in the room with the dying girl on the cross.

The recollection of the night spent under the breasts of this poor unfortunate never left his memory, mingling with the atrocious image of the imminent rotting, the melting away of that beautiful body that had once burned in his arms.

He covered his eyes with his hand in order not to see the dying martyr, but without relief he *heard* the spasms of her body on the cross.

At last, he looked. A great profusion of bloody threads intersected over her skin from the pins in her breasts to her curled up toes. Her head turned unceasingly. All her hair hung down her left side, drenched in blood, sweat and perfume.

"Aphrodisia! Can you hear me? Do you recognize me? It is I, Timon, Timon."

A stare, already nearly blind, captured him for an instant. But her head kept turning. Her body never stopped quivering.

Softly, as though he feared the noise of his footsteps might cause her pain, the young man approached the foot of the cross. He stretched out his arms and carefully took her head, gently and turning it between his brotherly hands, piously swept back from along her cheeks the hair pasted with her tears, and placed on her fevered lips a kiss of infinite tenderness.

Aphrodisia closed her eyes. Did she recognize he who had come to transform her horrible end by this gesture of loving pity? An inexplicable smile elongated her blue eyelids and with a sigh she surrendered her soul.

ENTHUSIASM

S O, the deed was done. Chrysis had the proof.

If Demetrios had decided to commit the first crime, the other two must have followed immediately. A man of his rank would have considered murder, even sacrilege, to be less dishonorable than stealing.

He had obeyed, now he was captive. This free, indifferent, cold man, also submitted himself to slavery, and his mistress, his despot, was Chrysis, Sarah of the land of Gennesaret.

Ah! To dream of it, to repeat it, to say it out loud, to be alone! Chrysis darted from the noisy house, and ran quickly, directly into a cool morning breeze, feeling refreshed at last.

She followed the street up to the Agora that led to the sea and at the end, clustered together like gigantic sheaves of wheat, were the masts of eight hundred ships. Then, she turned to the right onto the wide expanse of Drome Avenue, where she found the house of Demetrios. A shiver of pride went through her when she passed in front of the window of her future lover, but she was not tactless enough to look for him there right away. She traveled the long road up to the Canopic Gate and flung herself on the ground between two aloe plants.

He had done it. Without a doubt, he had done it for her, more than any lover had done for any woman. She did not tire of repeating it and reaffirming her triumph. Demetrios, Beloved One, the impossible and hopeless dream of so many feminine hearts, had exposed himself to every peril, every shame, every remorse, willingly and for her. He had even renounced the ideal of his philosophy, he had stripped his work of the magnificent necklace, and the dawning of a new day would see the lover of the goddess at the feet of his new idol.

"Take me! Take me!" she cried. Now, she adored him. She called out for him, she desired him. The three crimes, in her mind, had transformed themselves into heroic deeds, for which, in turn, she would never have enough affection, never have enough passion to give. With what an incomparable flame this unique love would burn, both equally young, equally beautiful, equally in love with one another and, after overcoming so many obstacles, joined together forever!

Together they would go from here, they would leave the city of the queen, they would sail for mysterious lands, for Amathus, for Epidaurus, or even for that unknown Rome, the second city of the world after Alexandria, that was attempting to conquer the Earth. What would they not do, wherever they went! What joy would be unfamiliar to them, what human happiness would not be envious of theirs and not pale before their enchanted voyage!

Chrysis got up in a daze. She stretched her arms out, raised up her shoulders, and inhaled deeply. A feeling of increasing tenderness and joy swelled up in her firm breasts. She began to walk again, toward home...

Opening the door of her room, she was startled to see that nothing under her roof had changed since the day before. The small objects for her grooming, objects on the table and the shelves, seemed to her inadequate to surround her new life. She smashed the ones that were too directly associated with old, useless lovers, for which she had taken on an unexpected hatred. If she spared the others, it was not because she cared more about them, rather she did not want to dismantle her room for fear that Demetrios had planned to spend the night there.

She slowly undressed. The leftovers from the orgy dropped from her tunic, bits of cake, hairs, leaves from the roses.

She managed, with one hand, to loosen her sash from around her waist and plunged her fingers into her hair, to lighten the thickness. But before going to bed, she had the desire to lay down on the tapestries on the terrace where the coolness of the air was so delicious.

She climbed up.

The sun had only risen a few moments before. It sat on the horizon like an enormous, swollen orange.

A large palm tree, with its curved trunk, let its mass of green leaves dangle over the edge of the terrace. Chrysis, with her breasts in her hands, took refuge under them and they tickled her bare body; she shivered.

Her gaze wandered over the town, that whitened, little by little. The deep-red mists of the dawn rose above the silent streets and dissipated into the clear air.

Suddenly, an idea sprang to her mind, gathered momentum, and won out, leaving her delirious: Demetrios, he who had already done so much, why should he not kill the queen, he who could be the king?

And then …

And then, that monumental ocean of houses, of palaces, temples, porticoes, colonnades, that floated before her eyes, from the Necropolis of the West to the gardens of the Goddess: Brouchion, the Hellenic town, sparkling and uniform; Rhacotis, the Egyptian town, in front of which the Paneion, bathed in light, rose straight up like an Acropolitan mountain; the Great Temple of Serapis whose facade was framed by two long rose-colored obelisks; the Great Temple of Aphrodite surrounded by the rustling of three hundred thousand palm trees and by countless streams; the Temple of Persephone and the Temple of Arsinoe, the two sanctuaries of Poseidon, the three towers of Isis Pharis, the seven columns of Isis Lochia, and the Theater and the Hippodrome and the Stadium where Psittacos had run against Nicosthenes, and the tomb of Stratonice and the tomb of the god Alexander —Alexandria! Alexandria! The sea, the men, the colossal marble Pharos whose reflections saved men from the sea; Alexandria! The city of Berenice and of eleven Ptolemaic kings, Physcon, Philometor, Epiphanes, Philadelphus; Alexander, the culmination of every dream, the crown of every glorious conquest since the three thousand years in Memphis, Thebes, Athens, Corinth, by the chisel, the reeds, the compass and by the sword! — farther yet, the Delta divided by the seven dialects of the Nile, Sais, Bubastis, Heliopolis; then, going up toward the south, the ribbon of fertile earth, the Heptanome, where, in graduated terraces along the banks of the rivers, stood twelve hundred temples to the gods; and further, the Thebaid, Dispolis, the Elephantine Isle, the insurmountable waterfalls, the Isle of Argo … Meroe … the unknown; and even, if the stories of the Egyptians could be believed, a land of fabulous lakes from which escapes the ancient Nile, so vast that the horizon is lost while spanning their purple waves and so high that on the mountains the stars draw near, reflecting there like golden fruits — all this, everything, would be the kingdom, the domain, the property of the courtesan, Chrysis.

She lifted up her arms, scarcely able to breathe, as though she thought she could touch the sky.

And at that moment, she saw to her left an enormous bird with black wings pass slowly by, flying toward the high seas.

BOOK FOUR

THE DREAM OF DEMETRIOS

HAVING returned to his house with the mirror, the comb and the necklace, Demetrios slept and a dream came to him; and this was his dream:

He is heading toward the pier, mingling with the crowd, on a strange night without a moon, without stars, without clouds, a night that had a glow all its own.

Without knowing why, or what attracts him, he is hurrying to get there, to be *there* as soon as he can, but he walks with difficultly and his legs meet the air with an inexplicable resistance, as if treading through deep water.

He trembles, he feels as though he will never get there, that he will never know towards whom he goes; in this clear obscurity he keeps walking, breathless and uneasy.

There are moments when the crowd disappears entirely — either it actually vanishes or he simply be ceases to aware of its presence. Then the crowd jostles each other again, more obtrusively, and they all go, go, go, with quick and resounding steps marching forward, faster than Demetrios ...

Then the human mass draws tightly together; Demetrios pales; a man shoves him with his shoulder; a woman's clasp tears his tunic; a young girl, pushed by the multitude, is so tightly squeezed against him that he feels as though the buds of her breasts bruise his chest, and she thrusts his face away with her frightened hands ...

Suddenly, he finds himself alone, the first one on the pier. And as he turns to look back, he catches sight of a white swarm in the distance; it is the entire throng suddenly drawn back to the Agora.

He understands that they will come no further.

The pier stretches before him with the allure of an unfinished path that would have ventured to cross the sea.

He wants to go to the Pharos, he keeps walking. His legs become unexpectedly light. A puff of wind from the sandy solitude sweeps him hurriedly toward the undulating solitude where the pier juts out. But with every step forward he takes, the Pharos recedes before him; the pier stretches out forever. Soon, on the top of the marble tower, a flaming crimson torch touches the plum-colored horizon, spurts, dims, subsides, and sets like another moon.

Demetrios still walks on.

Days and nights seem to have gone by since he left the great quay of Alexandria in the distance, and he does not dare to turn his head for fear of seeing nothing more than the traveled path: a white line extending into infinity and the sea.

Nevertheless, he turns back.

An island is behind him covered with magnificent trees with huge flowers, drooping down.

Did he blindly cross it or did it just loom up at that very moment, becoming mysteriously visible? He doesn't think of demanding an answer; he accepts the impossible as a natural event...

A woman is on the island. She remains standing in front of the door of the only house, her eyes half closed and her head bent over the bloom of a gigantic iris that grows to the height of her lips. She has thick hair the color of unpolished gold which must be of a marvelous length according to the voluminous swell of coiled hair that lay languidly on the nape of her neck. A black tunic covers the woman and a cloak, blacker still, is draped over the tunic, and, while closing her eyes, she smells an iris the color of the night.

Against this mourning dress, Demetrios only sees her hair, like a golden vase on an ebony column. He recognizes Chrysis.

A vague memory of the mirror, comb and necklace returns to him, but it is unreal; in this curious dream, only reality appears to him a dream...

"Come," says Chrysis. "Come in, follow me."

He follows her. She slowly climbs a staircase covered with white leather. Her arms dangle over the banister. Her bare heels float under her skirt.

The house is only one floor above the ground. Chrysis stops at the last step.

"There are four rooms," she says. "When you have seen them, you will never leave here again. Do you want to follow me? Do you trust me?"

But he would follow her anywhere. She opens the first door and closes it behind him.

The room is narrow and long. It has only one window letting in the light and it frames the whole sea. On both sides, two small shelves hold a dozen rolled volumes.

"Here are the books that you love," says Chrysis, "There are no others."

Demetrios opens them: they are the "Oeneus" of Chaeremon, "The Return" by Alexis, "The Mirror of Lais" by Aristippus, "The

Witch," the "Cyclops" and the "Bucolics" by Theocritus, "Oedipus at Colonus," "The Odes" by Sappho, and some other small works. In the midst of this perfect library, a young woman, silent, lies nude on some cushions.

"Now," murmurs Chrysis, drawing a single leaf of a manuscript from a long golden cylinder, "here is the only page of ancient verse that you never read without weeping."

The young man casually looks it over.

> *...who wailed while the women cried with them. And among the women, white-armed Andromache lamented, while in her hands she held the head of Hector, the slayer of men: "Husband, you have died young and left me a widow in your house. And the child is still little, child of ill-fated parents, you and me ..."*

He stops, glancing at Chrysis with a tender, surprised look:

"You?" he says to her, "you show this to me?"

"Ah! You have not seen everything. Follow me. Follow me quickly!"

They open another door.

The second room is square. It has only one window letting in the light and it frames all of the outdoors. In the middle, a wooden sawhorse holds a mound of red clay, and, in a corner, a young woman, silent, reclines nude on a curved chair.

"Here you will sculpt Andromeda, Zagreus, and the Horses of the Sun. As though you will have created them only for yourself, you will smash them before your death."

"It is the House of Happiness," says Demetrios under his breath.

And he drops his head into his hands.

But Chrysis open another door.

The third room is vast and round. It has only one window letting in the light and it frames all the blue sky. The walls are an open latticework of bronze, crossing at regular intervals, through which glides the music of flutes and lyres played in a melancholy tone by unseen musicians. And against the supporting wall, a young woman, silent, sits nude, on a throne of green marble.

"Come! Come!" repeats Chrysis.

They open another door.

The fourth room is a triangle, low, somber, and airtight. Heavy tapestries and furs adorn it so softly, from the floor to the ceiling, that nudity no longer astonishes, so that lovers can imagine having thrown off all their clothes in every direction on to the walls. When the door shuts, no one can tell where it was. There is no window. It is a confined world, beyond the world. A few locks of black hair dangle like wicks with tears of perfume, letting them slide into the air. And the room is lit by seven small stained-glass myrrhic panes, that give off a diversity of colors from the mysterious light of seven subterranean lamps.

"You see," the young woman explains in an affectionate and calm voice, "there are three different beds in the three corners of *our* room..."

Demetrios does not respond. And he wonders:

"Is this the last stage? Is this truly a goal of human existence? Have I traveled through the other three rooms in order to stop here? And could I, could I leave it if I lie here one whole night in the pose of a lover who stretches himself out as if on a tomb?"

But Chrysis speaks ...

*

* *

"Beloved, you have commanded me, I have come, take a good look at me ..."

She raises both her arms, lays her hands behind her head, elbows facing forward, and smiles.

"Beloved, I am yours... Oh! Not so quickly. I promised to sing to you, I will sing first."

And he can no longer look at her and he lies at her feet. She wears tiny black sandals. Four threads of bluish pearls twine between her slender toes and each nail has been painted with a crimson lunar crescent.

With her head slightly tilted, she strikes the palm of her left hand with the fingertips of her right, while slowly undulating her hips.

> *On my bed, during the night,*
> *I searched for the one whom my heart loves,*
> *I searched for him but I have not found him ...*
> *I implore you, daughters of Jerusalem,*
> *If you find my beloved,*
> *Tell him*
> *That I am sick with love.*

"Ah! It is the *Song of Songs,* Demetrios! It is the nuptial hymn of the women of my country."

> *I sleep, but my heart is awake,*
> *It is the voice of my beloved...*
> *He knocks at my door.*
> *Behold, he comes*
> *Leaping over the mountains*
> *Like a roe deer*
> *Or a young doe's fawn.*
> *My beloved speaks and says to me,*
> > *Open to me, my sister, my love,*
> > *My head is filled with dew.*
> > *My hair, with the drops of night.*
> > *Arise, my love,*
> > *Come away, beautiful woman.*
> > *Behold, the winter has passed*
> > *And the rain has come and gone;*
> > *Flowers spring up from the earth,*

Pierre Loüÿs

> *And the time for singing has come,*
> *The coo of the turtledove can be heard.*
> *Arise, my love,*
> *Come away, beautiful woman.*

She throws her veil far from her and remains standing in a
scanty cloth that clings to her legs and hips.

> *I have cast off my shirt;*
> *How will I put it back on?*
> *I have washed my feet;*
> *How will I soil them?*
> *The hand of my beloved passed over the keyhole,*
> *And my belly quivered in anticipation.*
> *I arose, opening to my lover.*
> *My hands dripped with myrrh,*
> *And from my fingers myrrh spread out*
> *Over the bolt of the lock.*
> *Ah! That he kiss me with the kisses of his mouth!*

She throws her head back, her eyes half closed.

> *Heal me,*
> *Comfort me,*
> *For I am love sick.*
> *Let his left hand be under my head,*
> *And his right to embrace me.*
> > *You have captured my heart,*
> > *my sister,*
> > *with one of your eyes,*
> > *with one small link from your necklace.*
> > *How fair is your love,*
> > *how sweet your caresses!*
> > *Better than wine.*
> > *The smell of you pleases me more*
> > *than all the fragrances,*
> > *more than all the spices.*

Your lips, all moist.
There is honey and milk under your tongue,
The smell of Lebanon is on your garments.
You are, Oh my sister,
a secret garden,
a spring pent up, a fountain sealed.
Awake, north wind!
Hasten, south wind!
Blow over my garden
That its perfumes flow out.

She extends her arms and offers her mouth.

Let my lover enter into his garden
And eat its precious fruits,

> *Yes, I enter into my garden,*
> *Oh my sister, my beloved,*
> *I gather my myrrh and my spices,*
> *I eat my honeycomb with its honey.*
> *I drink my wine with my cream.*

Set me like a seal on your heart,
Like a seal on your arms,
For Love is as strong as death.

Without moving her feet, without bending her clasped knees, she turns her torso slowly on her motionless hips. Above the sheath of her legs, her face and her breasts appear to be three magnificent flowers, roselike in a slender vase of cloth.

She dances thoughtfully, entwining her shoulders, her head, and her beautiful arms. She pretends to suffer in her tight-fitting garment and reveals more and more of the whiteness of her half-freed body. Her chest swells with every breath. Her mouth can no longer close. Her eyelids can no longer open. A growing fire reddens her cheeks.

Sometimes all ten fingers are brought together, interlacing in front of her face. Sometimes she raises her arms, stretching herself out deliciously. A long furtive groove separates her raised shoulders. Finally, a single flick of her hair that surrounds her face, and panting as though a wedding veil had been lifted up, she releases, trembling, the sculptured clasp that holds up the cloth around her loins and lets slip down to the carpet all the mystery of her charm.

Demetrios and Chrysis...

Their first embrace before lovemaking, is immediately so perfect, so harmonious, that they sustain the moment, so that they can know fully its many sensual pleasures. One of her breasts is squeezed under the arm that grasps her so forcefully. One of her thighs burns between two pressing legs and the other is brought back up, heavy and stretching. They remained like this, motionless, bound together but not penetrating, in the growing exultation of an unyielding desire that they can not satisfy. First, they make love only with their mouths. They intoxicate each other, face to face, with no cure for their painful virginity.

Nothing is viewed as intimately as the face of a woman loved. Seen from the extreme nearness of the kiss, the eyes of Chrysis appear enormous. When she closes them, two parallel folds remain on each eyelid and a color, evenly faint, extends from her shining eyebrows to the beginning of her cheeks. When she opens them, a green circle, fine like a thread of silk, lights a halo of color around the unfathomable black pupil, growing infinitely larger under her long, curved lashes. The small red flesh, from which tears flow, suddenly throbs.

This kiss will never end. It appears that under the tongue of Chrysis, there is not the honey and milk as written in the Scripture, but a liquor, liquid, lively, changing, and enchanted. And the tongue itself, of many shapes, hollows and rolls itself up, retreats and advances, more caressing than the hand, more expressive than the eye, the flower the rounds itself into a pistil or thins into a petal, the flesh that stiffens to shudder or softens to lick, Chrysis enlivens it with all her tenderness and her passionate fantasies ... These are the caresses that she prolongs and shapes. Just the ends of her fingers are enough to keep him in the grip of a web of quivering spasms that quicken along his sides and never completely disappear. She says she is only happy when aroused by desire or spent by exhaustion: the transaction terrifies her as though painful. As soon as her lover invites her there, she pushes him away with her outstretched arms; her knees shut, her lips plead. Demetrios coerces her by force.

...No spectacle of nature, not the flames of the setting sun, not the storm among the palm trees, not the lightning strike, not the mirage, not the great swelling up of the waters, seem worthy of astonishment to those who have seen, in their arms, the transfiguration of the woman. Chrysis becomes extraordinary. In turns, arched or falling back, her elbows rising over cushions, she grips the corner of a pillow, convulsing like a dying person, breathless, her head thrown back. Her eyes, brightened by discovery, riveted, their dizzied gaze to the side. Her cheeks are resplendent. The waves in her hair move disconcertingly. Two admirably muscular lines descend from her ear and shoulder, uniting under her right breast, cradling it like a fruit.

With a sort of pious awe, Demetrios contemplates this fury of the goddess in the feminine body, this transport of the whole being, this superhuman convulsion of which he is the cause, which he exalts or represses freely, and which, for the thousandth time, astonishes him. Beneath his eyes, all the forces of life exert and magnify themselves in order to create. The breasts have already taken on, to their exaggerated tips, the maternal majesty. And these moans, these lamentable moans, cry out before the birth! ...

THE CROWD

IN the morning, after the orgy at Bacchis' house had ended, a singular event occurred in Alexandria: rain fell.

Immediately, contrary to what ordinarily happens in less African countries, everyone went outside to welcome the shower.

The phenomenon was neither torrential nor stormy. Large tepid drops penetrated the air from the height of a violet cloud. The women felt the drops dampen their breasts and quickly tied up their hair. The men looked up at the sky with concern. Little children burst out laughing, tracking through the shallow mud in their bare feet.

Then, the cloud vanished into the daylight; the sky remained implacably pure, and, shortly after noon, the mud had returned to dust under the sun.

But this sudden rain had been enough for the moment. The town was invigorated. The men stood together on the flagstones of the Agora and groups of women mingled, while their voices grew increasingly louder.

Only courtesans were there, because the third day of the Aphrodisian Festivals were reserved for the exclusive devotions of the married women, coming to surrender themselves to the grand procession on the way to the Astarteion, leaving the square with only flowered robes and eyes adorned in black.

As Myrtocleia passed, a young woman named Philotis who was gossiping with several others pulled her over by the tie on her sleeve.

"Well, little one! Did you play at Bacchis' yesterday? What happened there? What did they do? Has Bacchis added a new enameled necklace in order to hide the valleys in her neck? Does she wear breasts ornaments of wood or copper? Did she forget to dye the tiny white hair on her temples before she put on her wig? Come speak, you pitiful minnow!"

"Do you think that I even looked? I arrived after the dinner, I played my part, I received my pay and I left, running."

"Oh! I know that you did not compromise yourself!"

"So that I stain my robe and get beaten? No, Philotis. Only rich women can afford the orgy. Little flute players only earn tears."

"When you do not want to stain your robe, leave it in the antechamber. When you are struck with a fist, make them pay double. It is that simple. You have no news for us, then? Not one affair, not one joke, not one scandal? We gag like the ibis. Invent something if you do not know anything."

"My friend, Theano, stayed after I left. When I woke up a few minutes ago, she had not yet returned. Perhaps the festival is still going on."

"It is ended," said another woman. "Theano is over there, leaning against the Ceramic Wall."

The courtesans ran in that direction, but stopped, with smiles of pity, after a few steps.

Theano, dizzy from intoxication of the most crude sort, stubbornly tugged at a rose, nearly stripped of its petals, whose thorns were caught in her hair. Her yellow tunic had red and white stains, as if the whole orgy had taken place on her. The bronze clasp, that held the gathered folds of cloth on her left shoulder, now dangled lower than her sash and left uncovered the shifting globe of a young breast, already sagging, that nursed two stigmata of crimson.

As soon as she saw Myrtocleia, she suddenly let out a distinctive burst of laughter that was known all over Alexandria, which had given her the nickname, the Hen. It was the interminable cackling of a laying hen, a cascade of gaiety that would descend when she was out of breath, then start up again with a piercing cry and continued like this, rhythmically, in the joy of the triumphant pullet.

"An egg! An egg!" cried Philotis.

But Myrtocleia gestured:

"Come, Theano. You must go to bed. You are not well. Come with me."

"Ah! Ha! ... Ah! Ha! ..." laughed the child.

And she took her breast in her small hand, crying in a troubled voice:

"Ah! Ha! ... the mirror ..."

"Come," Myrto repeated impatiently.

"The mirror ... it is stolen, stolen, stolen! Ah! Haaaa! I will never laugh so much again if I live longer than Cronos. Stolen, stolen, the silver mirror!"

The singer tried to drag her away, but Philotis had understood.

"Oh!" she cried to the other, gesturing with her arms in the air. "Come quickly! I have some news! Bacchis' mirror has been stolen!"

And they all exclaimed:

"Papaie! The mirror of Bacchis!"

In an instant, thirty women crowded around the flute player.

"What did she say?"

"What?"

"Someone stole Bacchis' mirror; Theano just said so."

"But when?"

"Who took it?"

The child shrugged her shoulders.

"How should I know!"

"You spent the night over there. You must know. This is not possible. Who entered her house? Surely someone told you about it. Try to remember, Theano."

"How should I know?...There were more than twenty people in the room...They had hired me as a flute player, but stopped me from playing because they did not like the music. They asked me to take on the role of Danaë and they threw gold pieces at me. Bacchis took them all from me ... And what more? They were crazy. The made me drink with my head down, from a huge overflowing bowl where they had poured from seven cups because there were seven wines on the table. My face was completely drenched. Even my hair and my roses were soaked."

"Yes," interrupted Myrto, "you are a very naughty girl. But the mirror? Who took it?"

"Exactly! When they put me back on my feet, the blood had run to my head and the wine into my ears. Ha! Ha! They began to laugh ... Bacchis sent for the mirror ... Ha! Ha! It was no more. Someone had taken it."

"Who? I am asking you, who?"

"Not me, that's all I know. They could not search me: I was completely naked. I could not have hidden a mirror, like a drachma, under my eyelid. It's not me, I know that. She crucified a slave, because of that ... When I saw that they were no longer looking at me, I picked up the Danaë coins. See, Myrto, I have five of them. You will buy some robes for the three of us."

*
* *

Little by little, talk of the robbery spread over the whole square. The courtesans did not hide their jealous satisfaction. A noisy curiosity excited the groups as they milled around.

"A woman did it," said Philotis. "Only a woman could pull off a coup like that."

"Right, the mirror was well hidden. A robber would have removed everything in the room and turned everything upside down without finding the stone."

"Bacchis had enemies, her former women friends above all. They know all her secrets. One of them could have lured her away and entered her house while the sun was at its hottest and the streets are nearly deserted."

"Could it have been one of her lovers? They say she takes on the porters now."

"Oh! Perhaps she sold her mirror in order to pay her debts."

"No, it's a woman. I am certain of it."

"By the two goddesses! It is well done."

Suddenly, an even more agitated throng pushed their way toward a spot on the Agora, following by a growing rumor that attracted all the passersby.

"What it is? What is it?"

And a piercing voice dominated the tumult, shouting over the agitated heads:

"Someone has slain the wife of the High-Priest!"

A violent emotion gripped the whole crowd. No one believed it. No one wanted to think that, in the midst of the Aphrodisian Festivals, a murder such as this had occurred, hurling the wrath of the gods onto the town. But from every corner, from mouth to mouth, the same words were repeated:

"The wife of the High-Priest was murdered! The festival of the temple is suspended!"

Quickly the news arrived. The body had been found, lying on a rose-colored marble bench in a secluded spot at the summit of the gardens. A long golden hairpin pierced her left breast; the wound did not bleed; but the assassin had cut off all the hair of the young woman and absconded with the antique comb of Queen Nitocris.

After the first cries of anguish, a profound stupor descended. The mass of people grew, minute by minute. All the town was there, a sea of bare heads and women's headdresses, an immense throng simultaneously emerged from every street filled with blue shadows into the dazzling light of the Agora of Alexandria. No one had seen its equal since the day Ptolemy Auletes was overthrown by the partisans of Berenice. Yet, the political revolutions appeared to them less horrifying that this sacrilegious crime on which the welfare of the town might depend. The men surrounded the witnesses, nearly crushing them, demanding new details and offering conjectures. The women informed the recent arrivals of the theft of the celebrated mirror. The most informed asserted that the two simultaneous crimes were committed by the same hand. But which one? Some women, who the day before had left their offerings for the coming year, were fearful that the goddess would no longer remember them, and they sat sobbing, their heads in their robes.

An ancient superstition had it that the appearance of two events would be followed by a third, more serious, one. The crowd expected something like this. After the mirror and the comb, what had the mysterious thief taken? A sweltering atmosphere, inflamed by the south wind, full of dust and sand, weighed heavily on the transfixed crowd.

Imperceptibly, as though this human mass were a single being, a shiver took hold and crescendoed into a terrifying panic. All eyes were fixed on the same spot on the horizon.

It was at the far end of the grand avenue that formed a straight line from the Canopic Gate, intersecting Alexandria, and lead to the Temple at the Agora. There, at the highest point of a gentle slope, where the pathway opened up to the sky, a second terrified throng had just appeared and ran down toward the first.

"The courtesans! The sacred courtesans!"

No one moved. No one dared to go and meet them for fear of learning of a new disaster. They arrived like a living deluge, preceded by the dull noise of their running over the ground. They raised their arms, shoving each other, appearing to flee from an army. They were recognized immediately, distinguished by their robes, their sashes, and their hair. Rays of light struck their golden jewels. They came closer. They opened their mouths. Silence waited.

"The necklace of the goddess was stolen, the True Pearls of the Anadyomene!"

A desperate clamor greeted the fatal words. At first, the crowds receded like a wave, then surged forward, striking the walls, filling up the road, driving back the terrified women onto the long avenue of the Drome, toward the desecrated sacred Immortal.

THE RESPONSE

A ND the Agora emptied out like a beach after the tide.

Not completely empty: a man and a woman remained, those alone who knew the secret of the great public outcry, and who, the one through the other, had caused it: Chrysis and Demetrios.

The young man was sitting on a marble block near the gate. The young woman was standing at the other end of the square. They could not recognize each other, but they sensed each other's presence. Chrysis ran under the heat of the sun, intoxicated by pride and, finally, by desire.

"You have done it!" she cried out. "You have done it!"

"Yes," the young man said simply. "I obeyed you."

She threw herself on his lap and engulfed him with a delirious embrace.

"I love you! I love you! Never have I felt like this. Gods! I know now what it is to be in love! You see it, my loved one, I give you more, me, more than I had promised the day before yesterday. I, the one who never desired anyone, I could never imagine that I would change so quickly. I had only sold you my body on the bed, now, I give you everything that I have that is good, everything that is pure, sincere and passionate, all of my virgin soul, Demetrios, think of it! Come with me, we will leave this town for a while, go to a hidden place, where there will only be you and me. There, we will have days like there have never been before on this earth. Never has a lover done for me what you have done. Never has a woman loved as I love; it is not possible! It is not possible! I can hardly speak, my throat is so choked with emotion. You see, I am crying. Now I know too what makes a woman cry: it is from too much happiness ... But you do not respond! You say nothing! Kiss me ..."

Demetrios stretched his right leg out, lowering his knee, which was growing a little tired. Then he made the young woman get up, and, raising himself, gave his garment a shake in order to remove the creases. With a slight, rather enigmatic, smile, he said softly:

"No... Farewell."

And he started to calmly walk away.

Chrysis, completely stunned, remained, her mouth opened, her hand dangling.

"What? ... what ... what did you say?"

"I say to you, farewell," he spoke without raising his voice.

"But... But then was it not you who ..."

"Yes. I had promised you."

"Then ... I no longer understand."

"My dear, whether you understand or not makes no difference to me. I leave this little mystery to your meditations. If what you have told me is true, it portents to be a lengthy contemplation. You have enough at the moment to occupy your thoughts. Farewell."

"Demetrios! What am I hearing? ... Where has this tone of yours come from? Is it indeed you who speaks? Explain it to me! I implore you! What has happened between us? It is like smashing my head against a thick wall ..."

"Must I repeat the same thing a hundred times over! Yes, I took the mirror; yes, I killed the priestess, Touni, to get the antique comb; yes, I stole the magnificent seven-strand pearl necklace from the neck of the goddess. I had to hand over to you the three gifts in exchange for only one sacrifice on your part. It was to be of great value, is that right? Now I have ceased to attribute such a considerable value to it and I ask you for nothing in return. Do the same and let us part. I wonder at your lack of understanding of a situation whose simplicity is so obvious."

"But keep them, your presents! How can I think of them! It is you that I want, only you ..."

"Yes, I know that. But once more, for my part, I no longer have the desire, and, since it is essential to have the consent of both lovers to have a love affair, our union greatly risks being left unrealized if I persist in my way of seeing things. I am trying to make you understand in the clearest words possible. I see that this clarity is inadequate, but since I cannot perfect it, I beg, with best wishes, for you to accept the fact gracefully and not to delve deeper into what appears obscure to you; particularly since you do not admit the possibility. I am eager to end this conversation that can result in nothing but perhaps compelling me to some unkind words."

"They talked to you about me!"

"No."

"Oh! I can guess it! They talked to you about me, don't say they didn't! They told you bad things about me! I have vicious enemies, Demetrios! You must not listen to them. I swear by the gods, they lie!"

"I do not know them."

"Believe me! Believe me, Beloved! What reason would I have in deceiving you since I expect nothing of you, just yourself? You are the first one that I have spoken to like this ..."

Demetrios looked her in the eyes.

"It is too late," he said. "I had you."

"You are delirious ... When was that? Where? How?"

"I'm telling you the truth. I had you in spite of yourself. What I waited for you to give me willingly, you have given me without knowing it. Last night, in a dream, you lead me to the country where you wanted to go and you were beautiful ... ah! You were beautiful, Chrysis! I have returned from that country. No human volition will force me to revisit it. No one ever finds happiness twice on the same small corner of the earth. I am not foolish enough to corrupt a happy memory. I owe you that, wouldn't you say? But since I have loved only your shadow, you will excuse me, precious one, from thanking your reality."

Chrysis clutched her head in her hands.

"This is abominable! Abominable! And he dares to say it! And he is in control of it!"

"You have become very precise quickly. I told you that I had dreamt: are you certain I was sleeping? I told you that I had been happy. Is it that happiness, for you, consists only in that crude physical quivering that you provoke so well? But you told me that you have no power to change your occupation and it is obviously the same for all those women who give themselves. No, it is yourself whom you diminish in taking on this improper behavior. You did not rein me in, knowing well all the bliss that is born from your walk. What makes the mistresses differ is that they each have individual ways of preparing and concluding an event which is, on the whole, as monotonous as it is necessary and merits no pursuit from my perspective, for all the trouble we take finding a perfect mistress. And in this sort of preparation and in this conclusion, you, among all women, excel. At least, I have had pleasure of imagining it and, perhaps you will grant me that, after having dreamed the Aphrodite of the Temple, my imagination has not had great trouble in representing the woman that you are? Once more, I will not tell you if it were a nocturnal dream or a waking delusion. Take satisfaction in knowing that, dreamed or created, your image appeared to me in an extraordinary setting. Illusion; but, above all, I will stop you, Chrysis, from stripping me of my illusions."

"And me, in all of this, what do you make of me, who still loves you in spite of the horrible things that I hear from your mouth? Was I conscious of your odious dream? Have I had half of the happiness of which you speak and that you have stolen from me! Has anyone ever heard of a lover who had an ego sufficiently appalling enough to take his pleasure from the woman, who loves him, without letting her share it? ... That confounds the mind. I will go mad."

Now Demetrios abandoned his ridiculing tone and said, in a slowly trembling voice:

"Did you concern yourself about me when you took advantage of my sudden passion and demanded, in a frenzied moment, three acts that could have shattered my existence, that will forever leave me with the memory of a triple shame?"

"If I have done that, it was in order to bind you to me. I would not have had you if I had given myself to you."

"Good. You have been satisfied. You have held me, not for long, but nevertheless you have held me in the slavery that you wanted. Left to suffer, I free myself today!"

"There is only one slave here, Demetrios. Me."

"Yes, you or me, but of the two of us, it is the one who loves the other. Slavery! Slavery! This is the true name of passion. All of you have only one dream, only one idea in your brain: to make your weakness break the power of man and your frivolity govern his intelligence! What you want, as soon as your breasts grow, it is not to love or to be loved, it is to tie a man to your ankle, humble him, bow his head and put your sandals on top of it. Then you can, according to your desire, rip away the sword, chisel or compass from him, smash all that surpasses you, emasculate all that frightens you, take Hercules by his nostrils and make him spin wool! But when you can neither bend his head nor his character, you adore the fist that strikes you, the knee that brings you to the ground, even the mouth that insults you! The man who has refused to kiss your bare feet, if he rapes you, he fulfills your desires. The man who does not cry when you leave his house can drag you there by your hair: your love is reborn from your tears, because only one thing consoles you for not inflicting slavery, amorous women! It is the submission to it!"

"Ah! Beat me if you want! But love me afterwards!"

And she embraced him so quickly that he had no time to turn his lips away. He freed himself from her arms.

"I detest you. Farewell," he said.

But Chrysis clung to his cloak:

"Do not lie. You adore me. Your soul is filled with me, but you are ashamed at having yielded. Listen, listen, Beloved! If you need only that to console your pride, I am ready to give still more, in order to have you, more than I asked of you. Let me make some sacrifice and after our reconciliation I will not complain about life."

Demetrios looked at her with curiosity; and like her, two nights ago on the pier, he said:

"What oath will you make?"

"By the Aphrodite, too."

"You do not believe in the Aphrodite. Swear by the Sabbath's Jehovah."

The Galilaean paled.

"No one swears by Jehovah."

"You refuse?"

"It is a terrible oath."

"It is the one I must have."

She hesitated for some time, then, in a subdued voice, said:

"I make the oath by Jehovah. What do you ask of me, Demetrios?"

The young man was silent.

"Speak, Beloved!" said Chrysis. "Tell me quickly. I am afraid."

"Oh! It is a little thing."

"But what?"

"I do not want you to give me three gifts, even if they were as simple as the first were rare. It would go against custom. But I can ask that you receive them, right?"

"Of course," said Chrysis joyfully.

"This mirror, this comb, this necklace, which you made me take for you, you did not expect to use them, did you? A stolen mirror, the comb of a victim and the necklace of the goddess, these are not jewels that anyone could display openly."

"How absurd!"

"No. I have thought a lot about it. Is it just from pure cruelty that you have driven me to ravish them at the price of three crimes, which have upset the whole town today? Ah, well, you are going to wear them."

"What!"

"You are going into the little closed garden where the statue of Stygian Hermes stands. The spot is always deserted and there is no risk of anyone bothering you. You will remove the left heel of the god. The stone is cracked as you will see. There, inside of the pedestal, you will find the mirror of Bacchis and you will take it in your hand; you will find the magnificent comb of Nitocris and you will plunge it into your hair; you will find the seven strands of pearls from the goddess Aphrodite, and you will put them around your neck. Adorned like this, beautiful Chrysis, you will walk through the town. The crowd will deliver you to the soldiers of the queen; but you will have what you wished for — I will come to you in your prison before sunrise."

THE GARDEN OF HERMES

THE first move Chrysis made was to shrug her shoulders. She would not be so naive as to keep her oath!
The second one was to go and see.

A growing curiosity drove her toward the secret place where Demetrios had hidden the three immoral spoils. She wanted to take them, touch them with her hand, make them sparkle in the sun, possess them for a moment. She felt that her victory would not be complete until she had held the plunder of her desires.

As for Demetrios, she would know how to recapture him with a ulterior maneuver. How could he believe that he had separated from her forever? The passion she thought he held was not the kind that extinguished itself easily without returning to the heart of a man. The many women whom he has loved form a selective family in his mind and when he encounters a former mistress, even hated, even forgotten, it awakens an insurmountable confusion where a little new love can spring. Chrysis would not ignore that. However ardent she was, however impelled she was to conquer the first man she had ever loved, she was not so foolish as to buy him at the price of her life when she saw so many other easier ways to seduce him.

And yet ... what a happy end he had proposed!

Under the gaze of an enormous crowd of people, to carry the antique mirror where Sappho had seen herself, the comb that had gathered up the royal hair of Nitocris, the necklace of sea pearls that had rolled around in the shell of the goddess, Anadyomene... Then, from one night to the next morning, to know, madly, all of the most passionate love that a woman can experience ... and at midday, dying effortlessly... What an incomparable destiny!

She closed her eyes ...

But no, she would not let herself be tempted.

She started walking up the street that led directly across Rhactois to the Great Serapeion. The route, opened up by the Greeks, looked out of place in this quarter of angular side-streets. The two populations intermingled with a bizarre promiscuity still tinged with hatred. Among the Egyptians, dressed in blue garb, the unbleached tunics of the Hellenes made a path of whiteness. Chrysis ascended rapidly, without listening to the conversations of the people, entertaining each other with the crimes committed for her.

In front of the steps of the monument, she turned right, taking a darkened street, then another, where the terraces of the houses nearly melted together, crossed over a small open area where, near a patch of sunlight, two very brown little girls were playing in a fountain, and, at last, she stopped.

*

* *

The garden of Hermes Anubis was a small cemetery abandoned long ago, the kind of desolate terrain where relatives no longer brought libations for the dead and passersby avoided going near. In the middle of the crumbling tombs, Chrysis stepped forward in great silence, fearful of the crunch of each stone under her feet. The wind, always filled with a fine sand, blew her hair from her temples and stretched out her scarlet silk veil toward the white leaves of the sycamores.

She discovered the statue between three funeral monuments that hid it from every side, enclosing it in a triangle. It was a well-chosen place for the burial of a mortal secret.

Chrysis slid herself, as best she could, into the narrow, stony passage way: when she saw the statue, she paled slightly. The god, with a head of a jackal, was standing, the right leg forward, his headdress falling and pierced with two holes where the arms came out. The head leaned over from the top of its rigid body, as if following the movement of its hands, gesturing like those of an embalmer. The left foot was loosened.

Looking slowly, fearfully, Chrysis assured herself that she was all alone. A small noise behind her made her shudder, but it was only a green lizard that scurried into a crack in the marble.

Then, she finally dared to take hold of the broken foot. She lifted it up at an angle, not without some difficulty because a part of the hollowed base, that rested on the pedestal, came with it. And under the stone she suddenly saw the gleam of the enormous pearls.

She pulled the necklace out. How heavy it was! She could hardly believe that pearls, not in settings, would weigh so heavily in her hands. The mother-of-pearl globes were all marvelously rounded, with a near lunar brilliance. The seven strands followed, one after the other, growing larger like concentric circles on a pool full of stars.

She put it around her neck.

With one hand, she straightened it, her eyes closed to better feel the cold of the pearls on her skin. She arranged the seven rows evenly along her naked breast and let the last slip down the hot interval between her breasts.

Next, she took the ivory comb, considered it for a while, caressed the small white figure, carved into the slender crown, and plunged the jewel in her hair several times before she placed it where she wanted it.

Then, she drew the silver mirror from the pedestal, looked into it and saw there her triumph, her eyes sparkling with pride, her shoulders adorned with the plunder of the gods ...

And, enveloping herself, even her hair, in her great scarlet veil, she left the cemetery without giving up the terrible jewels.

WALLS OF CRIMSON

WHEN the people had learned for the second time, from the mouths of the hierodules, the certainty of the sacrilege, it slowly coursed its way across the gardens.

The temple courtesans thronged by the hundreds along the paths lined with black olive trees. Some of them scattered ashes over their heads. Others bowed their heads into the dust, or pulled out their hair, or clawed at their breasts as a sign of misery. Many, their eyes covered by their arms, sobbed.

The crowd descended silently back into town by the Drome and along the quay. A universal mourning left the streets overwhelmed. The shopkeepers having returned hastily, feared for their multicolored shop windows and fixed wooden shutters

which succeeded each other like a monotonous stockade along the
ground floor of the shuttered houses.

Life in the port had come to a standstill. The sailors sat on the
railings, motionless, their cheeks resting in their hands. The vessels
nearing departure had lifted their long oars and furled their pointed
sails along the masts that balanced in the wind. Those who wanted
to drop anchor waited away off for the signal and some of their
passengers who had relatives at the queen's palace, believing it to
be a bloody revolution, made sacrifices to the gods of the Inferno.

At the corner where the island of the Pharos and the pier meet,
Rhodis recognized Chrysis among the crowd near her.

"Ah! Chrysis! Keep near me, I am afraid. Myrto is here, but
the crowd is so huge ... I am afraid they will separate us. Let us hold
hands."

"You know," said Myrtocleia, "you know what has happened?
Do they know who did it? Is he being tortured? Not since
Herostratus, has anyone seen anything like this. The Olympians
will abandon us. What will become of us?"

Chrysis did not respond.

"We have presented the doves," said the little flute player. "Will
the goddess remember that? The goddess must be incensed. And
you, and you, my poor Chrysis! You who should have been, today,
very happy or very powerful..."

"Everything is over," said the courtesan.

"How can you say that!"

Chrysis took two steps backward and raised her right hand
near her mouth.

"Look carefully, my Rhodis; look, Myrtocleia. What you will
see today, human eyes have never seen since the day the goddess
had descended on Ida. And until the end of the world, it will never
be seen again on this earth."

The two friends, bewildered, drew back from her, thinking
she was mad. But Chrysis, lost in her reverie, walked up to the
gigantic Pharos, a flaming mountain with six sides and eight marble

tiers. She pushed the bronze door open and, taking advantage of the distracted public, she closed it from the inside, lowering the resonating bars.

Several moments slipped by.

The crowd grumbled continuously. The living swell added its uproar to the rhythmic surging of the waves.

Suddenly, one cry rose up, repeated from a hundred thousand breasts:

"Aphrodite! — Aphrodite!!!"

A thunder of cries burst out. The joy, the enthusiasm of an entire people sang in an indescribable tumult at the foot of the thick walls of the Pharos.

The throng covering the pier flowed violently onto the island, swept over the rocks, climbed on the houses, up the signal masts, and onto the fortified towers. The island was full, more than full, and the crowd kept coming, becoming always more compressed, like a surge from an overflowing river, that pushed back the long human rows to the sea from the top of a steep cliff.

No end could be seen of this deluge of men. From the Palace of the Ptolemies to the wall of the Canal, from the Great Gate and from the Eunostos, the banks of the Royal Gateway overflowed with the compact mass, fed endlessly by the mouths of the streets. Above this ocean, stirring in immense eddies, foaming with arms and faces, the litter of Queen Berenice floated with its yellow veils like a small barge in peril. And from moment to moment, augmented by new mouths, the noise became terrible.

Neither Helen on the Scaean Gates, nor Phryne in the waves of the Eleusis, nor Thais inspiring the burning of Persepolis had known such a triumph.

Chrysis appeared at the west door on the first terrace of the reddened monument.

She was naked like the goddess, holding in each hand the corners of her scarlet veil which the wind unfurled in the evening sky, and the mirror, in her right hand, reflected the setting sun.

Languidly, with infinite grace and majesty, her head bowed, she climbed the outside ramp that formed a spiral band around the vermilion tower. A flame burned her half-closed eyes. The blazing sunset reddened the pearl necklace like a river of rubies. She walked in this glory; her gleaming skin took on all the magnificence of its flesh, the blood, the fire, the bluish carmine, the velvety redness, the vibrant rose, and, turning with the great, thick walls of crimson, she climbed towards the sky.

BOOK FIVE

THE SUPREME NIGHT

"**Y**OU are loved by the gods," said the old jailer. "If I, poor slave, had done a hundredth of your crimes, I would have seen myself tied to a trestle, hung by my feet, cut to pieces, and skinned with tongs. They would have poured vinegar in my nostrils, they would have piled bricks on top of me until I suffocated, and, when I had died from this suffering, my body would be food for the jackals of the burning plains. But you, who have stolen everything, killed everything, desecrated everything, for you, they reserve the gentle hemlock and give you a good room in the meantime. Zeus strike if I know why! You must know someone at the palace."

"Give me some figs," said Chrysis, "My mouth is dry."

Accordingly, the old slave brought her a dozen overly ripe figs in a green basket.

Chrysis remained alone.

She sat down and got up again, she went around the room, she hit the walls with the palm of her hand without thinking about what was happening. She let her hair down to freshen it, then, almost immediately she tied it back up.

They had made her put on a long garment of white wool. The cloth was hot. Chrysis felt completely bathed in sweat. She stretched her arms, yawned, and leaned on her elbows over the high window ledge.

Outside, the bright moon gleamed in the sky of transparent purity, a sky so pale and so clear that not one star could be seen.

It was on such a night, seven years ago, that Chrysis had left the land of Gennesaret.

She recalled ... There were five of them. They were ivory merchants. They had adorned the long-tailed horses with multicolored tassels. They had accosted her at the edge of a round well...

And before that, the bluish-lake, the clear sky, the light air of Galilee's country side...

The house was surrounded by pink flax and fruit trees. Thorny caper bushes pricked the fingers that were about to capture the moths ... She believed she saw the color of the wind in the undulations of the slender grasses ...

The little girls bathed in a clear stream where they found red shellfish under the tufts of flowering laurel; and there were flowers on the water and flowers all over the prairie and majestic lilies on the mountains, and the outline of the mountains was shaped like a young breast...

Chrysis closed her eyes with a faint smile, suddenly it was extinguished. The thought of death had just seized her. And she felt that she could no longer stop speculating until the end.

"Ah!" she said to herself, "what have I done! Why did I meet that man? Why did he listen to me? Why did I, in turn, let myself be enslaved? Why must it be that, even now, I regret nothing!

"Not to love or not to live, this is the choice that God has given me. What have I done to be punished?"

And a memory from her childhood returned to her, the fragments of sacred verses that she had heard recited.

For seven years she had not thought of them. But they returned, one after another, with a relentless precision, applying to her life and predicting her pain.

She murmured:
"It is written:

I remember your love
When you were young.
You have long since
Broken out of your chains,
And you said: I no longer want to be a slave;
But upon every rising knoll
And under every green tree
You bent down, like a prostitute.

"It is written:

I will follow my lovers
Who give me my bread, my water
My wool and my flax,
My oil and my wine.

"It is written:

How could you say: I am no longer stained?
Look at your footprint in the valley,
Confess what you have done,
Vagabond camel, wild ass
Panting and always in heat,
Who could have stopped you from satisfying your desire?

"It is written:

> **She was a courtesan in Egypt,**
> *She was set ablaze by lewd acts of one*
> *Whose member is like that of asses*
> *And his semen like that of horses.*
> *You recalled the crimes from your youth in Egypt,*
> *When he squeezed your breast because you were young.*

"Oh!" she cried to herself. "That is me! That is me!
"And it is written still:

> *You prostituted yourself to many lovers*
> *And you would come back to me! says the Eternal.*

"But my punishment is also written:

> *Behold: I incite your lovers against you.*
> *They will judge you according to their laws.*
> *They will cut off your nose and ears*
> *And what is left of you will fall by the sword.*

"And more:

> *It is done: she is stripped naked, she is led away.*
> *Her servants moan like doves*
> *And beat their breasts.*

"But I know what it said in the Scripture," she added, consoling herself. "Is it not written elsewhere:

> *I will not punish your daughters because they prostitute*
> *themselves.*

"And elsewhere in the Scripture does it not advise:

> *Go, eat, drink, because for a long time God let you prosper.*
> *At all times your vestments are white and perfumed*
> *oil always on your head.* **Enjoy your life with the**
> **woman that you love,** *throughout all the days of your*
> *futile life that God has given you in the sun,*
> *for there is neither work, nor thought,*

nor knowledge, nor wisdom, in death's dwelling
where you go."

She shuddered and repeated in a hushed voice:
"For there is neither work,
nor thought, nor knowledge, nor wisdom,
in death's dwelling **where you go.**

"The light is sweet. Ah! How wonderful it is to see the sun.
Young man, rejoice in your youth, give your heart over
to joy, walk in the ways of your heart
according to the vision of your eyes,
before you go toward your eternal dwelling place and
the mourners traverse the streets;
before the silver cord is broken, the golden lamp is
shattered, the jug is smashed on the fountain
the wheel is snapped in the rut,
before the dust returns to the earth
from which it was taken."

With another shiver, she repeated, more slowly:
"... before the dust returns to the earth from which it
was taken."

And, as she grasped her head in her hands in order to quell her thoughts, suddenly she felt without anticipating it the funereal form of her skull, transparent through her living skin: the sunken temples, the enormous orbits, the shortened nose under the cartilage and the jawbone jutting out.

Horror! This was what she was going to become! With a terrifying clarity, she saw the vision of her cadaver and with her hands she traced along her body this discovery so simple that until now had not occurred to her — she carried her skeleton in her, that it was not a result of death, of a metamorphosis, of a culmination, but a thing she controlled, an inseparable phantom of the human form — and the scaffolding for life is already the symbol of the tomb.

A fierce desire to live, to see everything again, to begin again, to do everything again, suddenly excited her. It was a revolt in the face of death; the impossibility to admit that she would not see the night of this day now being born; the impossibility to comprehend how this beauty, this body, this lively idea, this luxurious life of her flesh, full of passion, was going to cease to exist — and decay.

The door opened quietly.

Demetrios entered.

THE DUST RETURNS TO THE EARTH

"**D**EMETRIOS!**"** she cried out.

And she rushed forward ...

But, after having carefully closed the wooden latch, the young man had not moved, and he gave her a look so profoundly calm that Chrysis was suddenly frozen.

She had hoped for a spark, a movement of his arms, his lips, of something, an outstretched hand ...

Demetrios did not move.

He remained silent for a moment, with a perfect correctness, as if he wanted to clearly establish his detachment.

Then, seeing she asked nothing of him, he took four steps to the window, leaned on his elbow in the opening, and looked out at the awaking of the day.

Chrysis sat down on the low bed, staring straight ahead, dazed.

Then, Demetrios thought to himself.

"It is better," he thought, "it should be this way. Such games at the moment of death could be, finally, rather lamentable. I only marvel at her for not having had, from the very beginning, some inkling, and for her welcoming me this enthusiastically. For me, this affair is finished. I regret somewhat that it ended this way, because, considering everything, Chrysis did nothing wrong other than to express, very frankly, a desire that, without a doubt, most women have. If it had not been necessary to throw a victim to the indignation of the people, I would have been happy to banish this young, too passionate woman, and to free myself of her while leaving her the joys of life. But there was a scandal and no one can do anything about it. Such are the effects of passion. Sensual pleasure without thought, or the contrary, thought without pleasure, do not have these disastrous consequences. A man, aided by the gods, must have many mistresses to keep himself from forgetting that lips are all alike."

Having thus summarized, with this audacious aphorism, one of his ethical propositions, he went back unconstrained to his usual preoccupations.

He vaguely recalled an invitation to dine that he had accepted for the evening before, forgotten in the turmoil of events, and promised himself he would send an apology. He thought about the question of the sale of his slave, an old tailor, who was tied to the traditional cuts of the preceding reign and who had tried to perfect, without success, the bias-cut folds of the new tunics.

He even freed his mind so much that he drew on the wall, with the edge of his chisel, a quick study for his grouping of Zagreus and the Titans, a variation that changed the position of the right arm of the central figure. He had barely finished it when someone knocked gently on the door.

Demetrios opened the door slowly. The old executioner entered, followed by two helmeted foot soldiers.

"I bring the little cup," he said with a servile smile, addressing the royal lover.

Demetrios remained silent.

Chrysis, bewildered, raised her head.

"Come my girl," continued the jailor. "The time has come. The hemlock is ground up. The only thing left to do is to take it. Do not be afraid. You will not suffer at all."

Chrysis looked at Demetrios, who did not turn his eyes away.

With her gaze never leaving him, her large black pupils surrounded by a green halo, Chrysis held out her right hand, took the cup and slowly brought it to her mouth

She moistened her lips with the liquid. A honeyed narcotic had tempered the bitterness of the poison and the pain from the poisoning.

She drank half of the cup, then, either having seen this gesture at the theatre in Agathon's *Thyestes,* or it having sprung forth spontaneously, she held out the rest of it to Demetrios .... But with the wave of his hand, the young man declined this injudicious proposition.

Then, the Galilaean swallowed the rest of the drink, down to the green pulp at the bottom. And a wrenching smile arose on her cheeks where there had been a slightly contemptuous one.

"What should I do?" she asked the jailor.

"Walk around the room, my girl, until you feel your legs grow heavy. Then, lay down on your back and the poison will act by itself."

Chrysis walked to the window, leaned her hand on the wall, her forehead on her hand, and cast, toward the violet dawn, the last glance of a lost youth.

The east was drowned in a lake of color. A long pale band enveloped the horizon with a sallow sash like a sheet of water. Above it, many hues gave birth, the one from the other, to transparent layers of iridescent sky, sea-green or lilac, that gradually formed the foundation for the bluish-grey azure of the upper firmament. Then, these delicately tiered variations rose slowly; a line of gold appeared, began to climb, widening; a slender thread of crimson brightened this morose dawn, and, in a great swell of blood, the sun was born.

"It is written:

The light is sweet..."

She remained like that, standing as long as her legs were able to hold her. The soldiers were forced to carry her to the bed when she signaled that she was becoming unsteady.

Once there, the old man arranged the white folds of her robe along her outstretched limbs. Then, he touched her feet and asked her:

"Did you feel anything?"

She replied:

"No."

He touched her again, on her knees, and asked her:

"Did you feel that?"

She indicated that she did not, and, unexpectedly, moving her mouth and shoulders (because her hands were dead), revived by one last passion, and, perhaps, from the sorrow of this barren time, she lifted herself up toward Demetrios... But before he could have responded, she fell back, lifeless, her gaze extinguished forever.

Then, the executioner brought back, over her face, the upper folds of her clothing; and one of the assisting soldiers, supposing that a more tender past had one day brought together this young man and woman, cut off, with the tip of his sword, the last curl of her hair hanging over the slab.

Demetrios touched it with his hand, and, in truth, it was the embodiment of Chrysis, the surviving gold of her beauty, even the pretext for her name ...

He took the warm lock between his thumb and fingers, scattering it slowly, little by little, and, under the sole of his shoe, he mingled it with the dust.

IMMORTAL CHRYSIS

W HEN Demetrios found himself alone again in his red studio congested with marble statues, clay models, easels and scaffolding, he wanted to start back to work.

The chisel in his left hand and the mallet grasped in his right, he took up again, but without passion, a previous rough outline. It was the neck and shoulders of a gigantic horse destined to be in the temple of Poseidon. Under its roached mane, the skin of the neck, furrowed by a movement of its head, curved geometrically like the undulations on a river basin.

Three days ago, the detail of this classic muscle structure was the focus, in Demetrios' mind, of his everyday life; but on the morning of Chrysis' death, things appeared different. Not as calm as he wanted to be, Demetrios could not direct his preoccupied thoughts elsewhere. A kind of veil came down between the marble and himself, unable to be lifted. He threw his mallet down and began to walk among the dusty pedestals.

Suddenly, walking across the court, he called to a slave and said to him:

"Prepare the basin and the fragrances. You will perfume me after having bathed me, you will give me my white garments, and you will light the round incense-burners."

When he had finished dressing, he summoned two other slaves:

"Go," he said, "to the queen's prison; hand this lump of clay to the jailor and have him carry it into the room where the courtesan, Chrysis, lies dead. If the body is not already thrown into the pit, you will tell him that he should refrain from doing anything before I have given him the order. Run quickly. Go."

He put a roughing-chisel into the fold of his sash and opened the main door onto the deserted avenue of the Drome...

Suddenly, he stopped on the threshold, stunned by the vast light of the noonday sun over the African land.

The street and the houses should have been white, but the sun's perpendicular blaze washed the bright surfaces with such a fury of reflections that the limestone walls and the flagstone walks reflected simultaneously the immense incandescences of dark blue, red, green, raw ocher and hyacinth. The broad shimmering colors seemed to turn into air and only transparently cover the convolutions of the uneven facades. The shapes themselves were distorted behind this brilliance; the right wall of the street curved into the emptiness, floating like a sail and in certain places became invisible. A dog, lying close to a curb, was actually crimson.

Enthusiastic with admiration, Demetrios saw this spectacle as symbolic of his new existence. Long enough he had lived in the solitary night, in the silence and the stillness. He had taken, long enough, light for the moonlight, the ideal for the careless shape of an overly subtle gesture. His work was not virile. There was an icy shiver over the skin of his statues.

For the first time during the tragic experience that had just disoriented his thoughts, he had felt the full breath of life fill his chest. If he feared a second ordeal, if, leaving victorious from the battle, he swore to himself, before all things, to never again make himself yield his noble bearing in the presence of others, at least he had now come to understand — that it is only worthwhile to be creative, whoever, through marble, color or phrase, touches one of the deepest human emotions — and that ideal beauty is only an uncertain subject, always susceptible, through the expression of sorrow or of joy, to being transformed.

And as he finished this train of thought, he arrived in front of the prison door.

His two slaves were waiting for him there.

"We have brought the red clay," they said. "The body is on the bed. No one has touched it. The jailor welcomes you and appeals to your generosity."

The young man entered in silence, followed along the corridor, climbed some steps, and went into the chamber of the dead where he carefully locked himself in.

The cadaver was laid out, the head lowered and covered with a veil, the hands stretched out, the feet together. The fingers were laden with rings; two silver bracelets coiled themselves around the pale ankles and the nail of each toe was still red from the dust.

Demetrios' hand reached for the veil in order to lift it up; but he had barely taken hold of it when a dozen scurrying flies escaped through the opening.

He shivered to tips of his toes ... However, he held out the gauzy white wool, and folded it around her hair.

Chrysis' face had become illuminated, little by little, from that immortal expression that death bestows on the eyelids and the locks of hair of the corpse. The bluish whiteness of the cheeks showed a few small azure veins that gave the lifeless head an appearance of cold marble. The transparent nostrils flared above the delicate lips. Her frail ears had something ethereal about them. Never, not in any light, not even that of his dream, had Demetrios ever seen this more than human beauty and such radiance from the skin of the dead.

*

* *

And then, he recalled the words spoken by Chrysis during their first meeting: "You only know my face. You do not know how beautiful I am!" An intense emotion suddenly grips him. He wants to finally know. He can do it.

He wants to keep a memory of his three passion-filled days, something that will endure longer than himself — to position it like a model in the same ravished pose that he had seen in his dream, and to create from it a statue of Immortal Life.

He unfastens the clasp and the knot. He opens the cloth. The body lies heavy. He raises it up. The head falls back down. The breasts tremble. The arms collapse. He pulls off her robe and throws it to the middle of the room. The body falls back again, heavily.

With his hands under her cool armpits, Demetrios slides the dead woman to the head of the bed. He turns her head onto the left cheek, rearranges her hair and spreads it out again, radiating under her reclining back. Then, he raises her right arm, bends it above the forehead, clenches the fingers, still soft, onto the cloth of the cushion: two wonderfully muscular lines, descending from the ear and the elbow, come together under the right breast, cradling it like a fruit.

Next he arranges the legs, one stretching stiffly out to the side, the other its knee straight up, the heel nearly touching the buttocks. He adjusts a few details, bends the waist to the left, extends the right foot and lifts off the bracelets, the necklaces, and the rings, so as to not destroy, by a single discord, the pure and complete harmony of feminine nakedness.

The model kept the pose.

Demetrios throws the lump of damp clay he had brought onto the table. He kneads, shapes, stretches it out into human form: a sort of crude monstrosity is born from his fervent fingers; he stares at it.

The immutable corpse maintains her impassioned pose. But a slender thread of blood emerges from the right nostril, runs onto the upper lip, and, drop by drop, falls beneath the slack mouth.

Demetrios continues. The small clay model becomes alive, shapes itself, captures life. A wondrous left arm curves over the body as if it were embracing someone. The thigh muscles bulge with energy. The toes curl under.

*

* *

... When night grew over the earth and darkened the low room, Demetrios had finished the statue.

He had four slaves carry the clay model into his studio. That same evening, by the glimmering of the lamp light, he chipped away on a marble block from Paros, and, one year from that day, he was still working on the marble.

COMPASSION

"JAILOR, open up for us! Jailor open up for us!"
Rhodis and Myrtocleia were knocking on the closed door.

The door opened slightly.

"What do you want?"

"To see our friend," said Myrto. "To see Chrysis, the poor Chrysis who died this morning."

"That is not allowed, go away from here!"

"Oh! Let us, let us come in. No one will know it. We will not say anything. She was our friend, let us see her again. We will leave quickly. We will not make any noise."

"And if I am caught, my little girls? If I am punished because of you? It will not be you who will pay the price."

"You will not be caught. You are all alone here. There is no other prisoner. You have sent the soldiers away. We know all of this. Let us enter."

"All right! Do not stay long. Here is the key. It is the third door. Let me know when you leave. It is late and I would like to go to bed."

The good old man handed them the key of hammered iron that hung from his sash, and the two small virgins ran at once, on silent sandals, through the darkened passageways.

Then the jailor went back to his lodging and did not continue further the useless surveillance. The pain of imprisonment was not implemented in Hellenic Egypt and the little white house that it was the sweet old man's mission to guard, only served to house those condemned to death. In the intervals between executions, it remained abandoned.

At the instant when the huge key penetrated the lock, Rhodis stopped her friend's hand:

"I do not know if I dare to see her," she said. "I loved her so much, Myrto ... I am afraid ... Go first, will you?"

Myrtocleia shoved the door; but as soon as she had looked into the room, she screamed:

"Do not come in, Rhodis! Wait for me here."

"Oh! What is it? You are afraid too ... What is on the bed? Isn't she dead?"

"Yes. Wait for me ... I will tell you ... Stay in the corridor and do not look."

The body had remained in the ecstatic pose Demetrios had designed for the Statue of Immortal Life. But raptures of extreme joy touch very close to the excessive spasms of suffering, and Myrtocleia asked herself what dreadful pain, what martyrdom, what excruciating agony had arranged the cadaver in such a disorder.

She approached the bed on her tiptoes.

The trickle of blood continued to course down from the corpse's translucent nostril. The skin was perfectly white; the pale tips of the breasts were shrunken like frail navels; not one rosy reflection enlivened the reclining ephemeral statue, but a few emerald-colored spots softly tinted the smooth belly, signifying that millions of new lives were springing up on the barely cooled flesh and were demanding their turn.

Myrtocleia took the lifeless arm and lowered it along the hip. She wanted also to stretch out the left leg; but the knee was almost frozen in place and she could not extend it completely.

"Rhodis," she said in a pained voice. "Come. You can enter now."

The trembling child entered the room, her face drawn, her eyes wide open ...

As soon as they both understood, together they burst into endless sobs in each other's arms.

"Poor Chrysis! Poor Chrysis!" the child repeated.

They kissed each other on the cheek with a desperate tenderness that had nothing of the sensual, and the taste of the tears placed on their lips all the grief of their small benumbed souls.

They cried and cried, looking sorrowfully at each other and sometimes they spoke to each other in a voice, hoarse, torturous, the words ending in sobs.

"We loved her so much! She was not a friend for us, not a lover, she was like a very young mother, a small mother between the two of us ..."

Rhodis repeated:

"Like a little mother ..."

And Myrto, pulling her close to the corpse, said in a hushed voice:

"Kiss her."

They both leaned over, placing their hands on the bed and, with renewed sobs, touched their lips to the icy forehead.

And Myrto took the head between her hands, plunging them into the hair and she said this to it:

"Chrysis, my Chrysis, you were the most beautiful and the most adored of women, you look so much like the goddess that people took you for her. And here you are now, what have they done to you? You have lived to bestow joy graciously. There has never been fruit more sweet that your mouth, nor light more bright than your eyes. Your skin was a glorious robe that you did not want to conceal; sensual pleasure floated around it like an everlasting fragrance; and when you untied your hair, all desires escaped from it, and when you closed your bare arms, we prayed to the gods for death."

Crouched on the floor, Rhodis sobbed.

"Chrysis, my Chrysis," continued Myrtocleia, "yesterday, you were still alive and young, hoping to have a full life and now here you are dead, and nothing in the world can ever make you say one word to us. You have closed your eyes; we were not there for you. You suffered and you did not know that we wept for you behind the thick walls. While dying, you looked around for someone and your eyes did not meet our eyes, burdened with mourning and pity."

The flute player continued to weep. The singer took her by the hand.

"Chrysis, my Chrysis, you did tell us that one day, thanks to you, we could marry. Our union is made in tears and this is the sad betrothal of Rhodis and Myrtocleia. But sorrow more than love unites two clasped hands. They who have once wept together will never part. We will put your body into the earth, dear Chrysidion, and we will both cut all our hair off over your tomb."

She enveloped the beautiful cadaver in a coverlet; then she said to Rhodis:

"Help me."

They lifted it up gently; but it was a heavy burden for the small musicians and they placed it on the ground for the first time.

"We need to take off our sandals," said Myrto. "We must walk barefoot in the passageways. The jailor must have fallen asleep ... If we do not wake him up, we will go past, but if he sees us he will stop us ... As for tomorrow, that is of no concern: when he sees the empty bed, he will tell the queen's soldiers that he threw the body into the pit, as the law requires of him. Fear nothing, Rhodé ... Put your sandals into your sash like me. And come. Grab the body under the knees. Never mind the trailing feet. Walk without making a sound, slowly, slowly..."

PIETY

AROUND the bend of the second street, they lay the body down a second time in order to put their sandals back on. Rhodis' feet, too delicate to walk bare, were raw and bleeding.

The night was full of light. The town was full of silence. The iron-colored shadows stood squarely in the middle of streets, silhouetting the houses.

The petite virgins took up their burden again.

"Where are we going?" asked the child, "Where are we going to bury her?"

"In the cemetery of Hermes-Anubis. It is always deserted. She will be at peace there."

"Poor Chrysis! Would I have thought that on the day of her death I would be carrying her corpse, without torches, without a funeral chariot, secretly, like something stolen."

Then, both of them, mirroring each other, began to chatter, as if they were afraid of the silence, side by side with the cadaver. Chrysis' last day overwhelmed them with astonishment. How did it happen that she possessed the mirror, comb, and necklace? She herself could not have taken the pearls of the goddess: the temple was too well guarded for a courtesan to have entered it. Then, someone had acted for her? But who? They did not know her to have had a lover among the priests appointed to maintain the divine statue. And then, if someone had acted in her place, why had she not denounced him? And, at any rate, why these three crimes? What did they have to offer her, except to deliver her to punishment? A woman does not do these insane things without a reason, unless she was in love. Was Chrysis in love, then? With whom?

"We will never know," concluded the flute player. "She carried away her secret with her, and, even if she had an accomplice, he will never tell us."

Now Rhodis, who had already become unsteady, gasped:

"No longer, Myrto, I can no longer carry her. I am going to fall on my knees. I am broken from fatigue and grief."

Myrtocleia put her arm around her neck:

"Try again, my darling. We must carry her. It has to do with her life in the underworld. If she has no sepulchre and no coin in her hand, she will remain wandering forever at the edge of the river in the lower regions, and when, in our turn, Rhodis, when we descend to the dead, she will reproach us for our impiety and we will not know how to answer her."

But the child, faint, burst into tears in her arms.

"Quick, quick," replied Myrtocleia, "Here comes someone, at the end of the street. Put yourself in front of the body with me. Hide it behind our tunics. If anyone sees it, everything will be lost…"

She interrupted herself.

"It is Timon. I recognize him. Timon, with four women ... Ah! Gods! What is going to happen! He mocks everything and will make fun of us ... No, stay here, Rhodis, I will go and talk to him."

And, an idea suddenly took hold, she ran into the street ahead of the small group.

"Timon," she said, her voice filled with pleading, "Timon, stop. I beg you to hear me. I have important words to say. I must say them to you alone."

"My poor little one," said the young man; "how upset you are! Have you lost the knot from your shoulder, or has your doll broken her nose from a fall? That would be quite an irreparable event."

The young woman gave him a doleful look; but already the four women, Philotis, Seso of Cnidus, Callistion and Tryphera, had grown impatient with her.

"Come, stupid little thing!" said Tryphera, "if you have drained the breasts of your nurse, we can do nothing, we do not have any milk. It is nearly daylight, you should be in bed; since when do children wander around at night?"

"Her nurse?" said Philotis. "It is Timon she wants to take from us."

"The whip! She deserves the whip!"

And Callistion, an arm around Myrto's waist, lifted her up from the ground, while raising her little blue tunic. But Seso intervened:

"You are crazy," she shouted at her. "Myrto has never known a man. If she calls Timon, it is not to lie with him. Leave her in peace and have done with it!"

"See here now," said Timon, "what do you want from me? Come over here. Speak into my ear. Is it really serious?"

"Chrysis' body is there, in the street," said the young girl, still trembling. "We are carrying it to the cemetery, my little friend and myself, but it is heavy and we are asking you if you would be kind enough to help us ... It will not take long ... Soon afterwards, you will be able to join your women ..."

Timon gave a delighted look:

"Poor girls! And I laughed! You are better than we are …Certainly, I will help you. Go rejoin your friend and wait for me, I will come."

Turning toward the four women:

"Go to my place," he said, "by the street of the Potters. I will be there in a short while. Do not follow me."

Rhodis was still seated in front of the cadaver's head; she begged:

"Do not tell anyone about this! We have stolen it to rescue her spirit. Keep our secret; we will love you well, Timon."

"Do not worry," said the young man.

He took the body under the shoulders and Myrto took it by the knees, and they walked, silently. Rhodis followed with short, wavering steps.

Timon said nothing. For the second time in two days, human passion had just come to carry off one of the fugitives from his bed, and he wondered which extravagance carried away thus the souls outside the enchanted path that leads to happiness without shadow.

"Tranquillity!" he thought. "Temperance, calmness, oh voluptuous serenity! Who among men will appreciate you? Man excites himself, he struggles, he aspires, when one thing alone is precious: to know how to draw all the joy from the fleeting moment and only leave his bed as seldom as possible."

*

* *

They arrived at the door of the ancient desecrated cemetery.

"Where will we put her?" said Myrto.

"Near the god."

"Where is the statue? I have never been in here. I am afraid of tombs and grave markers. I do not know of the Hermes-Anubis cemetery."

"It must be at the center of the small garden. Look for it. I came here long ago when I was a child, when I was following a lost gazelle. Let us take the path through the white sycamores. We cannot fail to discover it."

In fact, they made their way straight to it.

The first faint violet light of day mingled with the moon over the marble slabs. A vague, distant harmony floated into the cypress branches. The rhythmic rustle of the palms, sounding like small drops of falling rain, gave out an illusion of coolness.

Timon opened a rose slab sunken into the ground with difficulty. The sepulchre was hollowed out beneath the funereal god whose hands made the gesture of the embalmer. It must have once contained a body, but they found nothing in the hole other than a pile of brownish dust.

The young man descended only to his sash and held his arms out in front of him:

"Give her to me," he said to Myrto. "I am going to lay her flat and we will close up her tomb ..."

But Rhodis hurled herself onto the body:

"No! Do not bury her so quickly! I want to see her again! One last time! One last time! Chrysis! My poor Chrysis! Ah! The horror ...What has she become!..."

Myrtocleia had just spread out the coverlet wrapped around the body and its face appeared to have changed so quickly that the young girls recoiled. The squared cheeks, the eyelids, the lips were swollen like six white cushions. Already the more than human beauty had vanished. They closed the heavy shroud; but Myrto slid her hand under the cloth, placing the obol destined for Charon in her hands.

Then, the two of them, shaking from intermittent sobs, put the folded inert body back into Timon's arms.

And when Chrysis was completely laid out in the sandy tomb, Timon opened the shroud once more. He fixed the obol securely into the small, loose bones of the fingers, he propped up the head with a stone slab; and, over her body, from her forehead to her knees, he spread out her long hair of shadow and gold.

Aphrodite

Then, he emerged from the grave and the musicians, kneeling in front of the gaping hole, cut each other's youthful hair in order to tie it up into a single bundle and bury it with the dead.

ΤΟΙΟΝΔ ΠΕΡΑΣ ΕΣΧΕ ΤΟ ΣΥΝΤΑΤΜΑ
ΤΩΝ ΠΕΡΙ ΧΡΥΣΙΔΑ ΚΑΙ ΔΗΜΗΤΠΙΟΝ

So ended the affair
between Chrysis and Demetrios.

Pierre Louÿs

THE SONGS OF BILITIS

This small book of antique love is respectfully dedicated to the young women of a
future society.   *-P. L.*

CONTENTS

PART 2

ELEGIES AT MYTILENE

PART 3

EPIGRAMS ON THE ISLAND OF CYPRUS

THE TOMB OF BILITIS

BIBLIOGRAPHY

Pierre Louÿs

LIFE OF BILITIS

Bilitis was born at the beginning of the sixth century (before our time) in a mountain village situated on the banks of the Melas, in the eastern part of Pamphylia. The country is harsh and forlorn, sombered by the darkness of an impenetrable forest, dominated by the enormous mass of the Taurus Mountains; mineral springs flow from its rocks, large salt lakes reside on its heights, and silence fills its valleys.

She was the daughter of a Greek man and a Phoenician woman. She apparently never knew her father for he plays no part in the memories of her childhood. Perhaps he died before she was born; that would explain why she had a Phoenician name — one only her mother could have given her.

In this nearly deserted land she lived a tranquil life with her sisters. Other young women, friends of hers, lived near there. The shepherds pastured their flocks on the wooded slopes of Taurus.

She awoke every morning to the crow of the rooster and went off to the stable, led the animals out to drink, and milked them. During the day, if it rained, she stayed in the women's quarters and spun woolen threads from her distaff. If it were a beautiful day, she would run in the fields and, with her friends, play a thousand different games about which she tells us.

Bilitis had a passionate devotion to the Nymphs. The sacrifices which she offered were almost always for their fountain. She often spoke to the Nymphs, although she seems never to have seen them. She hung on, with reverence, to every word of an old man who happened on them one day by surprise.

The end of her pastoral existence was saddened by a love about whom we know little, a love she alludes to, nevertheless, at great length. She stopped singing about it when the romance became unbearable. After she gave birth to a child, Bilitis abandoned her and left Pamphylia for mysterious reasons, never to return to the place of her birth.

We find her next at Mytilene where she had come by way of the sea, skirting along the beautiful coasts of Asia. Bilitis had barely turned sixteen at this time, according to the conjectures of M. Heim, who established the probable dates for her life from a verse that alludes to the death of Pittacus.

At the time, Lesbos was the center of the world. It was located midway between beautiful Attica and magnificent Lydia, and its capitol, Mytilene, was more enlightened than Athens and more corrupt than Sardis. Mytilene was built on a peninsula in view of the shores of Asia. A blue sea surrounded the city. From the top of the temples, the white thread of Atarnea, the port of Pergamus, could be made out on the horizon.

The narrow streets of Mytilene, always crowded with throngs of people, were resplendent in multicolored fabrics: tunics of crimson and hyacinth, veils of transparent silks, cloaks trailing in the dust made by yellow shoes. Dangling from the women's ears were impressive rings of gold inlaid with raw pearls and on their arms were massive silver bracelets roughly chiseled in relief. The men wore their hair glistening and perfumed with rare oils. The ankles of the Greek women were bare among the jingling of the ankle bracelets and large shiny metal serpents that dangled on their heels. The Asian women walked around in short boots made of soft tinted leather. In groups, passersby stood in front of shops, each store selling its displays of specialized wares — darkly colored rugs, blankets embroidered with golden threads, jewelry made of amber and ivory. The activities of Mytilene did not stop with daylight. There was never a time too late to hear, through open doors, the joyous sounds of music, the shouts of the women, and the noise from dancing. Pittacus himself, wanting to bring some order to this perpetual orgy, passed a law that forbid the employment of very young flute players at the nocturnal festivities. But this law, like all laws that make a pretense of changing the course of natural behavior, only ensured deception and disobedience.

In a society where the husbands are occupied at night by wine and dancers, inevitably the wives turned to each other for consolation in their forced solitude. From this, the women formed a delicate love that antiquity has given their name and that holds more true passion, whatever men think of it, than indecent groping.

At this time, Sappho was still beautiful. Bilitis knew her and speaks about her as Psappha, the name she used on Lesbos. Without a doubt it was this admirable woman who taught the little Pamphylienne the art of singing in rhythmic phrases and to preserve for future generations the existence of those dearest to her. Unfortunately, Bilitis gives us few details about Sappho, who today is not well known, and it is a cause for regret, for the slightest word about such an inspiring figure would have been precious. Instead, she left us about thirty elegiac songs telling of her friendship for a young girl of the same age named Mnasidika, who had lived with her. We already know the name of this young woman from Sappho's verse extolling her beauty, but the name itself was questionable and Bergh was almost convinced that she was simply called Mnais. The songs that we will read further on proves, however, that this hypothesis must be discarded. Mnasidika appears to have been a sweet, innocent girl, meant only to be adored — one of those charming creatures who is loved all the more because there is no effort on her part. Love without reason endures the longest; this one lasted ten years. It was finally shattered by Bilitis' intense jealousy and her inability to allow any changes.

When she felt that nothing kept her in Mytilene any longer except unhappy memories, Bilitis made a second voyage: she journeyed to Cyprus, an island as Greek and Phoenician as Pamphylia. It must have often reminded her of her birthplace.

It was there that Bilitis began her life for the third time, and in a manner that it will be more difficult for me to make acceptable without recalling again to what degree love was held sacred among the people of antiquity. The courtesans of Amathonte were not considered, like ours, as decadent creatures, exiled from all of mundane society. They were women from the best families of the city. Aphrodite had given them beauty and, in gratitude, they thanked the goddess by consecrating this beauty to the service of her cult. Every city that had a temple rich in courtesans like those of Cyprus gave these women the same respectful attention.

The legendary story of Phryne, as told to us by Athena, will give us some idea of the magnitude of a similar veneration. It is not true that Hyperides needed to present Phryne naked in order to influence the Areopagus. Yet, her crime was great: she had committed murder. The orator only tore off the top of her tunic, revealing her breasts. He then appealed to the judges, "Do not put to death this priestess inspired by Aphrodite."

Unlike the other courtesans who went out wearing transparent veils that displayed every detail of their bodies, Phyrne was accustomed to enveloping herself, even her hair, in one of those grand folded robes, whose elegance was preserved for us on the statues of Tanagra. No one, except her friends, had ever seen her arms or her shoulders, and she was never seen in the pool of the public baths. But one day something extraordinary occurred. It was the during the festival of Eleusis. Twenty thousand people had come from all parts of Greece and were gathered on the seashore when Phryne moved toward the waves. She took off her cloak, untied her sash, removed even the bottom half of her tunic and, "she let down her hair and went into the sea." And Praxiteles who was in the crowd, designed his "Aphrodite of Cnidus" after this living goddess, and Apelles caught a glimpse of the shape for his "Anadyomene." Admirable people, to whom naked Beauty could be seen without causing laughter or false modesty!

I wish that the story of Bilitis was as complete as that of Phyrne, because, while translating her songs, I have grown to love this friend of Mnasidika. Without a doubt, her whole life was also wonderful. I regret only that it was not spoken about more often and that the surviving writings of the ancient authors were so poor in giving information about her appearance. Philodemos, who plagiarized her twice, does not even mention her name. In the absence of such interesting anecdotes, I hope the reader will be contented with the details that she herself gives us about her life as a courtesan. That she was a courtesan is undeniable: even her last Songs bear witness to that; if she had all the virtues of her vocation, she also shared in its worst faults. But I want only to know of her strengths. She was pious and devoted. She lived a life true to the temple, so long as Aphrodite consented to prolong the youthfulness of her purest adorer. On the day she stopped being the loved one, she said she stopped writing. However, it is difficult to believe that her songs of Pamphylia had been written during the period of time they describe. How could a little shepherdess from the mountains learn to recite the complicated rhythms of Aeolian verse? It is more reasonable to assume that Bilitis, in her old age, found comfort in singing about those memories of her distant childhood. We know nothing of this last period of her life. We do not even know how old she was when she died.

Her tomb was discovered by M. G. Heim at Paleo-Limasso by the side of an ancient roadway, not far from the ruins of Amathus. During the last thirty years, the ruins have nearly disappeared; the stones from the house where Bilitis might have lived, today pave the quays of Port Said. But the Phoenician custom of building tombs underground had saved it from the plundering of treasure hunters.

M. Heim penetrated the depths of the tomb by way of a narrow shaft that had been filled with dirt. Near the end of the shaft, he encountered a door that had been walled-up, which he dismantled. The spacious low burial chamber, paved with slabs of limestone, had four walls covered by slates of a dazzling black granite on which, engraved in primitive capitals, were all of her songs we are about to read, apart from the three epitaphs that decorated the sarcophagus.

There she lay, the friend of Mnasidika, in a great terra cotta coffin, under a delicately-shaped clay figure bearing her death mask. Her hair was painted black, her eyes half-closed, with black lines drawn out to her temples as if she were living, and her cheek scarcely affected by a slight smile that grew from the lines of her mouth. No words are adequate to describe those lips, at the same time pure and clearly drawn, luxurious and delicate, united one to the other, as if intoxicated by their own touch.

When the coffin was opened, she appeared just as she must have twenty-four centuries earlier, when some pious hand had placed her there. Vials of perfume hung from the clay pegs and one of them, after so long a time, was still fragrant. The polished silver mirror where Bilitis had looked at herself, the brush that trailed the blue color along her eyelids, all were found in their place. A small nude statue of Astarte, a relic forever precious, forever watching over the skeleton decorated with all its gold jewelry — white like a snow-covered branch, but so soft and so fragile that, at the first touch, it mingled with the dust.

Pierre Louÿs
Constantinople
August, 1894

Pierre Louÿs

PART 1
PASTORAL POEMS FROM PAMPHYLIA

Sweet, too, is my music, whether I play on the pipe, flute, reed, or flageolet.

-Theocritos

THE TREE

I flung off my clothes, and climbed up the tree; my bare thighs embraced the smooth, moist bark; my sandals stepped on the branches.

At the top, but still covered by leaves and protected from the heat in their shadows, I sat astride a secluded bough, dangling my feet into the emptiness.

It had rained. Drops of water fell and trickled down over my skin. My hands were stained with moss and my toes were reddened from crushed flowers.

I felt the beautiful tree come alive as the wind swept through it; then I wrapped my legs even tighter and pressed my open lips on to the hairy nape of a branch.

PASTORAL SONG

We must sing a pastoral song, calling on Pan, the god of the summer wind. I watch over my flock as Selenis does hers, under the rounded shadow of a trembling olive tree.

Selenis lies on the meadow. She gets up and runs, or searches for cicadas, or gathers flowers and herbs, or splashes her face with the cool waters of the brook.

And I — I draw up the wool from the pale gold backs of the sheep to fill my distaff and I spin. The hours pass slowly. An eagle fades into the sky.

The shadow shifts away; let us move the basket of flowers and the jar of milk. We must sing a pastoral song calling on Pan, god of the summer wind.

MOTHERLY ADVICE

My mother bathes me in the darkness, she dresses me in the bright sunlight and arranges my hair by the lamplight; but if I go out in the moonlight she tightens my sash with a double knot.

She says to me:
"Play with virgins, dance with little children; do not look out of the window, shun the words of young men and fear the counsel of widows.

"One evening someone will come to take you, like all the others, into the midst of a grand procession of resounding drums and amorous flutes.

"On that evening, when you will go there, Bilitô, you will leave me three gourds of bile: one for the morning, one for midday, and the third, the most bitter of them all, the third for the days of the feast."

MY NAKED FEET

I have black hair that falls down the length of my back and a small round cap. My tunic is made of white wool. My firm legs are browned by the sun.

If I lived in the city, I would wear jewels of gold and tunics woven with golden thread and shoes made of silver ... I look down at my naked feet in their slippers of dust.

Psophis! Come here, little beggar! Carry me to the spring, bathe my feet in your hands and perfume them, with pressed olives and violets, over the flowers.

You will be my slave today; you will follow me and wait on me, and at the end of the day I will give you, for your mother, lentils from my mother's garden.

THE OLD MAN AND THE NYMPHS

An old blind man lives on the mountain. For having looked at the nymphs, his eyes have long since been dead. And, from that time on, his happiness is but a distant memory.

"Yes, I saw them," he told me. "Helopsychria, Limnanthis — they were standing near the edge in the green pool of Physos. The water sparkled higher than their knees.

"Their necks leaned forward beneath their long hair. Their nails were slender like the wings of the cicada. Their nipples were hollowed like the cups of hyacinths.

"They trailed their fingers over the water and gathered, from the invisible muddy bottom, the long-stemmed water lilies. Around their parted thighs, ripples slowly widened."

SONG

Torti-tortue, what are you doing here in our midst?
  I wind the wool and the thread of Miletus.
Alas! Alas! Why do you not come and dance?
  I am filled with sadness. I am filled with sadness.

Torti-tortue, what are you doing here in our midst?
  I cut a reed for a funeral flute.
Alas! Alas! Look at what has happened!
  I will not say anything. I will not say anything.

Torti-tortue, what are you doing here in our midst?
  I press the olives for oil to anoint the tombstone.
Alas! Alas! And who then is dead?
  Can you ask that? Can you ask that?

Torti-tortue, what are you doing here in our midst?
  He has fallen into the sea...
Alas! Alas! And how is that?
  From the backs of white horses. From the backs of white horses.

THE PASSERBY

In the evening, as I was seated in front of the door to the house, a young man passed by. He looked at me. I turned my head away. He spoke to me; I did not answer.

He wanted to come near me. I took a sickle from the wall and I would have slashed his cheek if he had taken one more step toward me.

Then, drawing back a little, he smiled and blew toward me, from his hand, saying, "Receive a kiss." And I cried out! And I wept! So much so that my mother rushed to me.

She worried, believing that I had been stung by a scorpion. I wept, "He gave me a kiss." My mother also kissed me and carried me away in her arms.

THE AWAKENING

It is already broad daylight. I should be up. But the drowsiness of morning is sweet and the warmth of my bed envelopes me. I want to remain lying here longer.

Soon I will go the stable. I will give the goats grass and flowers and a flask of fresh water drawn from the well where I will drink with them.

Then I will fasten them to the post and milk their soft, warm udders, and if the kids are not jealous, I will suckle with them from the supple teats.

Did not Amalthea feed Zeus? Therefore I will go. But not yet. The sun has risen too soon and my mother is not yet awake.

THE RAIN

The delicate rain moistened everything, very gently and silently. It is still raining a little. I will go out under the trees. Barefoot so I will not soil my shoes.

The springtime rain is delicious. The branches, laden with moist flowers, have a perfume that makes me giddy. I can see the sun glistening on the delicate skin of the bark.

Alas! How many flowers on the ground! Have pity on the fallen flowers. They must not be swept away and mingled with the mud, but saved for the bees.

The beetles and snails cross over the path between the puddles of water. I do not want to step on them or frighten the golden lizard that stretches out, blinking his eyelids.

THE FLOWERS

Nymphs of the woods and fountains, my beneficent friends, I am here. Do not hide from me, but come to my aid for I am burdened with many flowers.

I will choose, from out of all the forest, a poor wood nymph with raised arms and in her leaf-colored hair, I will insert my most voluptuous rose.

See — I have taken so many from the fields that I cannot carry them back with me unless you help me make a bouquet. If you refuse, beware.

The one with the orange hair. I saw her yesterday coupling like a beast with the satyr Lamprosathes, and I will denounce the shameless creature.

IMPATIENCE

I threw myself into her arms and wept; for a long time she felt the coursing of my hot tears over her shoulders, until my sorrow would let me speak:

"Alas, I am only a child; the young men do not look at me. When will I have, like you, a young woman's breasts to push out my robe and entice kisses?

"No one has curious eyes if my tunic slips. No one gathers up the flower that falls from my hair; no one threatens to kill me if my mouth gives itself to another."

She replied to me tenderly, "Bilitis, little virgin, you cry like a cat at the moon and are upset without reason. The girls who are the most impatient are not the first chosen."

Pierre Louÿs

COMPARISONS

Bergeronnet, bird of Cypris, sing with our first desires! The fresh bodies of young girls covered with flowers like the earth. The night of all our dreams approaches and we talk of it among ourselves.

Sometimes we compare, together, our beauties that are so different, our hair already long, our young breasts still small, our puberties rounded like quails hidden under nascent down.

Yesterday I competed with Melantho, my older sister. She was proud of her breasts which had grown in a month, and pointing to my straight tunic, she called me "little child."

No man could see us so we stripped naked before the girls, and if she was victorious on one point, I far surpassed her on the others. Bergeronnet, bird of Cypris, sing with our first desires!

THE FOREST RIVER

I bathed alone in the forest river. I am certain I frightened the water nymphs because I sensed them faintly, from afar, under the dark water.

I called them. To look more like them, I wove irises black as my hair and clusters of yellow gillyflowers behind the nape of my neck.

I made myself a green sash from a long floating grass and to see it, I pressed in my breasts and bent my head forward a little.

And I called, "Naiads! Naiads! Play with me — be kind." But the water nymphs are transparent and perhaps, without knowing it, I caressed their delicate arms.

COME, NAIADS

When the sun burns less fiercely, we will go and play on the river banks, we will do battle for a fragile crocus or for a dew-covered hyacinth.

We will fashion them into a necklace for the circle dance and a garland for the race. We will take each other by the hand and by the end of our tunics.

Come, Naiads! Give us honey. Come, Naiads! Let us bathe with you. Come, Naiads! Cast a sweet shadow over our sweat-covered bodies.

And we will offer you, beneficent nymphs, not shameful wine, but oil and milk and goats with twisted horns.

THE SYMBOLIC RING

The travelers who return from Sardis tell us about the necklaces and gemstones that adorn the women of Lydia, from the top of their hair to their painted feet.

The girls of my country have neither bracelets nor diadems, but wear a silver ring on their finger; its setting is engraved with the triangle of the goddess.

When they turn the point outward, it means, "Psyche is to be taken." When they turn the point inward, it means, "Psyche is taken."

The men believe this; the women do not. As for me, I do not even look which way the point is turned, for Psyche can free herself easily. Psyche is always to be taken.

DANCES IN THE MOONLIGHT

On the soft grass, in the night, the young girls with hair of violets danced together, one of the pair responding to the other as a lover.

The virgins said, "We are not for you." And, as if they were ashamed, concealed their virginity. The aegipan played the flute among the trees.

The others said, "You will come searching for us." They had fastened up their robes like the tunics of men and feigned to do battle, entwining their dancing legs.

Then, each saying she was vanquished, took her friend by the ears, like a cup with two handles, and bending her head, drank a kiss.

THE LITTLE CHILDREN

The river is almost dry; the brittle reeds are dying in the mud; the air burns and, far from the hollowed-out banks, a clear brook flows over the gravel.

There, from morning to evening, the little naked children come to play. They bathe only as high as their calves, for the river is low.

But they walk in the current, sometimes sliding on the rocks and the little boys splash water on the little girls who laugh.

And when a troop of merchants passes by, leading their enormous white oxen to drink from the river, the children clasp their hands behind their back and watch the great beasts.

THE STORIES

I am loved by the little children. As soon as they see me, they run to me and cling to my tunic or embrace my legs with their little arms.

If they have gathered some flowers, they give them all to me; if they have caught a beetle, they put it in my hand; if they have nothing, they caress me and make me sit before them.

Then, they kiss me on the cheek; they rest their heads on my breasts; they plead with me with their eyes. I know what that means.

What that means is: "Dear Bilitis, tell us again, for we are being good, the story of the hero Perseus or the death of the little Helle."

THE MARRIED FRIEND

Our mothers were pregnant at the same time, and this evening, Melissa, my dearest friend, got married. The roses still lie on the path; the torches have not yet burned out.

And I return, with Mother, by the same path, and I dream. Thus, as she is today, I too could have been. Am I not already a grown girl?

The procession, the flutes, the nuptial song, and the bridegroom's flowered chariot — all these festivities, on some other evening, will spread out around me amidst the branches of the olive trees.

At this same hour, like Melissa, I will unveil myself before a man. I will know love in the night, and later, little children will nourish themselves at my swollen breasts...

SECRETS

The next day I went to her house and we blushed as soon as we saw each other. She made me enter into her room so that we would be alone together.

I had many things to say to her, but when I saw her I forgot them. I did not even dare to throw my arms around her; I saw her high-knotted sash.

I was astonished that nothing in her face had changed, that she still looked like my friend, and yet, since the day before, she had learned so many things that intimidated me.

Suddenly I sat down on her lap, took her in my arms, and whispered quickly, anxiously, into her ear. Then she laid her cheek against mine and told me everything.

THE MOON WITH EYES OF BLUE

At night the hair of the women and the branches of the willows become lost in each other. I walked along at the edge of the water. Suddenly I heard singing: only then I knew that young girls were there.

I said to them, "To what are you singing?" They replied, "In honor of those who return." One awaited her father, another her brother, but the one who awaited her fiancé was the most impatient.

They had woven for them crowns and garlands, cut palms from the palm trees and lotuses pulled from the water. They clasped each other around the neck and sang, one after another.

I went along the river, sadly and very alone, but when I looked around me I saw, behind the tall trees, the moon with eyes of blue was guiding me home.

SONG

Shadow of the woods where she should have come, tell me, where
has my mistress gone?
>*She has descended to the plain.*

Plain, where has my mistress gone?
>*She has followed the banks of the river.*

Beautiful river who has seen her pass, tell me, is she near here?
>*She has left me for the path.*

Path, do you see her still?
>*She has left me for the road.*

Oh white road, road of the city, tell me, where have you led her?
>*To the street of gold that enters into Sardis.*

Oh street of light, touched you her naked feet?
>*She has entered the palace of the king.*

Oh palace, splendor of the earth, return her to me!
>*Look! She has chains upon her breasts and tassels in her hair, a
hundred pearls along her legs, two arms around her waist.*

LYKAS

Come, we will go into the fields, under the thickets of juniper; we
will eat honey from the hives, we will make snares for grasshoppers
with the stems of the asphodel.

Come, we will go to see Lykas who tends his father's flocks on the
slopes of the shadowy Taurus. Surely he will give us milk.

Already I hear the sound of his flute. He plays with great skill.
Here are the dogs and the sheep and he himself standing against a
tree. Is he not as handsome as Adonis!

Oh Lykas! Give us some milk. Here are figs from our trees. We are
going to stay with you. Bearded goats, do not leap, for fear of
exciting the restless bucks.

THE OFFERING TO THE GODDESS

This garland, woven with my own hands, is not for Artemis whom they adore at Perga, although Artemis is a good goddess who will protect me from difficult childbirth.

It is not for Athena whom they adore at Sidon, although she is of ivory and gold and carries in her hand a pomegranate which tempts the birds.

No, it is for Aphrodite whom I adore in my heart, for only she will give what my lips most need, if I hang my garland of delicate roses on the sacred tree.

But I will not ask aloud that which I beg of her. I will raise up on my toes and into a crevice in the bark I will entrust my secret.

THE COMPLAISANT FRIEND

The storm continued all night long. Selenis with the beautiful hair had come to spin with me. She remained for fear of the mud, and pressed up against one another, we filled my little bed.

When girls lie together, sleep remains at the door. "Bilitis, tell me, tell me, whom do you love?" She slid her leg over mine, caressing me softly.

And she said, close to my mouth, "I know, Bilitis, whom you love. Close your eyes, I am Lykas." Touching her, I responded, "Do I not see quite well you are a girl? You are joking, but it is not right."

But she replied, "Truly, I am Lykas if you close your eyes. Here are his arms, here are his hands ..." And tenderly, in the silence, she enchanted my dream with a singular illusion.

A PRAYER TO PERSEPHONE

Purified by ritual ablutions and dressed in violet tunics, we lowered our hands, filled with olive branches, to the earth.

"Oh Persephone of the Underworld, or whatever may be the name you desire, if this name is acceptable, hear us, oh Hairy-Creature-of-Darkness. Queen, barren and unsmiling.

"Kokhlis, daughter of Thrasymakos, is dangerously ill. Do not call her yet. You know she cannot escape you; one day, later, you will take her.

"But do not drag her not away so soon, oh Invisible Sovereign! For she weeps for her virginity; she beseeches you through our prayers, and, for her deliverance, we will give three unshorn black ewes."

THE GAME OF KNUCKLE-BONES

Since we both loved him, we played for him with the knuckle-bones. It was a great game. Many of the young girls looked on.

She led at first with the cast of Cyclops and I the cast of Solon. But then she threw the Kallibolos and I, feeling lost, prayed to the Goddess.

I played; I had the Epiphenon, she the terrible cast of Chios, I the Antiteukos, she the Triccas, and I the cast of Aphrodite which won the disputed lover.

But, seeing her pale, I threw my arm around her neck and said, close to her ear (so that she alone heard me), "Do not weep, little friend. We will let him choose between us."

THE DISTAFF

All day-long, my mother kept me in the women's quarters with my sisters whom I do not love and who talk among themselves in hushed voices. I, in a tiny corner, I spin my distaff.

Distaff, since I am alone with you, it is to you I will talk. With your wig of white wool you look like an old woman. Listen to me.

If I could, I would not be here, seated in the shadow of the wall and wearily spinning. I would be lying among the violets on the slopes of the Taurus.

Because he is poorer than I, my mother will not let him marry me. However, I say to you — either I will have no wedding day or it will be he who will lead me over the threshold.

THE FLUTE

For the day of Hyacinth, he gave me a panpipe made of carefully cut reeds united with white wax that is sweet as honey to my lips.

He is teaching me to play, seated on his lap, but I am trembling a little. He plays after me, so softly that I can hardly hear him.

We have nothing to say to each other, so near we are, one to the other; but our songs want to answer each other, and taking turns, our lips unite over the flute.

It is late. There is the song of the green frogs that begins with the night. My mother will never believe that I have stayed so long searching for my lost sash.

MY HAIR

He said to me, "This night I dreamt I had your hair around my neck. I had your locks wrapped like a black collar around the nape of my neck and over my chest.

"I caressed them and they were mine; and we were bound like this forever, by the same locks, mouth on mouth, like two laurels having only one root.

"And little by little, it seemed to me our limbs were so entwined — that I became you or that you entered into me like my dream."

When he had finished, he softly laid his hands on my shoulders and looked at me so tenderly that I lowered my eyes, shivering.

THE CUP

Lykas saw me come to him scantly-clad in a tunic, because the days were oppressive. He wanted to take a mold of my uncovered breast.

He took fine clay, kneading it with water, fresh and clear. When he laid it on my skin I thought I would faint, so cold was this earth.

From the form of my breast, he made a cup, rounded and navel shaped. He placed it in the sun to dry and painted it purple and ocher by pressing flowers all around it.

Then we went to the fountain that is consecrated to the nymphs and threw the cup into the current along with stalks of gillyflowers.

ROSES IN THE NIGHT

When the night ascends into the sky, the world belongs to us and to the gods. We go over the fields to the spring, through the dark wood to the clearings, wherever our naked feet lead us.

The small stars shine enough for little shadows like us. Sometimes, beneath the lower branches, we find some does.

But more charming than anything else in the night is a place known only to ourselves which lures us across the forest — a thicket of mysterious roses.

For nothing on this earth is as divine as the perfume of roses in the night. How is it that in those days when I was alone, I never felt their intoxication?

REMORSE

At first I did not reply; my cheeks flushed with shame and my breasts hurt from the pounding of my heart.

Then I resisted. I said, "No, no." I turned my head away and the kiss neither spread part my lips nor passion my clasped knees.

Then he begged my forgiveness. He kissed my hair, I felt his burning breath, and he left ... Now I am alone.

I look around the empty place, the deserted wood, the trampled earth. And I bite my knuckles until they bleed and smother my cries in the grass.

THE INTERRUPTED SLEEP

I was sleeping alone like a partridge in the heather ... The light breeze, the murmuring of the waters, the sweetness of the night, had kept me there.

Mistakenly, I went to sleep and I awoke with a cry, and struggled and wept. But it was already too late. What can the hands of a child do?

He did not leave me. Rather, more tenderly, he held me in his arms close to him, and I no longer saw the earth or the trees but only the gleam in his eyes...

To you, victorious Cypris, I consecrate these offerings still moist with the dew, vestiges of the pains of the virgin, evidence of my sleep and my resistance.

THE WASHER-WOMEN

Washer-women, say not that you have seen me! I confide in you — do not repeat it! I bring something to you between my tunic and my breasts.

I am like a little frightened hen ...I do not know whether I dare tell you...My heart pounds as though I would die ... It is a veil that I bring you.

A veil and the ribbons from my legs. You see, there is blood. By Apollo, it was in spite of me! I defended myself well, but the man who loves is stronger than us.

Wash them well; spare neither the salt nor the chalk. I will place four coins for you at the feet of Aphrodite. Even a drachma of silver.

SONG

When he returned, I hid my face with both my hands. He said to me, "Fear nothing. Who has seen our kissing?" — "Who has seen us? The night and the moon.

"And the stars and the first dawn. The moon, mirroring itself in the lake, told it to the water under the willows. The water of the lake told it to the oar.

"And the oar told it to the boat and the boat told it to the fisherman. Alas, alas! If that were all! But the fisherman told it to a woman.

"The fisherman told it to a woman — my father and my mother and my sisters and all Hellas will know about it."

BILITIS

One woman envelops herself in white wool. Another clothes herself in silk and gold. Another covers herself with flowers, green leaves and grapes.

Me, I would only know how to live naked. My lover, take me as I am, without robes or jewels or sandals. Here is Bilitis, bare.

My hair is black with its own blackness and my lips are red with their own redness. My curls float around me, free like feathers.

Take me as my mother conceived me in a night of love long past, and if I please you so, do not forget to tell me.

THE LITTLE HOUSE

The little house where he has his bed is the most beautiful on earth. It is made from the branches of trees, four walls of dried earth and a tresses of thatch.

I love it, for there we have slept since the nights have grown cool; and as the nights become cooler, they become longer also. When day comes, I finally feel weary.

The mattress lies on the ground — two coverlets of black wool enclose our bodies which warm each other. His chest presses against my breasts. My heart throbs...

He embraces me so tightly that he will bruise me, poor little girl that I am; but as soon as he is in me I know nothing more of the world, and you could cut off all my limbs without awakening me from my rapture.

THE LOST LETTER

Alas for me! I have lost his letter. I had placed it between my skin and my belt, under the warmth of my breast. I ran; it must have fallen out.

I am going to retrace my steps; if someone should find it they could tell my mother and I would be whipped in front of my jeering sisters.

If it is a man who found it, he will return it to me, or even if he wishes to talk to me in secret, I know the way to charm it from him.

If it is a woman who read it, oh Guardian Zeus protect me! Because she will tell it to the whole world, or she will take my lover from me.

SONG

The night is so profound that it penetrates my eyes.
You will not see the road. You will be lost in the forest.

The noise of falling waters fills my ears.
You would not hear the voice of your lover even if he were twenty steps away.

The perfume of the flowers is so powerful that I feel faint and I am going to fall.
You would not discern him if he crossed your path.

Ah! He is very far from here, on the other side of the mountain; but I see him and I hear him, and I smell him as if he touched me.

THE OATH

"Until the water of the river ascends again to the snow-covered peaks: until barley and wheat is sown in the wavering furrows of the sea:

"Until pines grow from the lakes and water-lilies from the rocks: until the sun becomes black, until the moon falls on the grass:

"Then, but only then, I will take another woman and I will forget you, Bilitis, soul of my life, heart of my heart."

He said that to me, he said that to me! What does the rest of the world matter: where are you infinite happiness which compares with my happiness!

THE NIGHT

Now I am the one looking for him. Each night, very quietly, I leave the house and I take a long path to his meadow to see him sleeping.

Sometimes I remain for a long time without speaking, happy merely to look at him. I draw my lips near to his and kiss only his breath.

Suddenly I stretch out over him. He wakes up in my arms and he can no longer get up, because I wrestle with him. He gives up and laughs and embraces me. We go on playing in the night.

...First dawn, oh wicked light, is it you already? In what nocturnal cave, on what subterranean meadow, can we love so long that we may lose memory of you...

LULLABY

Sleep. I asked Sardis for your toys and Babylon for your clothing. Sleep. You are the daughter of Bilitis and a king of the rising sun.

The woods, they are the palace that was built for you only and that I gave to you. The trunks of the pines are the columns; the lofty branches are the canopy.

Sleep. So that it not wake you, I would sell the sun to the sea. The breeze from the wings of a dove is not as light as your breath.

Daughter of mine, flesh of my flesh, you will say when you open your eyes if you wish the plain or the city, or the mountain, or the moon, or the white procession of the gods.

THE TOMB OF THE NAIADS

Along the length of the woods covered with white frost I walked; my hair before my mouth blossomed with tiny icicles and my sandals were heavy from the soiled, compacted snow.

He said to me, "What are you searching for?" "I follow the tracks of the satyr. His small cloven steps alternate like gaps in a loosely woven white cloak." He said to me, "The satyrs are dead.

"The satyrs and the nymphs also. For thirty years there has not been such a terrible winter. The track you see is that of a buck. But let us rest here, where their tomb is."

And with the iron of his hoe, he broke the ice from the spring where once laughed the water-nymphs. He lifted the large frozen pieces, and raising them toward the pale sky, he gazed through them.

PART 2
ELEGIES AT MYTILENE

Mnasidika is lovelier than the gentle Gyrinno.

- Sappho

TO THE SHIP

Beautiful ship that carried me here, along the shores of Ionia, I leave you to the shimmering waves and, with a nimble step, I leap onto the beach.

You will return to the country where the virgin is the friend of the nymphs. Do not forget to thank those invisible counselors and, as an offering, carry to them this branch picked by my hands.

You were a pine on the mountains, the vast flaming Notos shook your prickly branches, your squirrels and birds.

Boreos — now you guide and push gently toward the port this black ship, escorted by dolphins, at the pleasure of the benevolent sea.

SAPPHO

I rub my eyes ... It is already daylight I think. Ah! Who is this near me? ... A woman? ... By Paphia, I had forgotten ... Oh, Charites! How ashamed I am.

To what country have I come and what is this island where love is understood to be like this? If I were not so exhausted, I would think it some sort of dream...Is it possible that this is Sappho?

She sleeps ... She is truly beautiful, although her hair was cut like an athlete. But this extraordinary countenance, this virile chest, and these narrow hips...

I want to go before she wakes. Alas! I am against the wall. I must step over her. I am afraid of brushing against her hip and she will take me again as I pass.

THE DANCE OF GLOTTIS AND KYSE

Two little girls led me away to their house and, as soon as the door was firmly closed, they lit the wick of a lamp from the fire and wanted to dance for me.

Their cheeks were not painted and were as brown as their little bellies. They tugged at each other's arms and talked at the same time in an ecstasy of glee.

Seated on a mat supported by two raised boards, Glottis sang in a piercing voice and struck the beat with her sonorous little hands.

Kyse danced by fits and starts, then stopped, suffocated with laughter, and taking her sister by the breasts, bit her on the shoulder and threw her down like a goat that wants to play.

A PIECE OF ADVICE

Then Syllikmas entered and seeing us so intimate sat down on the bench. She took Glottis on her knee, Kyse on the other and she said,

"Come here, little one." But I stayed away. She continued, "Are you afraid of us? Come near; these children love you. They will teach you about something you overlook — the honey of a woman's caress.

"Man is violent and lazy. Doubtless you know this. Hate him. He has a flat chest, rough skin, close-cropped hair, hairy arms. But all women are beautiful.

"Only women know how to love — stay with us, Bilitis, stay. And if you have a passionate soul, you will see your beauty on the bodies of your lovers, as though in a mirror."

UNCERTAINTY

Glottis or Kyse, I do not know which one I will marry. They are not like each other, so one could not console me for the other, and I am afraid of making a bad choice.

Each one holds one of my hands and one of my breasts also. But to which one will I give my mouth? To which one will I give my heart and all that cannot be divided?

It is shameful to remain like this, all three of us in one house. They talk about it in Mytilene. Yesterday, before the temple of Ares, a woman who passed by did not say hello.

It is Glottis whom I prefer, but I cannot reject Kyse. What would become of her all alone? Will I leave them as they were, will I find another woman?

THE MEETING

I found her like a treasure in a field, under a bush of myrtle, enveloped from head to toe in a yellow cloak embroidered with blue.

"I have no friend," she said, "for the nearest city is forty stadia from here. I live alone with my mother who is widowed and always sad. If you wish, I will follow you.

"I will follow you to your house even if it were on the other side of the island and I will live with you until you send me away. Your hand is tender, your eyes are blue.

"Let us go. I carry nothing with me but this small naked Astarte that hangs from my necklace. We will put it near yours and we will give them roses to reward them for each night."

THE SMALL TERRA-COTTA ASTARTE

The little guardian Astarte that protects Mnasidika was modeled at Camiros by a skillful potter. It is large as a thumb and of pure yellow clay.

Her hair falls down and curls at her narrow shoulders. Her eyes are slit lengthwise and her mouth is very tiny. Because she is the Most-Beautiful.

With her right hand, she points to her delta which is perforated with little holes on the lower belly and along the groin. Because she is the Most-Amorous-One.

With the left arm she supports her heavy, rounded breasts. A pregnant belly protrudes between her wide hips. Because she is the Mother-of-All-Things.

DESIRE

She entered and, her eyes closed, passionately joined her lips to mine and our tongues discovered each other ... Never in my life was there a kiss like that one.

She was standing up against me, totally in love and willing. One of my knees, little by little, mounted between her hot thighs which gave way as though for a lover.

My hand wandered over her tunic seeking to discover the hidden body which in turn undulated and yielded, or arched and stiffened with every quiver of the skin.

With her eyes filled with ecstasy, she pointed toward the bed, but we had no right to make love before the wedding ceremony, and we parted abruptly.

THE WEDDING

In the morning we had the wedding-feast in the house of Acalanthis, whom she had adopted as a mother. Mnasidika wore the white veil and I the masculine tunic.

And then, in the midst of twenty women, she put on her festive robes. Perfumed with bakkaris, sprinkled with gold powder, her cool, lively skin enticed furtive hands.

In her room filled with greenery, she waited for me as her husband. And I carried her away on a chariot between myself and her brides-maid. One of her small breasts burned in my hands.

We sang the nuptial song and the flutes played, too. I carried Mnasidika under her shoulders and knees and we crossed over the threshold covered with roses.

THE PAST THAT SURVIVES

I will leave the bed as she has left it, unmade and rumpled, the covers intertwined, so the form of her body remains impressed beside mine.

Until tomorrow I will not go to the bath; I will not wear any garments, I will not comb my hair, for fear I might erase her caresses.

This morning I will not eat, nor this evening, and on my lips I will place neither rouge nor powder so that her kiss remains.

I will leave the shutters closed and I will not open the door for fear that the traces which she has left might take flight with the wind.

METAMORPHOSIS

Long ago I was enamored of the beauty of young men and long ago the memory of their words kept me awake.

I remember having carved a name in the bark of a plane tree. I remember having left a piece of my tunic on a path where someone passed by.

I remember having loved...Oh, Pannychis, my child, in whose hands have I left you? How, oh unfortunate one, have I abandoned you?

Today, and forever, Mnasidika alone possesses me. Let her receive in sacrifice the happiness of those whom I have deserted for her.

THE NAMELESS TOMB

Mnasidika, taking me by the hand, led me outside the gates of the city to a little uncultivated field where there was a marble monument. And she said to me, "This was the woman who was the lover of my mother."

I felt a great shiver and still holding her hand, I bent over her shoulder to read the four lines between the hollow cup and the serpent:

"It is not death which has carried me away, but the Nymphs of the fountains. I rest here under the light earth with the locks cut from the hair of Xantho. Let her alone weep for me. I tell not my name."

For a long time we remained standing and we did not pour a libation. For how could we call an unknown soul from among the throngs of Hades?

THE THREE BEAUTIES OF MNASIDIKA

So that Mnasidika may be protected by the gods, I have sacrificed to the Aphrodite-Who-Loves-Smiles two male hares and two doves.

And I have sacrificed to Ares two cocks armed for fighting, and to the sinister Hecate two dogs that howled under the knife.

And it is not without reason that I have called upon these three immortals, for Mnasidika carries on her countenance the reflection of their triple divinity:

Her lips are red like copper, her hair bluish like iron, and her eyes dark like silver.

THE DEN OF THE NYMPHS

Your feet are more delicate than those of silvered Thetis. Between your crossed arms you reunite your breasts and cradle them gently like the bodies of two beautiful doves.

Beneath your hair you hide your dewy eyes, your trembling mouth, and your ears like blushing flowers; but nothing will stop my gaze nor the hot breath of my kiss.

For, in the secret place of your body, it is you, Mnasidika, beloved, who conceals the den of the nymphs of which old Homer spoke, the place where the naiads weave their carmine linens.

The place where, drop by drop, flows the inexhaustible springs; where the North gate lets men descend and the South gate lets immortals enter.

THE BREASTS OF MNASIDIKA

Carefully, with one hand, she opened her tunic and offered her breasts to me, warm and sweet, in the same way a pair of lively turtle doves is offered to the goddess.

"Love them well," she said to me; "I love them so much! They are cherished little children. I look after them when I am alone. I play with them; I make them happy.

"I shower them with milk. I powder them with flowers. My delicate hair that rubs them is dear to their little points. I caress them, shivering. I put them to bed in wool.

"Because I will never have children, be their infant, my love, and because they are so far from my mouth, give them kisses for me."

THE DOLL

I gave her a doll, a doll made of wax with rosy cheeks. Her arms are attached by tiny pegs and her legs can bend.

When we are together, she lays her between us and she is our child. In the evening she cradles her and gives her a breast before putting her to sleep.

She has woven her three little tunics and we gave her jewels on the day of the Aphrodisian Festival — jewels and flowers, too.

She guards her virtue and does not let the doll leave without her; and certainly not in the sun, for the little doll would melt into drops of wax.

TENDERNESSES

Sweetly close your arms like a sash around me. Oh, touch, touch my skin like that! Neither water nor the breeze of noontide are softer than your hand.

Today, cherish me, little sister, it is your turn. Remember the tenderness that I taught you last night and kneel close to me, without a word, for I am weary.

Your lips descend from my lips. All your hair, undone, follows them like the caress follows the kiss. It glides over my left breast; it hides your eyes from me.

Give me your hand. It is hot! Press mine — hold it always. Hands better than mouths unite and nothing can equal their passion.

GAMES

I am a toy for her, more than her balls or her doll. With all parts of my body, she amuses herself like a child through the long hours, silently.

She loosens my hair and styles it according to her whim, sometimes knotting it under my chin like a thick cloth, or twisting it at the back of my neck, or braiding it to the end.

She looks with astonishment at the color of my lashes, the folds of my elbow. Sometimes she makes me kneel and place my hands on the coverlets:

Then, it is one of her games, she slides her small head underneath and imitates the trembling kid which suckles from the belly of its mother.

PENUMBRA

Under the cover of the transparent wool, we slipped, she and I. Even our heads were huddled together and the lamp illuminated the cloth above us.

This is how I saw her dear body in a mysterious light. We were very near, one to the other, more free, more intimate, more naked. "In the same shirt," she said.

To be even more uncovered, we had left our hair bound up, and into the close air of the bed the odors of two women ascended, of two natural potpourri.

Nothing in the world, not even the lamp, saw us that night. Which of us was loved, she and I alone could say. But men will know nothing about it.

Pierre Loüys

THE SLEEPER

She sleeps, in the midst of her loosened hair, her hands clasped behind her head. Does she dream? Her mouth is open; she breathes gently.

Without waking her up, I wipe off the perspiration from her arms, the fever from her cheeks, with a little white swan-like powder puff.

Very gently, I will get up; I will go to draw water, to milk the cow and ask for fire from the neighbors. I want to have my hair curled and be dressed when she opens her eyes.

Sleep, linger still longer between her beautifully curved eyelashes and continue the happy night with a dream that bodes well.

THE KISS

I will kiss, from one end to the other, the long black wings at the nape of your neck, oh sweet bird, captive dove, whose heart bounds beneath my hand.

I will take your lips in my mouth as an infant takes the breast of its mother. Thrill! ... for the kiss penetrates deeply and would satisfy love.

I will move my tongue from place to place, slowly along your arms and around your neck, and I will wind the lengthening caress of my fingernails along your sensitive torso.

Listen, roaring in your ears, all the rumors of the sea ... Mnasidika! Your gaze makes me suffer. With my kiss, I will close your eyelids, burning like lips.

JEALOUS CARE

You must not style your hair, for fear that the overheated iron burn the back of your neck or your curls. You will let it spread out over your shoulders and along your arms.

You must not dress yourself, for fear that the sash reddens the slender folds of your hips. You will remain naked like a little girl.

You must not even get up, for fear that your fragile feet be made sore from walking. You will lie on the bed, oh victim of Eros, and I will dress your poor wound.

Because I do not want to see any mark on your body, Mnasidika, other than the blemish of an overlong kiss, the scratch of a sharp nail, or the crimson imprint of my embrace.

THE DESPERATE EMBRACE

Love me, not with smiles, flutes, or braided flowers, but with your heart and your tears, as I love you with my breast and my lamentations.

When your breasts alternate with mine, when I feel your life touching my life, when your knees straighten up behind me, then my mouth, breathless, no longer even knows how to join with yours.

Embrace me as I embrace you! See, the lamp has died out. We roll over in the night, but I press your moving body and I hear your incessant plea ...

Moan! Moan! Moan! Oh, woman! Eros draws us into pain. You would suffer less on the bed when bringing a child into the world than when giving birth to your love.

MY HEART

Breathless, I took her hand and put it firmly under the moist skin of my left breast. And I turned my head here and there and I moved my lips without speaking.

My frantic heart, abrupt and hard, beat and beat my breast like an imprisoned satyr would pound, crumpled in a goatskin bottle. She told me, "Your heart is hurting you…"

"Oh, Mnasidika," I responded, "the heart of a woman is not here. Here is only a poor bird, a dove that stirs its feeble wings. The heart of a woman is more terrible.

"Like a small myrtle berry, it burns with a red flame and under an abundant foam. It is there that I feel myself bitten by the voracious Aphrodite."

WORDS IN THE NIGHT

We rest, our eyes closed; the silence is profound around our bed. Inexpressible nights of summer! But she, believing me asleep, lays her warm hand on my arm.

She murmurs, "Bilitis, are you asleep?" My heart throbs, but without responding, I breathe regularly like a woman lying in a dream. Then she begins to speak:

"Because you cannot hear me," she says, "ah! How I love you!" And she repeats my name, "Bilitis … Bilitis …" And she touches me with the tips of her trembling fingers.

"It is mine, this mouth! Mine alone! Is there another one more beautiful in the world? Ah! My happiness, my happiness! They are mine, these bare arms, this nape, this hair …"

ABSENCE

She went out, she is far away, but I see her, because everything in this room is full of her — everything is hers and I am like all the rest.

This bed still warm, where I let my mouth roam, is impressed with the outline of her body. On this soft pillow her small head slept surrounded with her hair.

This is the basin in which she has bathed; this is the comb that has penetrated the knots of her tangled hair. These slippers took hold of her naked feet. These folds of gauze contained her breasts.

But that which I dare not touch with my finger is this mirror where she viewed her fiery bruises and where, perhaps, the reflection of her moist lips still lives.

LOVE

Alas! If I think of her, my throat becomes parched, my head droops, my breasts grow hard and pain me. I shiver and I weep as I walk.

If I see her, my heart stops, my hands tremble, my feet grow cold, a fiery blush mounts to my cheeks, my temples throb painfully.

If I touch her, I become crazed, my arms stiffen, my knees quiver, I fall before her and lie like a woman about to die.

Anything she says to me wounds me. Her love is a torture and the passersby hear my lamentations ... Alas! How can I call her Well-Beloved?

PURIFICATION

There you are! Undo your ties and your clasps and your tunic. Remove even your sandals, even the ribbons around your legs, even the band around your breast.

Wash the black from your eyebrows and the red from your lips. Erase the white of your shoulders and uncurl your hair in the water.

For I want you completely pure, just as you were born on the bed at the feet of your fertile mother and before your proud father.

So chaste that my hand in your hand will make you blush to your lips and one word of mine in your ear will bewitch your fluttering eyes.

THE CRADLE OF MNASIDIKA

My little child, even though I am only a few years older than you, I love you, not as a lover but as though you had come forth from my laboring entrails.

When spread out on my lap, your two frail arms about me, you seek my breast, your mouth pursed, and press my nipples slowly between your palpitating lips —

Then I dream that at other times, I have truly nursed this delicate mouth, supple and wet, this crimson vase of myrrh in which the happiness of Bilitis is secretly ensconced.

Sleep. I will cradle you with one hand on my knee which rocks back and forth. Sleep so. I will sing you little mournful songs which bring sleep to the newly-born.

A WALK ALONG THE SEA

As we were walking on the seashore, without speaking and wrapped up to the chin in our drab wool robes, happy young girls passed by.

"Ah! Here are Bilitis and Mnasidika! See, the pretty little squirrel we have caught; it is soft as a bird and frightened as a rabbit.

"At Lydé's house we will put it in a cage, give it plenty of milk with lettuce leaves. It is a female — she will live a long time."

And the foolish girls set out running. As for us, we sat down without speaking, I on a rock, she on the sand, and we gazed at the sea.

THE OBJECT

Greetings, Bilitis, Mnasidika, greetings — *Be seated. How is your husband?* — Too well. Do not tell him you have seen me. He would kill me if he knew I had been here. — *Have no fear.*

And here is your bedroom? And your bed? Pardon me. I am curious. — *You know, however, the bed of Myrrhina.* — Very little. — *She is said to be pretty.* — And lascivious, Oh my dear! Let us not speak of it.

What did you want from me? — That you lend me... — *Speak.* — I dare not name the object. — *We do not have one.* — Really? — *Mnasidika is a virgin.* — Then, where can you buy it? — *From the harness-maker, Drakon.*

Tell me too, where you do buy your thread for embroidery? Mine breaks as soon as you look at it. — *I make my own, but Nais sells excellent thread.* — At what price? — *Three obols.* — That is expensive. And the object? — *Two drachmae.* — Farewell.

EVENING BY THE FIRE

The winter is hard, Mnasidika. Everything is cold except our bed. But get up and come with me, for I have made a large fire with dead branches and broken wood.

We will warm ourselves, crouching stark naked, our hair down our backs, and drink milk from the same cup and eat cakes made of honey.

How merry the crackling flame is! Are you too close? Your skin is reddening. Let me kiss it wherever the fire has made it burning hot.

I will heat the iron in the midst of the glowing embers and I will curl your hair. With the extinguished coals I will write your name on the wall.

PRAYERS

What do you want? Say it. If necessary, I will sell my last jewels so an attentive slave awaits the desire of your eyes and any thirst of your lips.

If the milk of our goats seems tasteless to you, I will hire for you, as for an infant, a nurse with swollen breasts who will suckle you each morning.

If our bed seems rough to you, I will buy you every soft cushion, every silk coverlet, every cloth, thick with feathers, from the Amathusian merchants.

Everything. But I must satisfy you, and even if we slept on the ground, it must feel softer to you than the warm bed of a strange woman.

HER EYES

Wide eyes of Mnasidika, how happy you make me when love blackens your eyelids and arouses you and drowns you in tears.

But how insane you make me when you turn elsewhere, distracted by a woman who passes or by a memory that does not include me.

Then my cheeks become sunken, my hands tremble, and I suffer… It seems to me that, in front of you, my life drains away in every direction.

Wide eyes of Mnasidika, do not cease to gaze at me! Or I will pierce you with my needle and then you will no longer see the terrible night.

ADORNMENTS

Everything, my life and the world, and the men, everything that is not her, is nothing. Everything that is not hers, I give to you, the passerby.

Does she know how much work I put into being beautiful before her eyes, with my hair and with my makeup, with my robes and my perfumes?

So, for as long as it takes, I would turn a millstone, I would wield the oar or plow the earth, if that would be the price to keep her here.

But make certain that she never knows it, Goddesses who watch over us. The day she learns that I love her, she will look for another woman.

MNASIDIKA'S SILENCE

She had laughed all day long and she even made fun of me a little. She had refused to obey me in front of several women whom we did not know.

When we returned, I pretended not to speak to her, and, as she flung herself around my neck, saying, "Are you angry?" I said to her:

"Ah! You are not like you used to be, not like the first day. I no longer recognize you, Mnasidika." She did not respond to me.

But she put on all the jewels she had not worn for a long time and the same yellow robe, embroidered with blue, as on the day of our first meeting.

A QUARREL

Where were you? — *At the flower merchant. I have bought some very beautiful irises. Here they are, I have brought them to you.* — It took you this long to buy me four flowers? — *The flower-woman kept me.*

Your cheeks are pale and your eyes are sparkling. — *It is fatigue from the walk.* — Your hair is moist and tangled. — *It is the heat and the wind that made it this way.*

Someone has untied your sash. I had made the knot myself, looser than this one. — *So loose that it became undone; a passing slave retied it for me.*

There is a spot on your robe. — *It is water that has fallen from the flowers.* — Mnasidika, my little soul, your irises are the most beautiful of any in all Mytilene. — *I know it well, I know it well.*

WAITING

The sun has spent all night among the dead while I have waited, seated on my bed, weary from watching. The wick of the empty lamp has burned to the end.

She will never return: here is the last star. I know that she will never return. I even know the name that I hate. Nevertheless, I still wait.

If only she would come now! Yes, if she would come, her hair disheveled, without roses, her robe soiled, spotted, rumpled, her tongue dry and her eyelids black!

As soon as she opens the door, I will say to her … But here she is … It is her robe that I touch, her hands, her hair, her skin! I kiss her with bewildered lips, and I weep.

SOLITUDE

Now for whom should I paint my lips? For whom should I polish my nails? For whom should I perfume my hair?

For whom are my breasts powdered with rouge, if they no longer tempt her? For whom are my arms washed with milk, if they are to embrace her never more?

How could I sleep? How could I go to bed? This evening throughout my entire bed, my hand could not find her warm hand.

I dare no longer return to my house, to the room so dreadfully empty. I dare no longer to open the door again. I dare no longer even to open my eyes again.

Pierre Louÿs

THE LETTER

That is impossible, impossible. I beg you on my knees, with tears, all the tears I have wept over this horrible letter, do not abandon me like this.

Consider how terrible it is to lose you forever for a second time, after having had the wondrous joy of hoping to reconquer you. Ah! My love! Can you not feel how much I adore you!

Listen to me. Agree to see me one more time. Do you want to wait at your door tomorrow at sundown? Tomorrow, or the day after. I will come for you. Do not refuse me that.

Perhaps for the last time, so be it, but this one more time, this one more time! I ask it of you, I cry it out to you, and consider that the rest of my life depends on your reply.

THE ATTEMPT

You were jealous of us, Gyrinno, a girl too ardent. How many garlands did you hang on the knocker of our door! You waited for us as we passed and you followed us in the street.

Now you are, true to your word, spread out on the loved place and your head is on the pillow from which floats the odor of another woman. You are taller than she was. Your body is different and it startles me.

See! I have surrendered at last. Yes, it is I. You may play with my breasts, caress my belly, open my knees. My whole body yielded to your tireless lips — alas!

Ah! Gyrinno! My tears also overflow with love! Wipe them with your hair; do not kiss them, my darling, and hold me even closer to calm my trembling.

THE EFFORT

Again! Enough of sighs and stretching arms! Begin again! Do you think then that love is a recreation? Gyrinno, it is a task and the most harsh of them all.

Awaken! You must not sleep! What do I care about your blue eyelids and the shaft of pain which burns your spindly legs. Astarte seethes in my loins.

We went to bed before the twilight. And here already is the wicked dawn; but I am not wearied with so little. I will not sleep before the second evening.

I will not sleep — you must not sleep. Oh! How bitter is the taste of morning! Gyrinno, enjoy it. The embraces are more difficult, more exotic and slower.

TO GYRINNO

Do not believe that I have loved you. I ate you like a ripe fig. I drank you like seething water. I carried you around me like a sash of skin.

I have amused myself with your body, because you have short hair, pointed breasts on your thin body, and nipples dark like two little dates.

Just as water and fruits are needed, a woman is also necessary, but already I have forgotten your name, you who have passed through my arms like the shadow of another adored one.

Between your flesh and mine, a burning dream has possessed me. I pressed you upon me as on a wound and I cried: Mnasidika! Mnasidika! Mnasidika!

THE LAST ATTEMPT

What do you want, old woman? — *To console you.* — It is useless. — *They have told me that since your parting, you go from love to love without finding forgetfulness or peace. I have come to offer you someone.*

Speak. — *It is a young slave, born at Sardis. She has no equal in the world because she is at once man and woman, although her chest, and her long hair and her clear voice are deceptive.*

Her age? — *Sixteen years.* — Her size? — *Tall. She has known no one here except Sappho, who is desperately in love with her and wanted to buy her from me for twenty minae. If you hire her, she is yours.* — And what will I do with her?

For twenty-two nights, I have tried in vain to escape my memories. . . . Agreed, I will take one more, but warn the poor little one so she is not frightened if I sob in her arms.

TORTUOUS MEMORY

I remember ... (what hour of the day is she not before my eyes!) I remember the manner in which She lifted her hair with her pale, slender fingers.

I remember one night that she spent, her cheek on my breast, so sweetly that happiness kept me awake, and the next day she had the mark of my rounded nipple on her face.

I see her holding her cup of milk and giving me a sidelong glance with a smile. I see her, powdered, her hair done, opening her wide eyes before her mirror, and retouching the red of her lips with her finger.

And, above all, if my despair is a perpetual torture, it is because I know, moment by moment, how she swoons in the arms of another, and what she demands and what she gives.

TO THE WAX DOLL

Doll of wax, cherished plaything that she called her child, she has left you, too, and has forgotten you as well as me, who, along with her, was your father or your mother, I know not which.

The pressure of her lips has discolored your tiny cheeks, and on your left hand here is that broken finger that made her weep so much. This little robe that you wear, it was she who embroidered it for you.

According to her, you knew how to read already. Nevertheless, you had not been weaned, and in the evening, bending over you, she opened her tunic and gave you her breast, "So you would not cry," she said.

Doll, if I wanted to see her again, I would give you to Aphrodite, as the most precious of my gifts. But, I want to think that she is really dead.

FUNERAL CHANT

Sing a funeral chant, muses of Mytilene, sing! The earth is gray like a vestment of mourning and the yellow trees shiver like cut tresses.

Heraios! Oh month melancholy and peaceful! The leaves fall gently like snow , the sun penetrates more deeply into the bare forest. . . . I no longer hear anything but the silence.

Now they have carried Pittacus, laden with years, to the tomb. Many are dead whom I once knew. And the one who lives is, to me, as though she were no longer.

This is the tenth autumn I have seen dying on this plain. It is time that I also fade away. Weep with me, muses of Mytilene, weep upon my footsteps!

Pierre Louÿs

PART 3
EPIGRAMS ON THE ISLAND OF CYPRUS

"… Crown my head with narcissus as I play the flute. Anoint me with saffron perfumed oils, wet my throat with wine from Mytilene, and join me with a virgin who will love the bed."

-Philodemos

HYMN TO ASTARTE

Mother inexhaustible, incorruptible, creature, first born, self-begotten, issued from yourself alone and who rejoices in yourself, Astarte!

Oh perpetually fruitful, Oh virgin and nourisher of all, chaste and lascivious, pure and pleasure-seeking, ineffable, nocturnal, soft, breather of fire, foam of the sea!

You who grants favors in secret, you who unites, you who loves, you who ignites a furious desire in the multiple races of savage beasts and joins the sexes in the forests!

Oh Astarte, irresistible, hear me, take me, possess me, Oh moon, and thirteen times each year draw from my entrails the libation of my blood!

HYMN TO THE NIGHT

The darkened masses of the trees move no more than the mountains. The stars fill an immense sky. A warm breeze, like a human
breath, caresses my eyes and my cheeks.

Oh Night, who brought forth the Gods! How sweet you are upon
my lips! How warm you are in my hair! How you enter into me
this evening and how I feel myself pregnant with all your spring-
time!

The flowers that are going to blossom are all going to be born of
me. The wind that breathes is my breath. The perfume that drifts
by is my desire. All the stars are in my eyes.

Your voice, is this the roar of the sea? Is this the silence of the plain?
Your voice — I cannot understand it, but it forces my head to my
feet and my tears bathe both of my hands.

THE MAENADS

Through the forests that dominate the sea, the Maenads stam-
peded. Maskale, with fiery breasts, shrieking, brandished the phallus
made of sycamore and smeared with vermilion.

All of them under the fox skin capes and the crowns of vine branches
ran and cried and leapt, the rattles clacking in their hands and the
sticks cracking the skins of the resounding drums.

Moist hair, agile legs, reddened and jostled breasts, sweated cheeks,
foaming lips, Oh Dionysus, they offer you, in return, the love you
have hurled within them.

And the sea wind lifting the red hair of Helikomis toward the sky,
twisted it like a furious flame on a torch of white wax.

THE SEA OF CYPRUS

On the highest promontory, I stretched myself out at the edge. The sea was dark like a field of violets. The milky way streamed out from the great divine breast.

A thousand Maenads slept around me on the shredded flowers. The long grasses were entwined in their hair. And here the sun was born in the waters of the East.

They were the same waves and the same shores that one day witnessed the white body of Aphrodite. . . Suddenly, I hid my eyes in my hands.

For I saw a thousand tiny lips of light flickering upon the water — the pure sex or the smile of Cypris Philommeides.

THE PRIESTESSES OF ASTARTE

The priestesses of Astarte make love at the rising of the moon; then they rise again and bathe in a vast pool edged with silver.

They comb their hair with their curved fingers and their hands, tinted with crimson, mingling with their black curls, seem like branches of coral in a dark and wavering sea.

They never pluck their hair, so that the triangle of the goddess marks their belly as a temple; but they paint themselves with brushes and perfume themselves with abundance.

The priestesses of Astarte make love at the setting of the moon; then in a room filled with carpets where a tall golden lamp burns, they lie down at random.

THE MYSTERIES

Within the enclosure three-times mysterious, where men never penetrate, we celebrated you, Astarte of the Night, Mother of the World, Fountain of the Life of the Gods!

I will reveal something, but not more than is permitted. Around a crowned phallus, a hundred and twenty women swayed, crying out. The initiates were dressed as men, the others in split tunics.

The incense from the perfumes, the smoke from the torches, floated between us like clouds. I wept burning tears. All of us, at the feet of Berbeia — we flung ourselves on our backs.

When the religious Act was consummated, and when they had plunged the crimson phallus into the Unique Triangle, then the mystery began, but I will say no more.

THE EGYPTIAN COURTESANS

With Plango I went among the Egyptian courtesans, to the highest part of the old city. They have clay amphoras, copper plates, and yellow mats on which they squat effortlessly.

Their rooms are quiet, without angles and without corners, for so many successive layerings of blue limewash have blunted the pillars and rounded the base of the walls.

They remain immobile, their hands resting on their knees. When they offer porridge, they murmur, "Happiness." And when thanked, they say, "Grace to thee."

They understand Greek and feign to speak it badly in order to laugh at us in their own tongue, but we — a tooth for a tooth — we speak Lydian and suddenly they are uneasy.

I SING OF MY BODY AND MY LIFE

Indeed I will not sing about famous lovers of the past. If they are no more, why talk about them? Am I not like them? Have I not enough to think about myself?

I will forget you, Pasiphae, although your passion was extreme. I will not praise you, Syrinx, nor you, Byblis, nor you, by the goddess select among all, Helen of the white arms!

If someone suffered, I scarcely feel it. If someone loved, I love more. I sing of my body and my life, and not of the barren ghosts of buried women lovers.

Oh my body, remain lying down according to your voluptuous mission! Savor everyday pleasures and passions as if there were no tomorrow. Leave not one pleasure unknown to regret until your dying day.

THE PERFUMES

I will perfume my skin all over so I will attract lovers. Into a silver basin, over my beautiful legs, I will pour the ointments perfumed with nard from Tarsus and bitter gum of Egypt.

Under my arms, crumpled mint; on my lashes and my eyes, sweet marjoram of cos. Slave, loosen my hair and fill it with the smoke from incense.

Here is oinathe from the mountains of Cyprus — I will let it flow between my breasts. The liqueur of roses that comes from Phaselis will perfume my neck and my cheeks.

And now, pour the irresistible bakkaris over my loins. It is more important for a courtesan to know the perfumes of Lydia than the customs of the Peloponnesus.

CONVERSATION

Good morning. — *Good morning to you.* — You are in a great hurry. —*Perhaps less than you think.* — You are a pretty girl. — *Perhaps more than you think.*

What is your lovely name? — *I do not tell it quickly.* — Do you belong to someone this evening? — *Always the one who loves me.* — And how do you love him? — *Any way he wishes.*

Let us dine together. — *If that is what you desire. But what will you give?* — This. —*Five drachmae? It is for my slave. And for me?* — You tell me. — *One hundred.*

Where do you live? — *In this blue house.* — What time can I send for you? — *At once if you wish.* — At once. — *Lead the way.*

THE TORN ROBE

Hold on! By the two goddesses, who is the insolent person who has put his foot on my robe? — *It is a lover.* — It is an idiot. — *I have been awkward, pardon me.*

Imbecile! My yellow robe is torn all down the back, and if I walk in the street like this, they will take me for a poor girl who serves Cyprus instead of the other way around.

Will you not stop? — I believe that he speaks to me still! — *Will you leave me so angry?... You do not answer? Alas! I dare speak no more.*

I must return to my house to change my clothes. — *And I cannot follow you?* — Who is your father? —*He is the rich ship owner, Nikias.* — You have beautiful eyes. I forgive you.

THE JEWELS

A diadem of gold latticework crowns my narrow white forehead. Five small gold chains follow the curve of my cheeks and chin and dangle from two large clasps in my hair.

On my arms, thirteen silver bracelets rise gradually, one over the other, which Iris would envy. How heavy they are! But they are weapons, and I know an enemy, a woman, who has suffered from them.

Truly, I am covered entirely with gold. My breasts are fortified with two breast plates of gold. The images of the gods are not as richly ornamented as I.

And around my heavy robe I wear a sash spangled with silver. There you can read this verse — "Love me eternally, but be not grieved if I betray you three times a day."

INDIFFERENCE

As soon as he entered my room, whoever he may be (what difference does it make?), "See," I say to my slave, "what a handsome man! And what a happy courtesan!"

I declare him Adonis, Ares or Hercules, according to his countenance, or the Old Man of the Sea if his hair is pale silver. And then, what disdain for fickle youth!

"Ah!" I say, "if I did not have to pay my florist and my goldsmith tomorrow, how I would love to say to you, I do not want your gold! I am your passionate servant!"

Then, when he has wrapped his arms beneath my shoulders, I see a ferryman from the port pass like a divine image over the starry sky of my transparent eyelids.

PURE WATER OF THE POOL

Pure water of the pool, serene mirror, tell me of my beauty.

Bilitis, or whoever you are, Tethys perhaps, or Amphitrite, you are beautiful, know that.

Your face bends downward beneath your thick hair, heavy with flowers and perfumes. Your soft eyelids scarcely open and your thighs are weary from the movements of love.

Your body, fatigued with the heaviness of your breasts, bears the delicate marks of fingernails and the blue blemish of the kiss. Your arms are reddened by the embrace. Each line of your skin was loved.

Clear water of the pool, your freshness brings peace. Receive me, who is truly wearied. Take away the rouge of my cheeks and the sweat of my belly and the memory of the night.

VOLUPTUOUSNESS

In the night, they left us on a white terrace, swooning among the roses. Hot sweat ran down like tears from our armpits over our breasts. Overwhelming sensual pleasure flushed our flung-back heads.

Four captive doves, bathed in four perfumes, fluttered above us silently. And drops of scent trickled down from their wings onto the naked women. I was inundated with the essence of iris.

Oh weariness! I rested my cheek on the belly of a young woman who enveloped herself in the coolness of my moist hair. The perfume of her saffron-colored skin intoxicated my opened mouth. She closed her thighs around my neck.

I slept, but an exhausting dream awakened me — the iynx, bird of nocturnal desires, sang distractedly from afar. I coughed, shivering. Little by little, like a flower, a languishing arm raised itself in the air toward the moon.

THE INN

Innkeeper, there are four of us. Give us a room and two beds. It is too late now to return to the city and rain has made the road impassable.

Bring a basket of figs, some cheese, and dark wine, but first remove my sandals and rinse my feet, because the mud tickles me.

You will bring two basins of water, a full lamp, a punch bowl, and goblets to the room. You will shake the covers and you will fluff up the cushions.

But the beds should be of sturdy maple and the planks noiseless! Tomorrow, you will not need to wake us.

DOMESTICITY

Four slaves guard my house: two robust Thracians at my door, a Sicilian in my kitchen, and a Phrygian woman, docile and silent, for the service of my bed.

The two Thracians are handsome men. Each has a staff in his hand to chase away poor lovers and a hammer to nail on the wall the wreaths as they are sent to me.

The Sicilian is a rare cook — I paid twelve minae for him. No one else knows how to prepare fried croquettes and corn poppy cakes like he does.

The Phrygian bathes me, combs my hair, and depilates me. She sleeps every morning in my room, and three nights each month, she takes my place next to my lovers.

THE BATH

Child, guard the door and let no passerby enter, for I and six girls with beautiful arms are secretly bathing in the warm water of the pool.

We only want to laugh and swim. Leave the lovers in the street. We will dip our legs in the water, and seated on the marble edge, we will play with knuckle-bones.

We will also play with the ball. Let no lovers enter — our hair is too wet, our throats have gooseflesh, and the ends of our fingers are wrinkled.

Moreover, he would be sorry who would surprise us naked! Bilitis is not Athena, but she shows herself only in her own time and chastises the eyes that are too ardent.

TO HER BREASTS

Flowering flesh, oh my breasts! How rich in sensuality you are! My breasts in my hands, you have the softness, the velvety warmth, the youthful fragrance.

Before, you were icy-cold like the breast of a statue and hard as the unfeeling marble. Since you are softening, I cherish you more, you who have been loved.

Your form, sleek and rounded, is the distinction of my brown torso. Whether I imprison you under golden mesh or whether I release you naked, you precede me with your splendor.

Therefore be happy tonight. If my fingers produce caresses, you alone will know them until tomorrow morning; for tonight, Bilitis has paid Bilitis.

MYDZOURIS

Mydzouris, little piece of dung, do not cry any longer. You are my friend. If the women insult you again, it is I who will answer them. Come here under my arm and dry your eyes.

Yes, I know that you are a dreadful child and your mother taught you early to prove yourself a woman of courage. But you are young and therefore you can do nothing that is not endearing.

The mouth of a girl of fifteen remains pure in spite of all. The lips of a hoary-headed woman, even virgin, are devalued — for the only disgrace is to grow old and be branded by our wrinkles.

Mydzouris, I admire your frank eyes, your impudent and bold name, your laughing voice and your slim body. Come to my house, you will be my assistant and when we go out together, the women will greet you.

THE TRIUMPH OF BILITIS

The people in the procession carried me in triumph, me, Bilitis, naked on a shell-like chariot where slaves, during the night, had plucked apart ten thousand roses.

I was lying down, my hands under the back of my neck, only my feet were clad in gold, and my body, languidly stretched out on the bed of my warm hair, mingled with the cool petals.

Twelve children, with wings on their shoulders, waited on me like a goddess — some held a parasol, others showered me with perfume or burned incense in the prow.

And around me I heard the roar, the intense clamoring of the crowd; meanwhile, the breath of desire drifted about my nakedness in the blue haze of the perfumes.

Pierre Louÿs

TO THE GOD OF WOOD

Oh venerable Priapus, god of wood, whom I had sealed in the marble edge of my bath — it is not without reason, guardian of the orchards, that you watch over the courtesans here.

God, we did not purchase you to sacrifice our virginities to you. No one can give something that is no longer, and the zealots of Pallas do not run about the streets of Amathus.

No. You once watched over the leafy hair of the trees, over the well-moistened flowers, over the heavy, savory fruits. That is why we have chosen you.

Today guard our blond heads, the opened poppies of our lips, and the violets of our eyes. Guard the firm fruit of our breasts and give us lovers who resemble you.

THE DANCING-GIRL WITH THE RATTLES

You attach the resounding rattles to your graceful hands, dearest Myrrhinidion, and barely naked out of your robe, you offer your lithe limbs. How pretty you are, your arms in the air, your loins arched and your breasts reddened!

You begin — your feet settle, one before the other, hesitate, and then glide softly. Your body folds like a scarf, you caress your quivering skin and sensual pleasure inundates your long, swooning eyes.

Suddenly, you strike the rattles together! Arch yourself, your feet pointed out, shake your loins, fling your legs and let your hands, filled with noise, call every desire in a ribbon around your twirling body.

Let us applaud with great cries, whether smiling over your shoulder you wiggle your buttocks, convulsing and muscular, or whether you undulate, stretched out, to the rhythm of your memories.

THE FLUTE PLAYER

Melixo, your legs together, your body bent, your arms forward, you slide your double flute lightly between your lips, moist with wine, and you play over the bed where Teleas still embraces me.

Indeed, am I not indiscreet, I who hire so young a girl to distract my laborious hours? I who show her thus naked to the curious looks of my lovers? Am I not inconsiderate?

No, Melixo, little musician, you are an honest friend. Yesterday, you did not refuse to change your flute for another when I despaired of completing a love full of difficulties. But you are trustworthy.

Because I know what you think. You await the end of this night that excites you cruelly and in vain, and at the first dawn, you will run in the street to your small tattered mattress with Psyllos, your only friend.

THE HOT SASH

"You think you no longer love me, Teleas, and for a month you have spent your nights at the table, as if the fruits, the wines, the honey could make you forget my lips. You think that you no longer love me, poor fool!"

Saying that, I untied my moist sash and I rolled it around his head. It was still quite hot from the heat of my belly; the perfume of my skin burst from its fine meshes.

He breathed it in slowly, his eyes closed. Then I felt him return to me and I saw very clearly his reawakening desires that he did not hide from me, but through cunning, I knew how to resist him.

"No, my friend. Tonight I belong to Lysippos. Farewell!" And I added as I fled, "Oh gourmand of fruits and vegetables! The little garden of Bilitis has only one fig, but it is good."

TO A HAPPY HUSBAND

I envy you Agorakrites, for having such a zealous wife. It is she who looks after the stable and in the morning, in place of making love, she waters the animals.

You can rejoice in that. How many others as you say, dream only of decadent pleasures, waking the night, sleeping the day, and still asking from adultery an immoral satiety?

Yes, your wife labors in the stable. They even say that she has a thousand tendernesses for the youngest of your asses. Ah! Ha! It is a beautiful animal. He has a black spot over his eyes.

They say that she plays between his hoofs, under his soft gray belly ... But those who say that are slanderers. If your ass pleases her, Agorakrites, it is without doubt because she recalls your look in his.

TO A STRAY

The love of women is the most beautiful one of all that mortals experience, and you would think so, Kleo, if you had a truly sensuous soul; but you dream only vanities.

You lose your nights in cherishing youths who are ungrateful to us. Look at them! How ugly those boys are! Compare their round heads with our vast hair; look for our white breasts on their chests.

Next to their narrow thighs, consider our luxuriant hips, a broad hollowed bed for lovers. Ask finally, what other human lips, except hers that they desire, so thoughtfully produce sensual delights?

You are sick, Oh, Kleo, but a woman can cure you. Go to young Satyra, the daughter of my neighbor Gorgo. Her buttocks are roses in the sun and she will not refuse you the pleasure that she herself prefers.

INTIMACIES

Oh, Bilitis, you ask why I have become lesbian? But what flute player is not, a little? I am poor; I have no bed. I sleep at the house of she who wishes me and I thank her with what I have.

As little children, we already dance naked. Those dances, you know them, dearest — the twelve desires of Aphrodite. We look at one another, we compare our nude bodies and we find them very pretty.

During the long night, we have passionately aroused ourselves for the pleasure of the spectators, but our fervor is not a pretense and we experience it so completely that sometimes, behind closed doors, one of us wins over her consenting neighbor.

How then could we love a man who is rough with us? He grabs us like common prostitutes and leaves us before the pleasure. You, you are a woman, you know what I mean. You can make love to another woman the same way as you do for yourself.

ORDERING

Old woman, listen to me. I give a banquet in three days. I need entertainment. You will rent every one of your girls to me. How many do you have and what can they do?

I have seven. Three dance the Kordax with the sash and the phallus. Nephele with the smooth armpits will mimic the love of doves between her rosy breasts.

A singer in an embroidered shawl will sing the songs of Rhodes accompanied by two flute players who will have garlands of myrtle coiling up their brown legs.

That is good. They should be freshly depilated, washed, and perfumed from head to foot, ready for other games if they are asked. Go give the instructions. Farewell.

THE ROLE OF PASIPHAE

In a debauchery that two young men and some courtesans arranged at my house, where love gushed out like wine, Damalis, in honor of her name, danced the role of Pasiphae.

She had made at Citium two masks, one of a cow and the other a bull, for herself and for Karmantidea. She wore fierce horns, and a hairy tail on her buttocks.

The other women, led by me, holding the flowers and the torches, turned ourselves around with shrieks and we caressed Damalis with the tips of our dangling tresses.

Our bellows, our songs, and the dancing of our loins lasted longer than the night. The empty room is still hot. I look at my reddened knees and the cups of Cos where the roses are floating.

THE JUGGLER

When first dawn mingled with the feeble glimmer of the torches, I sent into the orgy a flute player, wild and agile, who shivered a little from the cold.

Praise the little girl with the blue eyelids, short hair, and pointed breasts, clad only in a sash from which hung yellow ribbons and stems of black iris.

Praise her! For she was skillful and performed difficult tricks. She juggled with hoops through which she passed lightly like a grasshopper, without breaking anything in the room.

Sometimes she did cartwheels, over on her hands and feet. Or, with her two legs in the air and her knees apart, she curved herself backward and touched the ground, laughing.

THE DANCE OF THE FLOWERS

Anthis, a dancing girl from Lydia, has seven veils surrounding her. She unrolls the yellow veil; her black hair spreads out. The rose-colored veil slides from her mouth. The white veil falls, revealing her bare arms.

She frees her little breasts from the red veil that comes untied. She lets the green veil fall from her double, rounded buttocks. She draws the blue veil from her shoulders, but she presses on her puberty the last transparent veil.

The young men beg her; she jerks her head backward. Only at the sound of the flutes, she tears the last veil a little, then all of it, and gracefully, she plucks the flowers from her body.

While singing: "Where are my roses? Where are my perfumed violets! Where are my tufts of parsley! — Here are my roses, I give them to you. Here are my violets, will you have them? Here is my beautiful curled parsley."

VIOLENCE

No, you will not take me by force, do not count on that, Lamprias. If you have heard it said that someone violated Parthenis, know that she wanted him also, because no one enjoys us without being invited.

Oh! Do your best, make the effort. See, it is a failure. I scarcely defend myself. I will not call for help. And I do not even struggle, but I do move. Poor friend, it is a failure again.

Continue. This little game amuses me. The more so because I am sure to conquer. Again an unfortunate attempt, and perhaps you will be less disposed to prove to me your extinguished desires.

Butcher, what you are doing! Dog! You break my wrists! And this knee, this knee which eviscerates me! Ah! Go now. It is a glorious victory, that of ravishing on the ground a young woman in tears.

Pierre Louÿs

SONG

The first one gave me a necklace, a necklace of pearls, equal to a city with palaces and temples, treasures and slaves.

The second one composed verses for me. He said that my curls were as black as those of the night and my eyes as blue as those of the morning.

The third one was so handsome that his mother could not kiss him without blushing. He put his hand on my knees and his lips on my bare foot.

You, you have told me nothing — you have given me nothing, because you are poor. And you are not handsome, but it is you whom I love.

ADVICE TO A LOVER

If you want to be loved by a woman, oh young friend, whoever she may be, do not tell her that you desire her, but have her see you every day, then disappear, so that you can return again.

If she speaks to you, be amorous without eagerness. She will come to you on her own. Then know how to take her by force on the day when she intends to give herself.

When you welcome her in your bed, neglect your own pleasure. The hands of an amorous woman are trembling and without caresses. Excuse them from being zealous.

But you, do not rest. Prolong your kisses to breathlessness. Allow her no sleep, even though she begs for it. Always kiss that place on her body toward which she turns her eyes.

WOMEN FRIENDS AT DINNER

Myromeris and Maskale, my friends, come with me, for I have no lover tonight and, lying on beds of flax, we will chat over dinner.

A night of rest will do you good; you will sleep in my bed, without makeup and your hair a mess. Put on a plain woolen tunic and leave your jewels in their case.

No one will make you dance so as to admire your legs and the languid movements of your thighs. No one will ask the sacred Figures to judge whether you are amorous.

And I have not ordered two flute players with beautiful mouths for us, but two potfuls of browned peas, honey cakes, fried croquettes, and my last goatskin from Cos.

THE TOMB OF A YOUNG COURTESAN

Here lies the delicate body of Lyde, tiny dove, the most joyous of all courtesans, who more than all others loved orgies, flowing hair, luxurious dances and tunics of hyacinth.

More than all others she loved savory tongues deep in the throat, the caresses on the cheek, the games that only the lamp saw, and love that bruises the limbs. And now, she is only a small shadow.

But before putting her in the tomb, they styled her hair exquisitely and laid her in roses; even the stone covering her is impregnated with essences and perfumes.

Sacred earth, nurturer of all, welcome gently the poor dead — let her sleep in your arms, Oh Mother! And make spring up around her tombstone, not nettles and briars, but delicate white violets.

THE LITTLE ROSE MERCHANT

"Yesterday," Nais told me, "I was in the market when a little girl in red tatters, carrying roses, passed before a group of young men. And this is what I heard:

'Buy something from me. — *Explain yourself, little one, for we know not what you sell; yourself? Your roses? Or both at the same time?* — If you will buy all these flowers from me, you will have mine for nothing.

'And how much do you want for your roses? — I must have six obols for my mother, or else I will be beaten like a dog. — *Follow us. You will have one drachma.* — Then, I will go and fetch my little sister?'

"And both of them followed those men. They had no breasts, Bilitis. They did not even know how to smile. They trotted along like two kids that are being led to the butcher."

THE DISPUTE

Ah! By Aphrodite, behold you! Gore! Putrefaction! Monstrous woman! Sterility! Shrew! Good for nothing! Evil sow! Do not try to escape me; come closer still.

Now look at this woman of the sailors, who does not even know how to fold her garment on her shoulder, and who puts on such bad makeup that the black of her brows runs down her cheeks in rivulets of ink!

You are Phoenician: sleep with those of your race. As for me, my father was Hellene: I have a right over all those who wear a Greek hat. And even over the others if it so pleases me.

No longer stop in my street or I will send you to Hades to make love to Charon and I will say very justly, "Let the earth cover you lightly, so that the dogs can dig you out."

MELANCHOLY

I shiver; the night is cool and the forest all watery. Why have you led me here? My large bed, is it not softer than this moss strewn with stones?

My flowery robe will be stained with greenery; my hair will be tangled with twigs; my elbow — look at my elbow, already soiled with the damp earth.

Long ago, however, I followed into the woods a man who ... Ah! Leave me for a while. I am sad tonight. Leave me, without speaking, my hand over my eyes.

Really, can you not wait! Are we beasts to take each other so! Leave me. You will not open my knees or my lips. Even my eyes stay closed for fear of crying.

LITTLE PHANION

Stranger, stop; see who is beckoning to you — it is little Phanion of Cos. She is worthy of your choice.

See, her hair is curled like parsley, her skin is soft as the down of a bird. She is small and brown. She speaks well.

If you want to follow her, she will not ask for all the travel money you have; no, only a drachma or a pair of shoes.

At her home you will find a good bed, fresh figs, milk, wine, and if it is cold, there will be a fire.

INDICATIONS

Passerby, who is stopping, if you must have slender thighs, taut loins, a firm breast, and knees that grab, go to Plango; she is my friend.

If you seek a laughing girl, with exuberant breasts, delicate plump buttocks and arched loins, go to the corner of this street, where Spidhorodellis dwells.

But if long tranquil hours in the arms of a courtesan, soft skin, the warmth of the belly and the fragrance of hair please you, look for Milto — you will be happy.

Do not expect too much love, but profit from her experience. You can ask everything from a woman when she is naked, when it is night, and when the hundred drachmae are on the hearth.

THE MERCHANT OF WOMEN

Who is there? — *I am the merchant of women. Open the door, Sostrata, I offer you two opportunities. This is the first. Approach, Anasyrtolis, and bare yourself.* — She is a little plump.

She is a beauty. Besides, she dances the kordax and she knows eighty songs. — Turn around. Raise your arms. Show your hair. Present your foot. Smile. That is good.

Now this one. — She is too young! *Not at all; she was twelve years old the day before yesterday and you will teach her nothing more.* — Remove your tunic. Let me see? No, she is skinny.

I am asking only one mina. — And the first? — *Two minae, thirty.* — Three minae for the two? — *It is done.* — Enter here and bathe yourselves. And you, farewell.

THE STRANGER

Stranger, do not go any further into the city. You will not find anywhere else girls younger or more expert than mine. I am Sostrata, well-known beyond the sea.

See this one whose eyes are green as water in the grass. Do you not want her? Here are other eyes which are dark as violets and a head of hair three cubits long.

I have better yet. Xantho, open your robe. Stranger, her breasts are hard as quinces; touch them. And her beautiful belly, you see, carries the three furrows of Cypris.

I purchased her, along with her sister who is not yet of the age for love, but is a useful second. By the two goddesses! You are of a noble race. Phyllis and Xantho, follow the gallant knight!

THE REMEMBRANCE OF MNASIDIKA

They danced, one before the other, with a movement rapid and fleeting; they always seemed to be wanting to embrace, and yet never touched, unless with the tips of their lips.

When they turned their backs while dancing, they looked at each other, head on shoulder, and the sweat glistened off their lifted arms and their fine hair brushed over their breasts.

The languor of their eyes, the fire of their cheeks, the solemnity of their faces, were three passionate songs. They touched each other furtively — their bodies bent over from the hips.

And suddenly they fell, finishing the gentle dance on the ground ...Memory of Mnasidika, it was then that you came to me, and everything, other than your dear image, troubled me.

THE YOUNG MOTHER

Do not believe, Myromeris, having become a mother, you have lessened your beauty. See how your body, beneath your robe, has drowned its slim form in a voluptuous softness.

Your breasts are two large overturned flowers upon your chest, whose cut stems give out a milky sap. Your softened belly swoons beneath the hand.

And now consider the tiny child born of a quiver you had one night, in the arms of a passerby whose name you no longer know. Dream of her distant destiny.

These eyes that now scarcely open will one day be elongated by a line of black pencil, and they will sow in men sorrow or joy with one movement of their lashes.

THE UNKNOWN

He sleeps. I do not know him. He horrifies me. Nevertheless, his purse is filled with gold and he gave four drachmae to the slave while entering. I expect a mina for myself.

But I told the Phrygian to take my place in the bed. He was drunk and he took her for me. I would rather die in torment than stretch myself out next to this man.

Alas! I dream of the meadows of Taurus ... I was a little virgin ... Then I had a flat chest and I was so mad with jealousy that I hated my married sisters.

What would I not have done to obtain that which I refused to-night! Today my breasts are wrinkled and in my worn heart the bored Eros slumbers.

THE TRICKSTER

I awaken ... Is he gone! He has left something! No — two empty jars and some soiled flowers. The entire rug is red with wine.

I have slept, but I am still drunk... With whom then did I return? ... Still, we made love. The bed is still drenched with sweat.

Perhaps there were several; the bed is in such disarray. I no longer know... But someone saw them! There is my Phrygian. She is still sleeping across the threshold.

I give her a kick in the chest and I shout, "Bitch, you could not ..." I am so hoarse I can say no more.

THE LAST LOVER

Child, do not pass without loving me. I am still beautiful in the night. You will see how much warmer my autumn is than the spring-time of another.

Do not look for love from virgins. Love is a difficult art in which young girls are little versed. I have studied it all my life so that I can give it to my last lover.

My last lover will be you — I know it. Here is my mouth, for which a nation has paled with desire. Here is my hair, the same hair about which Sappho the Great has sung.

I will gather for you all that remains of my lost youth. I will even burn the memories. I will give you the flute of Lykas, the sash of Mnasidika.

Pierre Louÿs

THE DOVE

For a long time I have been beautiful; the day approaches when I will no longer be a woman. And then I will come to know the heartbreaking memories, the charred solitary desire, and the tears in my hands.

If life is a long dream, what good does it do to resist? Now, four and five times a night, I demand amorous pleasure, and when my loins are exhausted, I sleep wherever my body falls.

In the morning, I open my eyelids and I shiver in my hair. A dove is on my window. I ask her in what month we are. She says to me, "It is the month when women are in love."

Ah! Whatever the month, the dove speaks the truth, Cypris. And I throw both my arms around my lover and with great trembling I stretch my legs, still numb, to the foot of the bed.

THE RAIN OF THE MORNING

The traces of night are fading. The stars are moving away. Here the last courtesans have returned with their lovers. And I, in the morning rain, I write this verse upon the sand.

The leaves are laden with sparkling water. The rivulets, crossing over the footpaths, drag along the earth and the dead leaves. The rain, drop by drop, makes holes in my song.

Oh! How sad and alone I am here! The younger ones do not look at me; the older ones have forgotten me. That is all right. They will learn my verses, and the children of their children.

This is what neither Myrtale nor Thais nor Glykera will say to themselves the day when their plump cheeks become hollow. Those who will love after me will sing my stanzas together.

THE TRUE DEATH

Aphrodite — merciless goddess, you have willed that, for me also, the happy youth of luxurious hair shall disappear in a few days. Why am I not altogether dead!

I have looked at myself in my mirror; I no longer have smiles or tears. Oh sweet face that loved Mnasidika, I cannot believe that you were once mine.

Can it be that all is ended! I have not yet lived five times eight years; it seems to me that I was born only yesterday, and already I must say, "No one will love me any longer."

All my shorn hair I have twisted into my sash, and I offer it to you, Cypris eternal! I will not cease to adore you. This is the last verse of the pious Bilitis.

Pierre Louÿs

THE TOMB OF BILITIS

FIRST EPITAPH

In the country where the springs are born from the sea and where the bed of rivers is made of leaves of rock, I, Bilitis, was born.

My mother was Phoenician; my father, Damophylos, Hellene. My mother taught me the songs of Byblis, sad as the first dawn.

I have worshipped Astarte at Cyprus. I have known Sappho at Lesbos. I sang as I loved. If I have lived well, Passerby, tell it to your daughter.

And do not sacrifice a black goat for me, but in sweet libation, squeeze its teats over my tomb.

SECOND EPITAPH

Upon the somber banks of Melos, at Tamassos of Pamphylia, I, Bilitis, daughter of Damophylos, was born. I lie far from my native land, as you see.

As a child, I learned the loves of Adonis and of Astarte, the mysteries of the holy Seris, and the death and return to Her-of-the-Rounded Eyelids.

If I have been a courtesan, what is the harm? Was it not my duty as a woman? Stranger, the Mother-of-All-Things guides us. To ignore her is not prudent.

In gratitude to you who have stopped, I wish you this destiny: May you be loved, and never love. Farewell — remember, in your old age, that you have seen my tomb.

Pierre Loÿs

LAST EPITAPH

Under the dark leaves of the laurels, under the amorous flowering
of the roses, it is here that I lie, I who have known how to weave
the line into verse and make the kiss blossom.

I grew up in the land of the nymphs. I lived on the isle of women
lovers. I died on the isle of Cyprus. It is for this my name is illustrious and my tombstone polished with oil.

Weep not for me, you who stop; they performed glorious funeral
rites for me — the hired mourners tore at their cheeks; they laid in
my tomb my mirrors and my necklaces.

And now, over the pale meadows of asphodels, I walk, an intan-
gible shadow, and the memory of my earthly life is the joy of my
subterranean life.

BIBLIOGRAPHY

I. *The Songs of Bilitis*, issued in German, for the first time, with a Glossary, by G. Heim. Leipzig, 1894

II. *The Songs of Bilitis*, translated from the Greek, into French, for the first time, by P. L. Paris, 1895

III. "Six Songs of Bilitis," translated into verse, in French, by Madam Jean Bertheroy. *Revue pour les Jeunes Filles*, Paris, Armand Colin, 1896.

IV. "Twenty-Six Songs of Bilitis," translated, into German, by Richard Dehmel. *Die Gesellschaft*, Leipzig, 1896.

V. "Twenty Songs of Bilitis," translated, into German, by Dr. Paul Goldmann. *Frankfurter Zeitung*, 1896.

VI. "The Songs of Bilitis," by Prof. von Willamovitz-Moellendorf. *Goettingsche Gelehrte*, Goettingen, 1896.

VII. "Eight Songs of Bilitis," translated, into Czech, by Alesandre Backovsky. Prague, 1897.

VIII. "Four Songs of Bilitis," translated, into Swedish, by Gustav Uddgren. *Norisk Revy*, Stockholm, 1897.

X. "Three Songs of Bilitis," in French, set to music by Claude Debussy. Paris, Fromont, 1898.

Pierre Louÿs